Karen Saunders often gets asked where the inspiration for her character Suzy Puttock comes from. The truth is, she's a walking, talking disaster zone, just like Suzy. If you ever meet Karen, ask about her most embarrassing moments. She's got *loads*.

After Karen graduated with a degree in English Literature from Warwick University, she did lots of different jobs, like selling Christmas hampers, answering telephones and working in PR. She didn't like any of them much, so went back to university to complete an MA in Writing for Young People at Bath Spa University. She's been making up stories about ~~~~~~~~~~~~~~~~~ fairies, cars, ~~~~~~~~~~~~~~~~~~~~~~~~~ e.

Photo by www.griffithsphotography.co.uk

Suzy P. and the Trouble With THREE

Karen Saunders

xxx

templar

First published in the UK in 2014 by Templar Publishing,
an imprint of The Templar Company Limited, Deepdene Lodge,
Deepdene Avenue, Dorking, Surrey, RH5 4AT, UK

www.templarco.co.uk

MIX
Paper from
responsible sources
FSC® C020471

ISBN 978-1-84877-369-1

Printed and bound in Great Britain
by CPI Group (UK) Ltd, Croydon, CR0 4YY

For Ade and for Oliver,
who are made of awesome.

CHAPTER ONE

Oh thank you, thank you, *thank you.*

They're finally here. They're finally, finally here!

After weeks of waiting, school is done. Bring on the summer holidays, people!

It's going to be awesome. Six weeks of freedom. Six weeks of nothing to do but hang out with my bezzies.

No homework.

No snide comments from evil Jade Taylor and her equally evil sidekick Kara Walker.

There'll be lie-ins.

There'll be endless sun.

We'll busy ourselves making memories that last forever, and all that jazz.

It's going to be bliss.

Although, we *may* need to work on the blissful thing...

Because, instead of frolicking and showing off my bikini bod at the beach, playfully swatting an inflatable beach ball, I'm sitting in Tastee Burga, avoiding the rain.

Yarg. I *hate* this place.

Still, at least I'm hanging out with my fave peeps in the whole wide world – my best friend Millie, my boyfriend Danny, and Jamie, boyfriend of Millie and best friend of Danny. I just wish we'd gone to Bojangles, my favourite local café, for our end of term celebration, but Millie and I were outshouted by the boys and their noisy desire for meat.

But then, I wish for a whole heap of things. It doesn't mean any of them actually come true.

Like, I wish I was sophisticated and elegant, and not a walking disaster area who causes mayhem wherever she goes. Today alone, I've crushed a Year Seven after tripping down the stairs, been smacked in the chest by a netball resulting in still-sore boobage, and swallowed a midge while reading aloud in English, nearly choking to death.

I wish I had a better surname. Puttock? I mean, *really*? It's horrendous. *And* it rhymes with a body part nobody wants to be associated with.

I wish my hair was smooth and sleek, not coarse and untameable with a mind of its own. I also wish a product existed that could turn said coarse, untameable hair into beautiful ringlets. We're having the world's soggiest summer, and I'm permanently frizzy.

I wish my big sister, Amber, wasn't getting madder by the day. She's pregnant, and found out at her twelve-week scan it's twins. Now her levels of insanity seem to be increasing with her stomach size. I also wish her pregnancy insomnia would go away, and she'd stop wanting sisterly chats with me about random nonsense at 6 a.m. She and her husband Mark were supposed to be moving into their own place but with the babies on the way they can't afford it, so there's no end to the crack-of-dawn discussions in sight.

I wish my little sister, Harry, wasn't so flipping annoying. Having spent the last year being obsessed with practical jokes, she's now also completely fixated with magic. Blame Harry Potter. Her latest spell attempt is one to try to get me to disappear.

I wish Mum hadn't spent all of the family savings on Amber's wedding earlier this year, giving Dad a total nervous breakdown once he saw the final bill. The prompt implementation of the Puttock Emergency Budget has resulted in value-beans-on-value-toast for tea three times a week since. *And* we're not going away on holiday this year because we're so broke.

I wish I hadn't lost my school blazer, because Mum's going to throw the world's biggest wobbler when she finds out – it's the third one this year. Plus, the constant rain of this so-called summer means I keep getting wet without it, hence I'm sitting here in a soggy shirt.

I wish Millie would cheer up, because usually she's super fun and excitable, but right now she's as miserable as the weather. I haven't seen her eat a single jelly baby all day, and she's usually mainlining the things, so *something's* definitely going on.

I wish—

"Suzy!" Danny says, shaking my arm. "Come on, answer already. How much would it take for you to eat a moth? Twenty thousand quid?"

"Would you stop it? Pack it in, you're putting me off my fries," I say. Ever since Danny found out how much I loathe moths in a recent game of Truth or Dare, he's gone on and on about it.

The thought of having one in my mouth, that hairy body on my tongue, oh God, it's making me want to vom. I couldn't do it.

Even for stacks of cash.

Lately, Danny and Jamie have become obsessed with giving each other more and more outrageous challenges. Turns out, Danny would eat a tarantula for eighty thousand pounds, while Jamie, the human dustbin, would need half a million. I was surprised, I've seen him eat some terrifyingly out-of-date-stuff before.

"Come on, surely you'd eat a tiny little moth for twenty thousand," Danny says. "*Twenty thousand pounds. You'd hardly even notice it going down. One gulp and it's gone.*"

I shake my head. "Nuh-uh."

"Fifty thousand?" Jamie offers, his eyebrows waggling temptingly under his floppy dark fringe.

I think about the money. Oh, so much money... I could buy whatever I wanted. Get tickets to see The Drifting. Sort out my hair. Treat my family to an amazing holiday.

But the thought of a moth in my mouth... I put down my chip and grimace.

"Wow," Jamie says, shovelling in another spoonful of ice cream. "The stakes are getting high. Let's try one hundred thousand..."

"I don't want to play this stupid game," I say.

"Not for a hundred K? Then how much?" Danny asks.

"Shut up," I say.

"How much? How much?" Danny and Jamie chant, slapping their hands against the table.

"Would you two stop?" I say, although I'm laughing

now. "I guess… maybe a million?"

"A million?" chorus Danny and Jamie. "*Seriously?*"

"I can't believe you wouldn't do it for less," Danny says. "A harmless little moth. It'd be nothing."

"Yeah, well, that's how much it would take," I say. "Now let me eat in peace."

"Mills, you're up," Jamie says. But Millie's not paying attention. She's staring out of the window, twiddling the turquoise streak in her blonde bob as she watches people meandering through the shopping centre.

"Millie?" he says again.

"Hmm?" Millie says.

"Ready for your dilemma?"

"I'm not playing," Millie says.

"Not an option," Danny tells her. "Right…" He thinks for a moment. "How much to give a full body massage to a skunk? No gloves."

"Good one," Jamie says.

"I told you, I'm not playing," Millie says.

"All right, grumpy. Can I have that burger if you're not eating it?" Jamie asks, pointing to her untouched food.

"Sure," Millie replies, pushing it across the table.

"Are you okay?" I ask.

"Yup," Millie says.

"Really?"

"Yes, really," Millie says, standing up. "I'm going to the loo. Back in a minute."

"What's up with her?" I ask, watching her walk towards the toilets.

"She said she was fine," Jamie says.

"I'm not so sure," I say. "I'll go and talk to her."

"If she says she's fine, she's fine," Jamie calls.

Pfff. Shows how much boys know.

I wait for Millie by the sinks. Eventually, she flushes and emerges. Her eyes look all puffy.

"Have you been crying?" I ask.

"I've got something in my eye," Millie says, splashing cold water onto her face.

"In both your eyes?" I say.

"Weird, huh?" Millie says. "Hey, I want to go and see if Pink Panda have got the top I saw on their website. I'm going to celebrate summer by treating myself. You coming with, or staying here?"

"I'll come," I say, even though I'm skint.

"Great," Millie says, grinning as she leans over to give me a big hug. "Let's go!"

Maybe I was wrong about her. After all, Millie doesn't really get upset. She's always super perky and upbeat. Admittedly, most of it's sugar-fuelled, but she's always been that way, the whole time I've been her best friend.

Which is forever.

"We're going shopping," Millie announces when we return to the boys, who immediately look dismayed.

"Nooooo," moans Jamie.

"I'm not going to any clothes shops," Danny says. "Besides, there's a documentary on tonight about the making of the first *Star Wars* trilogy. I'm getting the next bus back."

My boyfriend is cute, with amazing blue eyes, short blondey-brown hair and kissable lips that curve into the warmest, happiest smile. My boyfriend is sweet and funny, and really kind. I love him to pieces. But – and this is a big but – he is way, way too obsessed with *Star Wars* for my liking.

"I'll come with you, mate," Jamie says. He gives Millie a kiss as Danny leans over and kisses me goodbye too.

"Mmm, fruity," he says, sniffing enthusiastically at my neck.

"Gerroff," I push him away, laughing. "It's a perfume Amber gave me. She's not wearing any while she's pregnant."

"How come?" Millie says.

"In case the babies don't like the smell or something."

"You what?" says Danny. "How can they smell anything?"

"I know. Insane," I say. "I'll ring you later."

"Only after the documentary's finished," Danny

instructs. "No calls will be answered until ten."

I roll my eyes as I agree, because I know he's deadly serious.

Millie's still kind of quiet as we're walking through the shopping centre.

"Does Danny talk to you much about when his parents were getting divorced?" Millie suddenly asks, taking me by surprise.

"Um... not really," I say. "It was a couple of years ago now, I think he's kind of over it."

"Was he upset?"

"Uh... yeah. I guess. You would be, wouldn't you, if your parents split up? But I think the fact they've stayed friends helps, even though his mum moved away. It's not like they're slagging each other all the time or anything. Why?"

"No reason," Millie says, hurriedly. "Just, you know, wondering. Oooh, look at him," she says, grabbing my arm and pointing excitedly. Up ahead there's a seriously cute lad giving out flyers.

"Check out those cheekbones," Millie says dreamily. "And that mouth, mmm... Couldn't you imagine kissing it?"

I shake my head and laugh. Millie's such a minx. She's a total flirt, but way too into Jamie to do anything about any of her crushes. She just enjoys looking. And Jamie knows exactly what she's like. It doesn't seem to bother him. Whereas me… well, I'm more wary about eyeing up other boys these days, after what happened earlier this year with Zach, a guy from our school. I briefly broke up with Danny to be with Zach, but it was the biggest mistake of my life.

I shudder. I was such an idiot to think he was better than Danny. I hate being reminded how close I came to throwing everything away.

"Come on, you," I say, steering Millie towards Pink Panda. They don't really sell the kind of clothes I'm into – I'm not brave enough to wear half their stuff – but Millie loves it. She's got fantastic dress sense, and a real knack for putting crazy, bright items of clothing together. They'd look ridiculous on most people (me included), but on her they look great. I think it's partly about the accessories she uses. She's very good at accessorising, is Millie. It's almost an art form.

Millie lets go of my arm and darts through Pink Panda's doors, grabbing items – including the coveted top – like she's doing a trolley dash, squealing with joy as she goes. I follow behind more slowly. I've got less than a tenner left which needs to last me for the rest of the week *and* pay for my bus home. If I do find something I like, it'll have to be in the sale, or being given away for free.

Flicking through the clothes on the sale rail, I can see a few tops that are quite pretty, but most importantly, cheap, although probably still out of my budget. I grab a couple, then come across a dress that's the ugliest thing I've ever seen in my life. It's a rainbow tartan minidress, with frills and ruffles around the sleeves and hemline.

Delightedly, I pick it out to show to Millie.

I catch up with her queuing by the changing rooms. "Check this out," I snigger, holding up the dress.

Millie's eyes widen. "Oh. My. God. That's outrageous. You have to try it on."

"Hah. No chance," I say.

"Please," Millie says.

"No way, it's disgusting! And I don't wear dresses. Ever since that gross thing Amber made me wear as bridesmaid, I've vowed never, ever again. Swore an oath and everything."

"Please," Millie begs, holding her hands together in prayer position. "Please, please, pretty please with a cherry on the top. It'll be hilarious. I'd laugh for a week."

"Oh, all right," I relent. It *would* be pretty funny to see what I look like. I check the label and see that it's too small for me, so chances are I'm not going to fit more than a toe inside anyway.

"How many items?" a bored assistant asks. She leads us, and two other girls who arrived in front, to the cubicles at the end of the corridor. The girls are tall and slim in their private school uniforms, which they're wearing with heels. I'm not allowed to wear heels as Mum says my feet haven't finished growing yet, and if I wear heels regularly I'll be wheelchair-bound by my twenties, or something. Apparently I'll thank her for it one day.

I'm not convinced.

"They're our age, can you believe it?" Millie whispers, tilting her head towards the girls. "I heard them talking before you came over. They look loads older, right?"

The pair have flawless, perfectly made-up faces and matching hairstyles: blonde and long with toffee highlights and not a strand out of place. They're also carrying what look suspiciously like Mulberry handbags. *Mulberry!*

The only reason I know what a Mulberry bag looks like is because Amber has shoved every picture she's ever seen of one in my face. She's desperate for the kind her celebrity icon, Conni G, has. But they're crazy expensive. Like, hundreds of pounds. Thousands, sometimes.

I think it's fair to say if I had a Mulberry, chances are I'd trash it in seconds by squishing banana in it, or spilling lemonade over it, but still. Imagine being the kind of girl with a bag like that. Life would be different if I was a Mulberry girl, all rich and elegant.

I sigh enviously.

"Make sure you show me what that dress looks like," Millie says, swishing the curtain behind her. "No chickening out."

I wriggle out of my clothes and attempt to squeeze into the dress, pulling the zip up as far as I can. It only gets halfway up my side. I'm not exactly big, but the dress is so tight there are little rolls of fat appearing all over the place. Plus it's so short you can practically see my knickers, and so tight I can only walk in teeny-tiny Geisha girl steps.

My blotchy corned-beef skin teamed with forgotten-to-shave pits don't exactly help the overall look, either.

"I'm not coming out, you're going to have to come in," I call to Millie. There's no way I'm risking anyone seeing me.

Millie sticks in her head and cracks up. "That is too horrendous," she says, fumbling for her phone. "Let me take a photo for the boys…"

"Er, no flipping way," I say, clasping my trousers in front of me with one hand to cover up as much of my body as I can, while swatting Millie away with the other.

"You've seen it now, I'm taking it off," I say, but when I pull at the zip nothing happens.

I tug again.

And again.

Tug. Tug. Tug.

Nothing.

Oh God. I'm completely and utterly stuck!

Millie's laughing so hard there are tears streaming down her cheeks.

"This isn't funny," I say, although I'm giggling too.

Millie's still doing her utmost to nab a photo when her phone rings. "Hi, Soph," she answers hesitantly, greeting her older sister. "Uh huh, uh huh, oh no, really?" Millie's tone is serious. I can make out Sophie's voice, high and stressed, although I can't hear exactly what she's saying. After a couple of minutes, Millie says, "I'll be home as soon as I can," and hangs up.

"Everything okay?" I ask.

"Um, yeah, fine. I've got to go. Sorry."

"You can't, I need your help to get the dress off," I call, as Millie rushes away. She's not even stopping to buy the top she wanted so much.

"Millliieee," I howl in despair. "You can't just leave me here."

"Sorry," Millie calls over her shoulder.

"Ladies and gentlemen, the store will be closing in five minutes. Please take your purchases to the till," a voice announces over the intercom.

This can't be happening.

What am I supposed to do now?

CHAPTER TWO

I think I'm about to hyperventilate.

I'm stuck in the world's most disgusting dress and the shop's about to close. As far as I can make out, I've only got two choices – reveal myself looking this way and ask the shop assistants for help, or stay here all night.

Neither option is particularly appealing.

Don't panic, Suze. Just don't panic.

I can't believe Millie left me here like this!

Think, for goodness sake. There's got to be *something* you can do.

But I can't come up with anything. Not one single solution, other than... I'm going to have to go onto the shop floor and ask for help.

As much as I don't want anyone to see me like this, I can't stay in this changing room until morning.

I grab my stuff and hold it up like a protective shield, trying to cover as much of me as possible before I creep out.

Fortunately the shoppers have gone and there are only two assistants left, pulling down the shutters and fiddling with the till. I shuffle awkwardly in their direction. They're engrossed in a conversation about a bar they're going to after work.

"Uh, excuse me?" I say.

The assistants turn, and when they catch sight of me, they're unable to disguise their horrified expressions. Their name badges tell me they're called Abi and Lou.

"She's wearing that dress," I hear Lou mutter. "You owe me a fiver. I knew someone would buy it one day."

"We're closing, I'm afraid," says Abi. "If you want to buy that, you'll have to come back tomorrow. We've shut the tills."

"Yeah, that's sort of the problem," I say awkwardly. "I tried this dress on and now I can't get it off."

Lou snorts loudly and ducks down behind the counter.

"You're stuck in the dress?" Abi's lips are twitching dramatically, like they're doing some kind of dance.

"Uh huh," I say, lifting up my arm to show them the zip, straining halfway down my side.

Oh, this is mortifying. Now they're getting a full close-up view of my once-white-now-grey bra and bristly armpit.

Abi yanks at the zip. "Wow, this really is jammed. Lou, give me a hand, would you?"

Lou manages to compose herself enough to join us.

"You hold the material down here," instructs Abi, "I'll pull here, and..."

Several minutes later they're still heaving and pulling at the zip.

"Have you seen the time?" Lou hisses. "We're meeting the guys soon."

Lou straightens up and checks her watch. "Okay, tell you what, we'll mark the dress down as damaged and unsaleable and you can wear it home. You can cut it off later."

"What? No!" I say in horror.

They can't be serious... can they?

I honestly didn't think there'd be anything worse than revealing myself in this dress to the shop assistants. Turns out there is – revealing myself to the world.

"Can't we cut it off here?" I plead.

"Sorry," Abi says. "Not enough time. We need to go, we've got an important stock meeting."

"But she said you were going to meet some guys," I point out indignantly.

"To discuss stock," Lou says. "And we can't be late. Haven't you got a coat or something?"

"No," I say, once again cursing my lost blazer. "Just my school shirt and trousers."

"You could put the shirt over the top," Abi says. She checks the tag in the dress, and makes a note of the barcode number. "I'll scan that through in the morning, but now, it's all yours."

"Thanks," I say gloomily as I wriggle into my shirt, and slip on my shoes, which don't go with the dress *at all*. I can't even put my trousers on underneath – the dress is too clingy for that to be an option, and putting them on top would look weirder.

"At least you got a free dress out of it," Lou says, as she escorts me to the exit. The dress is so tight I can only take teetering penguin steps.

As the door closes behind me and the shutters drop down, the last thing I see in the shop is Lou and Abi, bent double with laughter.

Gnargh.

Standing outside Pink Panda, and yanking at my hem with my free hand, trying to cover more than a millimetre of thigh, I frantically dial home.

If nobody can come and get me, things are rapidly going to get worse, as my only choice will be to walk through the shopping centre and get on the bus.

Pick up, pick up, I pray. People are staring curiously

as they pass, but I'm doing my best to ignore them.

There's no answer. The phone rings and rings, until the answerphone kicks in. Rats!

"You've reached the Puttock household," Dad's voice recites. "You probably don't want to speak to me, but to one of the women I live with. If so, ring their mobiles. That's why I pay all those damn phone bills. Otherwise, leave a message after the tone."

"Mum, Dad, it's Suzy," I say. "Um, I've had a bit of an incident in town, and I need you to call me as soon as you can. It's urgent, okay?"

I ring both their mobiles next, but they're switched off. Pulling the bus timetable out of my bag, I scan it quickly. To my dismay, the last bus home is leaving in ten minutes and I've not got enough cash for a taxi. If Mum and Dad don't get my message, I won't be able to get home.

Which means I'm going to have to head for the bus stop.

Pushing my shoulders back, I decide the only way to carry this off is with an air of panache and fake confidence. I start to strut through the shopping centre, but the people laughing and pointing are somewhat off-putting. My confidence fizzles away until soon I'm doing a tottering waddle, head down, tugging my hem every painful step of the way.

One last check of my mobile, and I try the house phone again, but no joy. Nobody's around.

Flipping marvellous.

So that leaves getting the bus, then. As I join the crowd of people waiting for the number 16, I hear stifled giggles, and realise the Mulberry girls are leaning up against a wall, watching me and sniggering.

It's at this point I realise I am never going to be as glamorous and sophisticated as those two. Ever. I bet nothing like this happens to them.

I busy myself trying to find some money in my purse, but fumble with the zip so the coins end up falling everywhere. It's impossible to bend down elegantly in this stupid dress, but I scrabble around on the ground for the ones within reach and pray I'm not showing my pants.

My face is now burning so hotly I may spontaneously combust.

After the bus arrives I sink down into a free seat. The Mulberry girls glide past and settle themselves behind me. They get stuck straight into a discussion about summer holidays. One's going to the family home in 'Barbs' (takes me a minute to figure out she means Barbados – hey, haven't we all got a place in the Caribbean?) while the other's looking forward to popping in to see her personal shopper in Selfridges at the weekend before heading off to Australia.

I sigh enviously. I *knew* life was better for Mulberry girls.

After the world's longest bus ride, I finally make it to the house. Mrs Green, who lives next door, gets quite the surprise when she sees me scuttling past.

"You'll catch your death, love," she calls after me.

"Hello?" I say apprehensively, once I'm safely inside. No answer. In the middle of the kitchen table there's a note, saying everyone's gone to the nursing home to see Aunt Lou.

Missing out on a visit to Great Aunt Lou has to be the one high point of this pretty pants afternoon. Also known as Aunt Loon, she's as vicious as a viper and has an equally poisonous tongue.

And there's another bright side. Because now I suppose at least I can get out of this dress without anyone seeing me. Harry would have a field day if she clocked me looking like this. I'd never hear the end of it.

Now where are the scissors? I seriously need to get this dress off. The kitchen ones aren't sharp enough, so I grab Mum's dressmaker's scissors from the drawer in the sitting room, and try to cut past the zip, but it's no good. I can't get the angle right, and after stabbing myself in the ribs, drawing blood, I realise I'm going to have to wait for someone to come and free me. So I wait. And I wait.

28

I text Millie, but she doesn't answer. She's not online either. I ponder ringing Danny, but his documentary's on and if I try to speak to him all I'll get is a few huffy grunts. It'll be too late by the time the Star Wars fest is finished for him to come over and free me.

I eat tea, which makes the tight dress even tighter and more uncomfortable. Eventually, I give up on waiting for someone to come home and go to bed.

Still wearing the dress.

CHAPTER THREE

I wake with a start the next morning as Amber lands on the end of my bed. The mattress practically tilts over as she lowers her vast bulk onto it. I stare at her through bleary eyes, then at the alarm clock.

6.30 a.m.

Really? It's the first day of the summer holidays. I want to sleep! I'm knackered, as I was jerking awake all night long, panicking I was dying. This stupid dress kept making me feel like I was suffocating.

"Oooh, goody, you're up," Amber says.

"Well, I am now, because you woke me," I say, grumpily. "But now you're here, you can help me with something..."

"I couldn't sleep," Amber says, like she's not even heard me. Will nobody help me out of this flipping frock? I don't think she's even *noticed* I'm not in my PJs.

"I needed someone to talk to," she continues.

"You have a husband," I remind her. "Who sleeps in

your room, in your bed, right next to you. Every. Single. Night. Can't you speak to him instead?"

"Oh, you know Markymoo, he's such a heavy sleeper," Amber says. "And besides, I wanted you, Suzypoos. You're much better at talking baby stuff than he is. You can't really talk about that kind of thing with boys."

Hmm. Well, I suppose it is kinda awesome becoming an aunt to twins. It's a shame they're not identical, that would be cooler than cool, but twins of any sort are still pretty amazing. And I am much more tolerant towards my sister these days, ever since she helped me and Danny get back together after our break-up at the beginning of the year.

"What about Mum?" I say, giving up on getting any help from Amber and snuggling under the duvet. "She can chat babies morning, noon and night. Didn't you try her?"

"I did," Amber says regretfully, "but Dad kicked me out and told me if I didn't leave he'd lock me in the wardrobe. As if I'd fit. That's no way to talk to your pregnant daughter, if you ask me."

Dad still hasn't quite recovered from the shock of hearing that his eldest is expecting twins. There's the possibility there could be two more females in there waiting to invade his territory, and he's not dealing with the prospect particularly well. Amber and Mark have been majorly strong-willed about refusing to find out the sexes of the babies. We all thought Amber would be dying to know, but she's decided she wants a surprise.

"Budge up and let me get in," Amber says.

"This is a single bed," I protest, as Amber leaves me with about a millimetre of space and hanging dangerously off the edge.

She huffs and puffs for ages, trying to get comfortable, then admits defeat and sits up instead, leaning against the headboard and rubbing her bump. "Oh, Babyboos, you do make Mummy so uncomfy, don't you?" she says. "I'll be glad when I can get some sleep again."

"You do know you're having twins, right?" I say. "I think it's going to be years before that happens."

"Shush," Amber says. "These two are going to be perfect angels. Now, look at this Conni G column." She thrusts a pregnancy magazine in my face. Amber worships Conni G, who had a baby recently and now writes a column about it. Apparently a fake-tanned, botoxed, silicone-breasted airhead is exactly the person to turn to for parenting advice.

Our future generations are doomed.

"You know how Conni called her baby Pashmina?" Amber says.

I nod my head warily. Amber's name suggestions have got weirder and weirder as the pregnancy's gone on.

"Well, I've been thinking about clothes-themed names for my babies. What about Scarf and Kaftan? Really unusual, don't you think? And it wouldn't matter if they were boys or girls..."

Scarf and Kaftan Mycock? *Seriously?*

"Um... I'm not sure that would work," I say. It is way too early to be tactfully negotiating this level of mental. "Wouldn't they get bullied?"

"You think?" Amber's genuinely surprised. "Nobody seems to like any of my choices." She pouts, but her face brightens as the door is nudged open. "Oooh, look, here's Crystal Fairybelle," Amber squeals in delight as her Chihuahua takes a flying leap at the bed. She covers him in kisses, pulling the duvet off me as she does so.

"Why are you wearing a dress?" Amber asks, once she's finished the Crystal love-fest.

It took her long enough to notice.

"Long story," I say, grabbing the dressmaking scissors from the bedside cabinet. "Cut me out, would you?"

"Cut you out? No way. That dress is amazing. Is it a new style you're trying? Much better than your normal look which is, well, kind of blah."

"Charming, thanks."

It's not my fault all I can afford is Primark and Mum's totally tight with my clothing budget.

Amber laughs. "You know what I mean. You look the same as everyone else. Be more like Millie, stand out from the crowd."

"I'm happy blending in, thanks," I tell her. "Now, please chop. The zip's stuck and I can't wear it any more. I really, really, need to breathe."

"There's got to be a way to free you without ruining it," Amber says, fiddling with the zip, but eventually giving up. "Nope. You're stuck fast. You're sure you want me to cut it?"

"I really, really am."

As Amber snips the dress away, my whole body sags with relief.

Ahh, I feel so free!

I chuck the dress into the corner of my room, then wriggle into my PJ bottoms and sweatshirt, Amber watching enviously. "Look at you, you're so slim..."

"Yeah, well, I'm not seven months pregnant, am I?"

"True," Amber concedes. "Although actually, I'm nearly thirty-two weeks now. Ooh, one of the babies is moving." She grabs my hand and places it on her stomach.

Wow. As I feel the persistent kicks, I marvel again that my sister is actually growing two teeny tiny people inside her. It blows my mind while at the same time completely terrifying me.

I'm not sure the world is ready for mini Amber and Mark hybrids.

I'm certainly not.

"That's got to be a boy, hasn't it, kicking like that?" I ask.

"Who knows?" Amber says, nuzzling her Chihuahua. "But whatever happens, you're going to be godmother, aren't you, Crystal? Or, rather, dogmother. You'll share the responsibility of the babies with me, won't you, doggy-woggy? Conni was talking about balancing careers and babies in her column this week," Amber informs me solemnly. "She says it's very difficult to juggle both. It's a big sacrifice for me to give up my job and be a full-time mother."

Amber 'works' as an aromatherapist. She has one client, her friend Fleur, who she treats in her bedroom once a fortnight. She's hardly what you'd call a high-flyer.

"I'm sure it'll be fine," I reassure her.

"I guess. Mmm, I'm so tired," Amber says, with a huge yawn.

I close my eyes and, although I'm still precariously close to tipping off the bed due to Amber and Crystal hogging most of the available space, eventually I doze off.

We wake up again at a much more civilised time.

"Breakfast?" I say.

35

"Definitely," Amber says. "I'm starving."

As Amber and I make our way downstairs, I hear the letterbox clatter, and detour to grab the post. Nothing for me, but there are about eight baby product catalogues for Amber and a letter for Mum, with a gorgeous handwritten envelope. The stamp is foreign, and as I peer more closely, I see that the letter's come from Italy. Must be from Caro, Mum's super glam, super rich friend who lives out there.

In the kitchen, Mum leaps up from her chair, dashes over to Amber, and takes her arm to lead her over to the table. "Come on, love, you sit down. Take the weight off."

"Yeah, fatty," says Harry, taking a huge bite of toast.

"Harry, that's not kind," Mum says.

"Am I getting too big, Mum?" Amber asks, her bottom lip starting to wobble. "I know I've put on a lot of weight, but everyone says you do with twins…"

"You look wonderful," Mum says. "You're blooming. Absolutely blooming. Isn't she, Chris?"

"Blooming massive," Dad mutters to Harry and they both crack up.

"Stop it, you two," Mum says.

"I *am* massive, though," Amber says. "Even my feet are fat."

She waves a swollen elephant foot in the air dramatically. Over the last few months, my once slender sister has been swallowed up by babies and water retention. She's lived in baggy clothes and flip-flops since she passed the five month stage, as nothing else fits. If she keeps growing at this rate, she'll need her own postcode soon.

"Ignore them," Mum says, rubbing Amber's shoulders. "You look beautiful. Now, can I get your breakfast?"

"Yes, please," Amber says. "Could I have some fresh fruit with honey and Greek yogurt, then maybe a full English with extra hash browns? Ooh, and if it's not too much trouble, some pancakes with chocolate spread and maple syrup?"

Hmmm. Eating like this could possibly be why Amber's looking a little, erm, bloated.

"You're going to eat *all* that?" Dad says.

"I'm hungry," Amber says. "Plus, I'm eating for three."

"Coming right up," Mum says. "You have to give those babies all the nutrients they need."

"I'll have some toast, if you could stick in a couple of pieces of bread, please," I ask.

"Can you do it yourself, love? I'm busy," Mum says, bustling around, pulling things out of cupboards. "And don't use that bread, it's Amber's," she says, whisking the organic seeded loaf out of my hands and replacing it with the value white sliced.

Flipping charming.

"We need to start thinking about buying things for the babies, Mum," Amber says.

"Things? What things?" Dad says, his eyes narrowing suspiciously.

"Cots, buggies, nappies, clothes, changing table, monitors..." Amber starts.

"But you're paying for that, aren't you?" Dad says, alarmed.

"Yes, Daddy," Amber says. "Mark's been doing lots of overtime. But Mum needs to come and help me choose it all. Now, what do we think of the names Twinkle and Tootle for the twins?"

There's a deathly silence.

"No?" Amber says. "I think Twinkle and Tootle are cute. Only for girls, though, obviously."

"Which they're not going to be," Dad says.

"Um, a letter came for you, Mum," I say, realising a speedy change of subject is in order. I slide the envelope across the table.

"Careful," Mum says. "Don't get it mixed up with my competition notes."

By the side of Mum's plate there's a huge stack of scrap paper and Post-its. Ever since Dad enforced the Puttock Emergency Budget, Mum's become obsessed with entering competitions, convinced she's going to win our way out of trouble.

She hangs out in the newsagent's for ages, flicking through papers and magazines, making notes of all the competition email addresses. I think the newsagent's on the verge of banning her, to be honest. She's not good for business, especially as she frequently ends up engrossed in the magazines while she's there, right under the huge sign that says *Please don't read unless you intend to buy*.

Mum's aiming high, hoping for a holiday win or a new TV for the lounge. So far, she's won a year's supply of cat food (we don't have a cat) and a pack of dishcloths. Hardly ground-breaking stuff. But still, Mum makes her notes all week, then boots everyone off the computer every Saturday morning so she can email in her entries.

Mum places the first course of Amber's breakfast down, carefully moves her stuff onto the counter, then rips open her letter.

"Who's it from?" Harry asks.

"Caro," Mum murmurs distractedly.

"Who's Caro?" Harry asks.

Mum doesn't answer, but turns the paper over and keeps reading.

"You know, Mum's old friend from college," I say. "She lives in Italy."

Mum's eyebrows are furrowed as her eyes flick across

the words. Finally she puts the letter down and takes a long drink of coffee.

"Can't she just email, like a normal person?" Dad says.

"Well, you know what Caro's like, flatly refuses to embrace any kind of technology. She's not having an easy time by the sounds of it," Mum says. "She's still living in Italy, but she's coming back to England soon. She's getting divorced from Luca."

Dad snorts. "Surprise, surprise. That's, what... divorce number three, now?"

"Mmm. She's asking if Isabella can come and stay with us. It won't be a problem, of course, but we'll need to get some things ready for her," Mum muses.

Dad starts to choke on a mouthful of tea. "Isabella's coming to stay?"

"That's what this letter's about," Mum says. "The divorce is getting a bit messy and Caro's sending Isabella on ahead while she sorts out the final bits and pieces. She's lost touch with most of her other friends here and thought it would be nice for Isabella to come and see us."

"Who's Isabella?" Harry asks.

"Caro's daughter," I explain. I vaguely remember them visiting us, years ago, after divorce number two. Isabella spent the whole time hiding behind Caro's legs, and wouldn't play in the den I'd built.

"How long's she coming for?" Dad asks.

"Only a couple of weeks," Mum says.

"*A couple of weeks?*"

"Why have we never met her?" Harry interrupts again.

"You have," Mum says. "You were very young at the time. Caro's a bit... flighty. She's moved around a lot, and been in and out of touch. There are photos of her and Isabella around somewhere. I'll go and see if I can find them."

Mum disappears off into the dining room. A few minutes later she returns, waving a photo triumphantly.

"Found it," she says. "This is Isabella and Caro. Look."

We all lean in to peer at the picture of a young, geeky girl, with big glasses and neatly tied dark hair pulled into bunches. She's smiling warily at the camera, in front of a forest backdrop, next to a blonde, glamorous woman wearing the tightest pair of white jeans I've ever seen, a fierce pout and gigantic sunglasses.

"The last thing this house needs is anyone else moving in," Dad says. "We're full to bursting already, and we're getting two new recruits any day—" He stops short at Mum's expression. "Oh, for Heaven's sake. When's Isabella arriving?"

"A week Thursday," Mum says. "I'll give Caro a call

after breakfast to confirm the details."

"Calling Italy? How much is that going to cost?" Dad asks.

"I won't be long," Mum soothes, when we all know full well that once she gets on the phone she won't be off again for at least an hour. "It'll be lovely to spend time with Isabella. You're all to be nice to her. Especially you, Suzy."

"Hey! Why wouldn't I be nice?" I ask.

"Just making sure, because she'll be staying in your room," Mum says, ignoring my splutters of indignation. "I'm sure you'll get on brilliantly. Caro and I used to have such fun together..." Her eyes glaze over as she's transported to some distant time.

"Why does she have to stay in my room?" I ask.

"Because you're about the same age and you'll be the best of friends by the time she goes home," Mum says.

"Do I get any say in this?"

"Nope," Mum says, getting up to mix the pancake batter. "Now, finish your breakfast. Anybody else want pancakes?"

As Harry and Dad shout that they do, I fold my arms and sit back in a huff.

Fan-flaming-tastic. Now I'm stuck sharing my room with some random for weeks.

It's my room! My space! My summer!

I don't even *know* this girl.

Thanks for nothing, Mum.

42

CHAPTER FOUR

Later that morning, I'm sitting with my mates in Millie's room, listening to The Drifting's new album. Danny's spinning around on Millie's desk chair, Jamie's flicking Millie's fairy lights on and off and Murphy, Millie's ginormous dog, is chewing on a slipper.

Millie's attempting to see how many jelly babies she can get into her mouth at once, and I'm helping her keep count.

Yeah, we're bored.

Completely and utterly out-of-our-skulls bored.

It's crazy, we always look forward to the holidays so much, then they get here and we can't think of anything to do.

Happens every. Single. Time.

There is no summertime magic, just summertime tragic.

"Anyone fancy getting the bus into town and going to Tastee Burga?" Jamie asks.

"I'm up for that," Danny says, at the exact moment Millie and I groan.

"No. No more Tastee Burga," Millie says firmly, through her mouthful of sweets.

"Why not?" Jamie asks.

"Because I'm fed up of that place," Millie says. "It's grim. There are loads of other things we could do. We could go to the park and play frisbee, or have a picnic, or take Murphy for a walk..."

"Yeah, if it was anything like a summer out there," Jamie says, peeing rather effectively on her chirpy bonfire. "But it's freezing. And raining."

"Yes, but it shouldn't be," Millie protests. "It's summer. Where's the *sun*?"

From downstairs, there's a sound of shouting, then a loud crash. Millie freezes.

"What's that?" Danny asks.

"Nothing," says Millie. Her good mood has evaporated in a flash and now her face is tense. "It's probably Sophie."

"It sounds like your parents," Jamie says, listening at the door. "Wow. It *is* your parents. And they're really going for it."

Millie laughs awkwardly. "God, they're so embarrassing.

Jamie, stop earwigging, would you?" She turns up the volume on her stereo, drowning out the sounds of the yells from downstairs.

Jamie attempts to speak, but nobody can hear him over the music.

"You what?" Danny bellows.

"Maybe we should go out," Jamie shouts. "Bojangles for hot chocolate?"

My friends look at each other and shrug their agreement.

"Let's go," I say.

Millie turns off the stereo, and all of a sudden it's quiet. No music. No shouting. No crashes. She smiles with relief.

As we file down the stairs, I can see Millie's dad out in the garden, hacking angrily at the soggy hedge. I'm kind of surprised to see him – he's always at work these days. Then, as we pass the kitchen, we see Millie's mum, Clare, sitting at the table, hands clasped around a mug of tea, staring at the fridge.

"We're going out, okay?" Millie says.

Clare doesn't answer. She just keeps staring.

She's been acting really weird since she lost her job a couple of months ago. They shut down the company she worked for, due to 'tough economic times' or something, and it's made Clare proper miserable. It's horrible, because Millie's house has always been a fantastic place to hang out before. Not only does it look amazing – it's full of art and sculptures and colourful walls – but Clare used to make us little treats to eat when we went over, or got us movies that she knew we'd want to watch. We haven't had anything like that for ages.

"Mum?" Millie tries again.

Clare turns and sees us standing in the doorway. Her eyes are red and her cheeks are blotchy but she forces a smile.

"Sorry, lovely, did you say something?"

"We're going to Bojangles," Millie says.

"Okay. Have a nice time," Clare says. "If you want, I'll give you a lift back. I'm heading to the supermarket in a bit."

"Whatever," Millie shrugs.

I look at my friend in surprise. Millie and Clare have always been really close; I've never heard her sound so off with her mum before.

As Danny and Jamie walk on ahead up the road, Millie's unusually quiet. What *is* going on with her?

"Everything okay?" I ask.

"Yeah, fine," Millie says. "Why?"

"Dunno. You seem a bit stressed. Like you did the

yesterday. What was all that about, anyway? You left me in the shop stuck in that hideous dress. Don't think I've forgiven you yet, you know."

Millie flushes guiltily. "I'm so sorry. I still feel terrible about it."

"Meh, it's all right," I say. "I've been through worse. I'll just add it to the ever-growing list of embarrassing things I've done to myself. So why'd you have to dash off?"

"No reason."

I frown. "Are you sure? Sophie sounded pretty upset, and I've hardly heard from you since."

"I'm sure."

"So there's nothing bothering you?" I press.

"I guess… um… I guess I'm just worried about Mum and Dad," Millie says.

"What? Why?"

"They're rowing a lot, and I dunno…" Millie's voice trails off.

"That thing this morning? It was just an argument," I say dismissively. "My parents bicker constantly, you know what they're like."

"Yeah, but it's been happening all the time."

"Well, they're probably tense because your mum lost her job. It'll be better when she gets a new one."

Millie forces a smile. "I suppose. It's just..."

"You're freaked about nothing, I promise," I say, flinging my arm around her shoulders. "You should try living with my parents. Then you'd have something to stress about."

Millie slowly breathes out. "Maybe. So, um, how are things in the house of Puttock? What's the goss?"

"There's a girl coming to stay with us," I announce, loud enough that Danny and Jamie turn around.

"A girl?" Millie asks, as we wait at the crossing.

"What sort of girl?" Danny asks.

"And how old are we talking here?" Jamie says.

"Some daughter of an old friend of Mum's," I say. "She's our age, from Italy."

"An *Italian* girl," Jamie says. "That means she's going to be hot."

"Oi," Millie says, mock indignantly. "It does not."

"It does," Jamie says. "All Italian girls are gorgeous, everyone knows that. Just like Australian girls are sporty, and Swiss girls are excellent skiers and cow-milkers."

"I'm not entirely sure that's true," I say, as the green man appears and we start to walk across the road.

"Don't shatter my illusions," Jamie says. "It's true. I know it. So why is this divine creature coming?"

"Her parents are getting divorced," I say.

Millie makes a strange, strangled noise.

"Sorry," she says, blushing. "Um, I was thinking that must be hard for her. Coming to a foreign country to stay with a family she doesn't know that well."

"It's not a foreign country because she's English, she's just been living in Italy for ages," I explain. "But Caro — that's her mum — is moving back because of the divorce. It's all been getting a bit full-on so she's sending Isabella back over early to come and stay with us. Says she needs to take some time out to relax or something."

Everyone bursts out laughing.

"I know, it's bonkers," I say. "Dad's stressy about money, Mum's obsessed with babies, Amber's pregnant, and Harry will probably try to saw her in half within an hour of her arriving. Our house is about as relaxing as a war zone."

"Hey," Danny protests. "Your family's not that bad."

Danny is crazily protective of my family. Everyone can see they're stark raving loonies except Danny, who thinks they're merely eccentric. He's an only child who lives with his dad, so I think he has sibling envy.

Plus, he doesn't have to flipping live with them.

"You're seriously deluded," I say. "Would you want to spend a fortnight with us? Really?"

"Good point," Danny says. "Two weeks *is* quite a long time."

"Are we going to get to meet her?" Jamie asks. "Is she going to come and hang out with us?"

"I guess," I say.

"Then let's hope she's nice," Danny says. "And that she likes hanging out in Bojangles, because I predict it's where we'll spend most of our summer. Especially if the weather doesn't improve."

"Mmmm, Bojangles hot chocolate with whipped cream and marshmallows," I say dreamily, reaching my hand out to push open the café door.

Bojangles is one of my favourite places in the world. They serve the best hot chocolate and cake I've *ever* tasted. I often go to sleep dreaming of it, that's how good it is. The only benefit to this cold and rainy summer is that I can keep drinking my favourite bevvy.

"Hi, guys," says Hannah, Bojangles' new owner, from behind the counter.

When Bojangles went up for sale recently we were all dead worried, wondering how things were going to be different. It was a huge relief to find out that Hannah's lovely and she hasn't changed the place at all.

We nab our favourite table, the one in the window.

Jamie and Danny grab the menus, but I don't know why because we're here all the time and know everything they serve. I know exactly what I'm going to have. Hot chocolate

50

with cream and marshmallows, and a slice of Death by Chocolate cake.

I'm reaching down to get my bag when I remember I've not got much money left. Less than a fiver, after the bus ride of shame yesterday and a magazine I had to pay Mum back for.

I open my purse, hoping a twenty pound note will have magically appeared, but nope. There's only a couple of quid and a handful of coppers. Rats. That's not even enough for a hot chocolate.

"What can I get you?" Hannah says, appearing at the table with a pen poised over her notebook.

I let everyone else place their orders first.

"Suzy?" Hannah says.

"Um, a glass of water, please," I mumble.

"Is that all?" Hannah says.

"I thought you'd been dreaming about a hot chocolate?" Danny says. "With cream and marshmallows?"

"Yeah, um, I changed my mind," I shrug, trying to look all casual.

"Liar," Danny says. "Did you forget your purse again?"

"Nope, it's here," I say, showing him. "I'm, uh, a bit broke."

"I'll treat you," Jamie says. His parents run their own

51

design business and are never around, the lucky so and so. They buy Jamie's affection to alleviate their guilt at never seeing him (that's what he says, anyway) so Jamie's always loaded. Fortunately, he's really generous and never minds sharing his cash. "Do you want that hot chocolate?"

"Are you sure?" I ask

"Course," Jamie says.

"And you can share my cake," Danny says. "See what sacrifices I'm prepared to make for you?"

"I appreciate it greatly," I say solemnly. "Thanks, guys."

My friends are officially the greatest ever. Trufax.

"So what are you lot up to this summer?" Hannah says, when she gets back with our drinks and food. "You going away?"

"Chance would be a fine thing," I say.

"Nor us," Millie says.

"We're going to the States in August, but that's forever away," Jamie says, to groans of envy from the rest of us. He is *so* lucky. He's going to Florida with his parents, and they're visiting the theme parks and the Everglades. It sounds *amazing*.

"I'm heading to Cornwall for a bit to stay with Mum," Danny says.

"Sounds good," Hannah says, setting down the drinks and sliding the cakes across the table to us. "Enjoy."

"I can't believe you guys get to go away and we don't," I grumble as I stab a huge chunk of Danny's chocolate cake with my fork. "It's so unfair."

"It's not our fault you're stuck here," Jamie says, sucking half his smoothie in a single gulp. "You guys usually go on holiday, why not this year?"

"Too broke," I say. "The Puttock Emergency Budget plan is still in effect, ergo no Puttock can spend more than ten pence without Dad's express permission. And he says there's no cash for holidays."

"Why aren't you going away, Mills?" Danny asks.

Millie shuffles uncomfortably. "Dad couldn't get the time off."

"He's working loads at the moment, isn't he?" Jamie says.

"He says he needs the extra hours since Mum lost her job."

"Well, that sucks," Jamie says. "No holidays for the girls, then."

"Yeah, and what are we supposed to do while you guys are away?" I say.

"I'm sure you'll think of something to keep yourselves entertained," Danny says, popping a piece of chocolate flake into my mouth. "We won't be gone for long. And we're not going at the same time, anyway."

"I still don't think it's fair," I say.

"Ah, but you get the fun of a sexy Italian staying with you," Jamie says, grinning wolfishly. He dodges out of the way, laughing hard, as Millie aims a thump at his thigh.

"She's not Italian!" Millie reminds him.

"When's she coming?" Danny asks.

"Next week sometime," I say.

We eat. We drink. We chat. Then Danny flips his wrist over to look at his watch. "I need to get back," he says.

"I have to go too," Jamie says. "I'm meeting the lads in the park for a kick-about."

"See you," Millie and I chorus as the boys clatter out of the café.

"Want to come back to mine and hang out?" I ask Millie.

"Sure," she says. "I'll text Mum and tell her to pick me up from there instead."

Millie produces a pack of jelly babies and starts munching away happily as we walk back. As we approach my house, I stare in confusion at the parking space to the side of it.

Because there's a massive caravan sitting on it.

And I mean *massive*.

"I didn't know you had a caravan," Millie says.

"We don't," I say. "I have no idea what that's doing there."

When I open the front door, I can hear Harry screaming

with excitement as she runs out of the kitchen to greet us. This in itself is pretty alarming, as Harry is *never* pleased I'm around.

"Did you see it, Suzy?" she whoops.

"The caravan? I could hardly miss it, could I? Did you pull it out of that magic hat of yours or something?"

"Ha ha," Harry says. "No. It's ours!"

"What're you talking about, idiot child? We don't own a caravan."

"We do now, and don't call your sister an idiot," Mum says, following Harry out from the kitchen. "Hi, Millie, good to see you."

"Mum, have you been shopping again? That must've cost a fortune. Dad's going to kill you."

"I didn't buy it. I won it. Can you believe it?"

"You won a *caravan*?"

Mum nods happily. "They delivered it about ten minutes ago. Apparently they rang about it during the week, but I didn't get the message."

"It's not my fault I forgot to tell you," Harry says. "And all they said was they were dropping something off. I didn't know it'd be a caravan, did I?"

"The fact they were calling from Caravans4U might have been enough of a clue for most people, but never mind," Mum says.

"What are we going to do with a caravan?" I ask.

"We're going to go on a wonderful holiday," Mum says, beaming. "Camping is great fun. I used to go all the time with my parents when I was younger."

Am I actually going to be forced to stay in that thing, for days at a time, mere centimetres away from my parents and sisters?

Oh dear Lord. What a horrifying thought.

Outside I hear several cross expletives before Dad charges through the front door.

"Who's left that bloody caravan on the drive?" he fumes. "Can you believe the nerve of some people? A chuffing caravan, of all things. Do you know which of the neighbours it was, Jen?"

"It's ours," Mum says.

"Ours?" Dad says, freezing on the spot. "What are you talking about, ours?"

"I won it!" Mum tells him proudly.

"You won it?" Dad says.

"Yes, from one of my magazines," Mum says.

"So that thing actually belongs to us and we have to keep it?"

"Yes!" Mum says.

"Oh God," Dad groans, rolling his eyes upwards. "What do we want with a caravan, for heaven's sake? Can you send it back? No, wait. I suppose we could always sell it. The money would come in handy." His face brightens. "I'll go and see what kind of price those things go for on eBay."

"Dad, no," Harry says. "I want to keep it."

"I'm not selling it, Chris," Mum says. "Not until we've used it at least once, anyway. Just to try it, and see if we like it. It'll be a cheap holiday. You're the one who's always banging on about us saving money, saying that we can't afford to go anywhere. Well, now we can. And soon."

Dad wanders off, muttering darkly.

"Knock, knock," calls Clare. She walks over to Mum and kisses her cheek. Sometimes it blows my mind that they're such good friends. They're so different.

Clare isn't exactly what you'd call a traditional mother. She's really cool, with cropped-short hair and wears super fash clothes. Each of her ears is pierced a billion times and she accessorises with large funky jewellery and these gorgeous floaty scarves. It's easy to see where Millie's love of colour and fashion come from. She's also got loads of amazing stories about ghosts she's seen *and* reads tarot cards.

I regularly have serious mum-envy.

Clare's usually round and smiley, but looking at her now, she's slimmer than normal. She must be on a diet. And she looks kind of tired, with these bags under her eyes I've not noticed before.

"It's been too long," Mum says, releasing her from the embrace.

"Ah, you know what it's like," Clare says, shaking her head. "I've been job hunting, which is a full-time job in itself."

Mum makes a sympathetic face. "How's it going?"

"Don't ask. The market's completely dead. Sorry I'm early, Millie, but we need to pick up Sophie from her friend's house."

Millie ignores her.

"How's Martin?" Mum asks. "We should meet up soon."

"He's always at work," Clare says, shrugging dismissively. "Anyway, what's new with you? I see you're getting all geared up for a holiday." She nods out of the window. "I didn't know you were caravanners."

"We're not," Mum says. "Well, not yet." She goes into the speech about how she won the caravan, holidays to remember, yada yada.

"You're so lucky," Clare says. "I'd kill for any kind of break at the moment, even one on a campsite."

"Well, why don't you come with us?" Mum says. "The caravan's a six berth, we've got plenty of room. We'd need to put the girls in a tent, but that wouldn't be a problem.

We're not sure when we're going yet – we need to find a campsite – but the offer's there if you want it."

Maybe my sanity can be saved if Millie comes along too. I look over at her, wide-eyed with hope.

"Well, Sophie's going away to summer school for a month, so she wouldn't be coming. And there's no way Martin would take time off," Clare says. "But we could go. What do you think, Millie?"

Millie and I exchange an excited glance.

"I'll chat to Martin, but in principle, yes, that sounds great, thanks," Clare continues. "Right Millie, we need to get going, I want to grab some petrol before we pick up Sophie. I'll ring you later, Jen, to talk through the details."

"Fantastic," says Mum. "We'll have a lovely time. I'm sure Isabella will enjoy it, too. Give her a taste of a traditional British holiday."

Oh yeah. Isabella. I'd forgotten all about her.

"Isabella?" says Clare.

"I'll tell you on the way," Millie says.

As Clare and Millie leave, with Millie promising to call me later to discuss holiday outfits, Dad wanders back, flicking the kettle on.

"Clare's joining us on holiday," Mum calls from the hall.

Dad's face brightens. "Brilliant. That means Martin is coming, right? He'll balance up the male to female ratio somewhat."

"I don't think so," Mum says. "As far as I know, it'll only be Millie and Clare. I don't know about Mark. I'll ask him and Amber when they get back."

Dad swallows as he does the quick calculations in his head. "So I'm going to be on holiday with seven women?" he says weakly. "Seven women and Mark?"

"Absolutely," Mum says. "You'll have a wonderful time."

"Can't I stay at home?" Dad asks. There's excitement in his eyes as he ponders the prospect of time to himself, with nobody bothering him.

"No chance," Mum says firmly. "We need someone to tow the caravan."

CHAPTER FIVE

It's not long until our fate is sealed.

Much internet research and several phone calls later, Mum has booked us into a place called Bluebell Campsite, in west Wales.

I'm not even getting to go in the stupid caravan but will be sleeping under canvas, because Dad said seeing as how he's sharing with Mum, Amber, Mark and Clare – not forgetting Crystal Fairybelle – there was no room for anyone else. Millie's bringing a tent, so we'll share that, and Harry and Isabella can have the awning.

With the climate getting colder and soggier by the day, we're going to freeze to death.

But at least Millie's coming. Silver lining and all that.

"They have professional musicians," reports Harry, returning from her online nosy into where we're going to be staying.

Hmm. Well, I suppose that doesn't sound *too* bad.

I mean, if professional musicians go there, it must be pretty cool, right? Maybe The Drifting will turn up to do an impromptu gig or something.

Yeah, yeah, I know, it's a long shot. But I'm still hopeful.

"Right, we're off to get Isabella from the train station," Mum says.

"Do I have to come?" asks Dad. "I don't need to be there. I'm sure she'd much rather meet you by herself. And the darts is on..." He stares longingly in the direction of the lounge, and the TV.

"You're coming," Mum says. "Anybody else joining us?"

"I'm going for a lie down," Amber says. "I'm not feeling too great."

"Do you need anything?" Mum says. "We can take you back to the hospital if you think something's wrong."

"They said everything was fine when they saw her yesterday. And the day before. And the day before that, too," Dad says.

"I know, but she needs to be careful," Mum says. "It's no trouble to run you back in if you want to be checked over," she tells Amber.

"I'll look after her, don't worry," Mark says, putting a reassuring hand on Amber's back. "She's tired, that's all. The babies were dancing a jig in there all night."

"Go and have a lie down then, it's important you rest,"

Mum says. "Suzy and Harry, you're staying here. Suzy, I want your packing started and your room spotless by the time we get back, with the camp bed made up. Harry, your packing needs doing too."

"My room's tiny," I complain. "There'll be no room with a camp bed in there."

"It's not for long," Mum says. "And there'd be a darn sight more room if you'd tidy it properly. And I mean *properly*. Not shoving everything into the wardrobe and forcing the doors shut. As for your packing, there's a suitcase on our bed you can take."

"And you're only taking one case," Dad says. "I know what you lot are like – clothes for every occasion with a few spares in case. We haven't got room to take everything everyone's ever worn. Are you listening, Suzy?"

"Uh huh," I say, not really listening.

Mum checks the time. "Right, we need to go. Isabella's train is getting in soon."

As Mum hustles Dad out of the door, I huff back up the stairs. Stacked outside is the bedding for Isabella and the camp bed, ready to go into my room next to the desk. Talk about a squash. Isabella won't have any space down there. It feels really weird, thinking about sleeping so close to a complete stranger. I know I've met her before, but it was about a hundred years ago.

My room really is a pigsty. I've got tons of clothes lying everywhere – some waiting to be washed, some waiting to be packed – plus there are bowls, mugs, a pile of sweet wrappers from the last time Millie was here and about six half-finished books littering every available surface.

My phone goes with a text from Millie.

> **12 skirts, 8 jeans and 5 shorts shd b enuf, yes?**
> **& 9 pairs shoes? All my tops, obvs. She there**
> **yet?**

I tap back:

> **Def enuf. No. Pars gone to get her.**

I lie on my bed to flick through a magazine for a bit, then decide I may as well get on with the tidying. Mum will only go nuts if I don't, and who needs the hassle? I chuck all my dirty clothes into the corner of the room, before grabbing the suitcase from Mum and Dad's room, and dumping it onto the bed.

We're going for ten days. So how many pairs of jeans should I take? Probably best to take them all. And a few pairs of shorts, on the off chance the sun comes out at any point. My leggings – black, navy, brown, grey and charcoal. And then tops, and jumpers because it's guaranteed to be cold, so my snuggly hoody, even if not the most fash, is definitely going in.

Plus I also need my hair-taming equipment (practically

a suitcase's worth by itself) and make-up and jewellery...
Okay, there is no way everything is going to fit into this
ridiculously small case.

I swap it for the larger one and carry on packing.
It's still one case, so Dad can't complain. Swimming
costumes, books, a couple of bags, oh and shoes, mustn't
forget shoes – trainers, trusty Converse, boots, pumps,
a couple of pairs of sandals and flip-flops... That's the
trouble with this stupid British summer, you never know
what the weather's going to be like. You have to take
clothes for every eventuality – rain, shine or hurricane.

Finally I'm done. And actually, it's *a lot* tidier in here,
probably because ninety per cent of everything I own
has been crammed into the case, but never mind. So
now I'll chuck my dirty clothes into the washing basket
and I'll be done.

Oh dear God.

There is a massive, creepy moth nestled on top of my
dirty clothes, giving me the stink eye.

My breathing gets quick and my chest tightens.

I could squish it with a magazine, but it's resting on
a top I don't want covered in moth guts. What if I grab
the clothes and shake them out of the window? Then
the moth will fly off on its merry way and I won't have
to go that near to it.

I just need it out of my room. Now.

It's more scared of you than you are of it, I repeat in my head, not that it helps. As I open the window and see our car pulling up, I realise I need to act fast. I was under strict orders that everything had to be in place before Isabella got back, and the bed still isn't in the room or made up. My eyes flick onto Isabella for a moment, and see that, wow, she's *seriously* pretty.

Actually, no.

She's *stunning.*

Long, dark hair and a gorgeous outfit. But I don't have time to take much in before my attention returns to the problem at hand.

The moth.

I gingerly seize the pile of clothes.

Don't want to get too close... Now, don't start moving, moth. Stay there, nice and still... Oh God, it's flapping!

I shriek and drop the bundle in alarm. The moth flutters back down again. Luckily it's still on the clothes, but now it's hugging my bra and stinky socks. With any luck, it'll die from the toxic fumes.

Nervously, I gather the clothes again and make my way to the window, where I lean out and start to shake them.

Mothy doesn't budge.

I shake harder.

And harder.

Will you just *get off*…

Mum, Dad and Isabella are coming now, walking up the path.

"Suzy?" Mum says, glancing up in bewilderment. "What are you doing?"

I give another violent shake, but it's too hard and the bundle of clothes falls out of my grasp. The moth flies away, the clothes fall through the air, and my bra lands on Isabella's dark head.

She seems seriously unimpressed as my B-cups flap round her cheeks in the breeze.

Way to make a first impression, Suze.

"Um, hi," I say, waving weakly. "Sorry about that."

Isabella mutters something darkly in what I suspect is Italian as she plucks at the bra disdainfully, holding it between her thumb and forefinger while stepping over the dirty socks and pants littering the path.

"You'll have to excuse my daughter," Mum says, grabbing the bra and shoving it into her handbag. "That's Suzy. You'll be sharing her room."

"Really?" Isabella says, sounding deeply unenthusiastic. She stares up at where I'm still hanging out of the window. "I can't wait."

Once Isabella's inside, I quickly start to realise she's one of *those* girls.

A Mulberry girl.

She has that frosty, groomed, detached look about her. She's not the geeky girl from the photo any more. Her hair falls in a lustrous curtain down her back. She's got huge blue eyes, with amazing olive-y coloured skin. She's wearing a dress (a *dress*! As casual wear!) with these gorgeous grey pumps and her luggage has got the Louis Vuitton logo all over it. That can't be genuine... can it? No wonder she was a bit narky at having my cheap and cheerful H&M bra dangling around her chops.

Wow. Do I ever feel inferior now. God knows what she must think of me in my hoody, baggy jeans and scragged-back hair.

How did Mum ever think this was going to work, me and this girl sharing such close quarters? She's coming away on holiday with us and everything.

I suspect Isabella's having the same thoughts.

She's clutching her bag to her chest, staring around warily. Mum mentioned their house being a villa on a lake or something. This place must be a bit of a let-down. It kind of needs redecorating, and some of the carpets are really threadbare, although Mum's tried to cover them up with colourful rugs.

"Make yourself at home, Isabella," Mum says, going to put the kettle on. Dad disappears off into the lounge and soon the sound of the sports channel echoes through the house.

I guess I should say something to her. Try to make friends. Make amends for the bra.

"Did you have a good journey?" I ask.

"I guess," Isabella shrugs.

"Cool. And, um, did you mind travelling by yourself? You weren't worried you'd get lost or anything?"

The thought of travelling all the way to Italy by myself is pretty scary.

Isabella shoots me this look like I'm a complete imbecile. "Nope. I've been travelling alone since I was ten."

"Here's a cuppa for you," Mum says, pressing a mug into Isabella's hands. "I'll shout the other girls. Amber! Harry! Come and meet Isabella, please."

Harry comes clattering into the kitchen.

"Hi," she says. "I'm Harry."

"Hi," Isabella replies.

"Want to see a magic trick?" Harry asks.

"Er, okay," Isabella replies.

"This is my assistant, who'll be helping," says Harry, holding up Hagrid, her pet rat, in her cupped hands.

Hagrid's pink nose twitches eagerly in Isabella's direction.

Isabella squeals and backs away. "Keep that thing away from me. I'm allergic."

"You're allergic to rats?" I ask.

"Yes," Isabella says. And then she sneezes.

It sounds awfully fake to me.

"Isabella, I had no idea, I'm sorry. Harry, put Hagrid back in his cage, please," Mum says.

"But I want to show Isabella my trick..." Harry says.

"Go. Now," Mum says.

Harry sulks away as Amber lumbers in, clutching Crystal Fairybelle.

"Oh, what a gorgeous dog," Isabella says, rushing to stroke the Chihuahua.

"So you're allergic to rats but not dogs? How does that work?" I ask.

"Different kind of fur," Isabella tells me, still fussing over the dog. "She's the cutest. Can I hold her?"

"Sure. Although he's actually a boy." As Amber passes Crystal to Isabella, and they get involved in a long conversation about how he was bought by Mark as a wedding present for Amber, Mum sidles over.

"Is your bedroom tidied?" she whispers.

"Yes," I whisper back.

"And you've put up the bed?"

"I was about to do it when you came back."

"Oh, honestly," Mum sighs in exasperation. "Isabella, do you want to follow me and I'll show you where you're sleeping? We just need to get your bed sorted."

Mum leads us up the stairs, and Isabella stands in the doorway of my bedroom.

"This is a very small room," Isabella says. "There's hardly any space. Isn't there anywhere else I could go?"

"I'm afraid not," Mum says.

"Your house is tiny," Isabella says, matter-of-factly.

Mum's slightly taken aback, but quickly recovers. "I suppose it's a lot smaller than what you're used to. But we're going on holiday in a couple of days so don't worry, you'll only be staying here for a night or two."

Isabella brightens. "A holiday?"

"Yes," Mum says. "I won a caravan, so we're going to a campsite in Wales."

Now Isabella looks confused. "In a caravan?"

"Yes," Mum says. "That one out on the drive." She points out of my window.

"We're staying in *that*? On a *campsite*?" Isabella asks, the colour draining from her face.

It's hard not to laugh at her expression of pure horror.

She's clearly as delighted about the prospect as me. Maybe we've got more in common than I thought.

"Oh no. You're not staying in the caravan," Mum says and Isabella breathes with relief. "You're going to be in the awning," Mum continues, and Isabella freezes.

"Mum didn't say anything about camping," Isabella says carefully. "I think there must be some sort of misunderstanding. Maybe I can go and stay in a hotel or something."

"Don't be silly," Mum says. "You're coming with us and that's that. We can't pack you off to a hotel by yourself, Caro would kill me! We'd love to have you join us."

Isabella glances at me, and I shake my head slightly, rolling my eyes. For a moment, I think I see the start of a smile twitching around her lips.

"Now, let me get your bed set up," Mum says, hauling the camp bed in. She disappears off down the corridor and appears a moment later with a brand new bedding set that she shakes out of its packaging.

"Is that for Isabella?" I ask.

"Yes, and I'm not supposed to be spending any money, so don't tell your father," Mum hisses, shooting me a look that says 'don't discuss this in front of the guest'.

"How come she gets a new duvet cover and I don't?" I ask. "I've been asking for one for ages. Mine has massive holes in since Hagrid ate it."

"You can have this one after Isabella's gone home,"

Mum says. "Now help me put it on, would you?"

"She's got a new duvet too?" I howl indignantly, as Mum removes another plastic wrapper.

"Shhh!" Mum scowls and glances over at Isabella, but she's not listening, she's far too engrossed in checking her phone. "Hagrid ate the spare too and I couldn't put her in half-chewed bedding, could I?"

"You've put me in half-chewed bedding," I point out.

"You know full well that's different," Mum says. "Right, Isabella, here we go. You're all set."

"Thanks," Isabella says. She catches sight of my massive suitcase on the bed and raises an eyebrow. Mum sees what she's looking at and makes a cross noise. "Suzy, that's not the case I left for you. That's the one for me, your father and Harry to share."

"I couldn't fit everything I needed into that other one," I protest.

"Then you're taking too much," Mum says. "Isabella, can you help her? You didn't bring much. Teach Suzy the value of a capsule wardrobe."

As Mum leaves, I turn to Isabella, to see what words of wisdom she'll share about packing, but she's lying down on the bed, iPod out and headphones in, texting.

CHAPTER SIX

When I wake up the next morning, my throat is dry and there's a revolting taste in my mouth. I push myself up from the pillows onto my elbows, and stare down at the floor. Isabella's lying there, wide awake and sending a text message. Annoyingly, she looks as perfect as she did when she arrived, hair flowing over the pillowcase like Sleeping Beauty and her face flawless.

Whereas I'm guaranteed to have crazy bed head and mascara streaked halfway down my cheeks.

"Morning," I say, with a cheery smile. "Sleep okay?"

"Not really. You were snoring," Isabella says.

That explains the grim taste in my mouth, then. I probably slept with it gaping open all night.

"Sorry. Who are you texting?" I ask.

"Uh, just a friend," Isabella replies.

Oh. Clearly she's not up for sharing much personal info just yet. Never mind. We'll get to know each other a bit better soon enough. Today she's off with Mum, who's taking her round Collinsbrooke to show her the sights.

Which will take about five minutes, because all there is to see is the local church, a clock tower and a covered market street.

Mum wanted me to go with them, but I pointed out it was my last day with my boyfriend until we got back from holiday, so I was let off. There was a dodgy moment where it looked like Mum was going to send Isabella to join us, but the need to do something cultural and worthy with our visitor won out.

"Do you want breakfast or something?" I ask.

"I think I'll go and have a shower," Isabella says.

"Go ahead," I tell her. "I'm starving. I need to eat."

The rest of my family are already in the kitchen, Amber eating her usual mountain of food, while Crystal Fairybelle sits under the table. Every now and then, Amber slips pieces of sausage or bacon under the chair.

"That dog will get fat," Dad warns.

"Don't say that," Amber screeches, scooping the dog onto her lap and covering his ears. "You'll give him a complex."

"We don't talk about weight issues in front of the dog," Mark says solemnly.

"Morning," Mum says, spotting me in the doorway as the phone starts ringing.

"Want me to get that?" I say.

"No, I'll go. It might be the campsite."

At the mention of the word campsite, Mark's face crumples. "I can't believe you're going away," he says.

"And I can't believe you're not coming," Amber wails, also starting to cry.

After days and days of painful deliberation, Mark's decided he's not coming with us, as he needs to save his holiday time for after the babies arrive. But Amber needs a break, and Mum wants to keep an eye on her, so they've agreed to be separated.

From the fuss the pair of them are making you think they're about to be parted for all eternity. They haven't stopped crying for days.

As I ponder whether to brave the value cornflakes (which taste of sawdust) or value branflakes (which taste of cardboard), I can hear Mum on the phone.

"Oh hello, Sarah. Everything okay? Aunt Lou well?"

It's not the campsite, then. It's the carer from Aunt Lou's nursing home.

"We did?" Mum says on the phone. "I don't think so. We've got someone staying at the moment. I don't remember saying anything about that. Is Aunt Lou sure?

She is. Right. And she's very upset. Well, that puts me in quite a difficult position... No, I understand it puts you in a difficult position too, I know what she's like. Okay then, we'll be over after lunch. She's expecting us sooner? Right. In that case, we'll see you at about ten. See you then. Bye, Sarah."

She replaces the handset with a sigh so heavy it practically echoes around the hall. As she walks back into the kitchen, Dad puts down his mug with an ominous thud and glowers.

"Don't say it..."

"Aunt Lou's expecting us at the nursing home this morning," Mum says.

Dad groans. "I'm supposed to be helping Ian mend his fence today. We were only there a couple of days ago. You didn't really tell her we'd go, did you?"

Mum shakes her head. "Of course I didn't. I'm supposed to be showing Isabella around this morning. But you know what Aunt Lou's like. She's apparently moaning on to Sarah that her family have abandoned her, nobody comes to see her, and is very distressed. I can't leave her like that."

"She's so manipulative, that woman," Dad says, as he loads his crockery into the dishwasher. "I wish we *could* abandon her, nasty old trout."

"Don't say things like that," Mum protests, but she's laughing. "Yes, she's impossible, but what can we do? Suzy, could you take Isabella out with your friends today and show her around?"

"Do I have to?"

It's not that I don't want to. It's just it's the last time Millie and I are going to get to be with our boyfriends until we get back from holiday.

Which means it's our last time as a foursome for ten whole days.

Anyone else with us would be weird. It wouldn't be the same.

"Can't you take her out with you?" I ask. "I'm sure they'd love her at the nursing home."

"No, we can't," Mum says. "She's a teenage girl. She doesn't want to be hanging around with old people. She'll have a much better time with you and your friends."

"That's so unfair," I mutter, crossly sloshing milk onto my cereal.

"Do you need anything, Isabella?" Mum asks.

I turn to see Isabella standing in the doorway, wrapped in an expensive-looking satin dressing gown with a towel on her head and a fierce scowl on her face.

"Do you have an adaptor for my hairdryer?" she asks.

"No, but you can borrow mine. I'll go and get it for you,"

78

Mum says, steering Isabella from the room. "There's been a bit of a change of plan for today. You're going to be spending the day with Suzy and her friends."

I don't hear Isabella's reply.

Darn you, Aunt Loon, I think. *This is all your fault, you evil old bat.*

As soon as Isabella's finished getting ready and had breakfast, we head off out. While we walk, I've got that horrible prickly feeling of awkwardness and an uncomfortable silence hangs over us. I'm getting the impression that Isabella would rather be anywhere else in the world than hanging out with me and my mates.

"Erm, it's not far to the coffee shop," I say, desperate to make conversation.

Silence.

"Bojangles is great. I think you'll like it," I continue, starting to babble nervously. "It's probably not as nice as the cafés you have in Italy. I expect they have great places there, don't they, with really fancy coffee and stuff, but Bojangles is still pretty cool..." My voice fades away.

This is so totally awkward.

Isabella's only response is to pull her phone out of her bag and scan it. She's permanently attached to the thing.

All the way here she's been sending texts and laughing at secret messages she doesn't want to share.

"There are my friends." I point to where Danny, Millie and Jamie are messing around on the street corner, waiting for us. Jamie's throwing a football at Danny's head. Danny's trying to head it back, but keeps missing.

"Hi, Suze." I see the boys checking Isabella out and trying not to stare. Danny blushes a bit and chews at the corner of his thumb, something he always does when he's nervous.

Yup, Isabella is *seriously* pretty. Even my utterly unobservant boyfriend's noticed.

"This is Isabella," I say, gesturing to her. "Isabella, this is my boyfriend, Danny, my best friend, Millie, and Jamie, who's Millie's boyfriend."

"Hey! And your friend too," Jamie says.

Isabella forces a smile and we all stand around, nobody quite knowing what to say. "Shall we go?" I ask. "That's Bojangles up there, Isabella."

"It's amazing," Millie enthuses. "They do the best cake in the world."

"We hang out there a lot," I explain.

"Are you sure it's open?" Jamie asks. "It's kind of dark."

"Course it is," Millie says confidently, reaching out her hand to push the door. "Bojangles is always open... Oh. It's locked."

"Look, how unobservant are you?" Danny says. "There's a sign up. What does it say?"

"Oh no!" Millie says, reading the notice. "It's from Hannah. She says a pipe burst yesterday, it flooded the café, and now it's closed for renovations. It's going to be shut indefinitely until they get it all sorted. This is the worst news ever!"

"How can it be closed indefinitely?" I say. "It's the *holidays*. Where are we supposed to hang out now?"

We peer through the window. Through the gloom we can just about see inside and it does look a real mess. Half the ceiling has fallen in, and there are water marks up the walls.

"Tastee Burga?" Jamie says hopefully.

"No," I say. "Enough with the Tastee Burga already. How many burgers can one boy eat, anyway?"

"My capacity for meat is all-encompassing," Jamie says proudly.

"You're not kidding," I say.

"There's another coffee place just there," Isabella says, pointing to the sign of a well-known coffee chain.

"We don't go in there," Jamie says. "Millie started boycotting them a couple of months ago."

"What about the park?" I offer.

"The park?" Isabella says, looking up at the ominous

grey clouds above our heads. "Isn't that for kids?"

"Anyone got any better ideas?" I ask.

Nobody has.

So we head to the park, where Millie and I huddle down onto a bench (Isabella refuses to sit on the soggy wood in case she gets her very expensive-looking coat dirty), and Jamie and Danny start messing around with the football again.

"So, are you liking being back in England?" Millie asks Isabella.

Isabella shrugs. "I only just got here. But I have to say, this place is dead."

Millie laughs. "Tell me about it. You're going to London in a couple of weeks, aren't you?"

"Yeah. But I'd much rather be going back to Italy. It's cold here," Isabella says. "Isn't it supposed to be summer?"

We stare at the grey sky. You'd hardly know it was July.

Millie sighs. "Rubbish, isn't it? I've got a ton of new summer clothes I want to wear, but it's too cold."

"I love what you're wearing now," Isabella says.

Is the ice queen thawing? That's the nicest thing I've heard her say since she arrived. Although, to be fair, Millie does look great. She's wearing a gorgeous red pinafore dress with purple pockets over a long-sleeved turquoise T-shirt and zebra print tights. On top she's got her vintage cream mac. I don't know how she does it. Anyone else would look like they randomly grabbed some clothes and threw them on, but Millie's got the confidence to rock any outfit. It's hard not to feel invisible next to her sometimes.

"Thanks," Millie says. "I love your look too. Is it designer?"

"Mmm-hmm," Isabella says, then starts rattling off a list of names. Millie's engrossed, and soon they're jabbering away about clothes.

"She seems nice," Danny whispers, after the boys join us at the bench. "Your text said she was a bit frosty."

"She has been with me," I whisper back.

Wow. Isabella's said more to Millie in the two minutes since they met than she has to me in the whole time since she arrived.

"So what's Italy like?" Jamie asks.

"Pretty. Warmer than here," Isabella says.

"That's not hard, though, is it?" Danny says dryly, having finally worked up the courage to speak to Isabella.

Everyone laughs.

"I've got some photos, if you want to see," Isabella says. She skims past the first photo on her phone with a dismissive, "Ugh. My mum and stepdad. Well, soon to be ex-stepdad. You don't want to see them." She sounds flippant, but I'm sure a flicker of sadness crosses her face.

"Okay, here we go," she says. "This is where I live, although I suppose it's *lived*, now."

When I see the photo, I have to try not to gasp. It's huge. Like, properly, properly massive. Surely they can't own all that building... can they?

"In, like, a flat or something?" Millie says, tentatively.

"Nope," Isabella says. "The whole thing is ours. Well, I say ours, it's my stepdad's, really. It's got, like..." She counts for a moment on her fingers. "Ten bedrooms. I think. But that's only one of our houses. We have another in Rome. But that's just an apartment. Although it's still pretty big, I guess. And we have a holiday place at Lake Como, too."

No wonder she thought our place was tiny. Our entire house is probably the same size as her toilet.

And when she shows us the holiday villa, it's clear why she was horrified at staying in a caravan. The luxury villa is ginormous.

Crikey. Her stepdad must be seriously, seriously loaded.

Then she flicks through a load of photos showing her and her friends, hanging out together, pulling faces at the camera, having a great time. They're all absolutely stunning, like they've wandered off the set of some Californian TV show. The Isabella in these pictures seems like a ton of fun.

Her life is *amazing*.

84

"Are you moving to London for good now?" Millie asks.

Isabella's face darkens. "Yeah. Mum dumped me here while she gets the divorce finalised. She and Luca have been fighting loads."

"That's got to be tough," Millie says.

Isabella shrugs, but her eyes go all watery and she gazes off into the distance for a moment. "It's fine," she says, dismissively. "I don't care."

Millie scooches next to Isabella. "Jelly baby?" she offers.

"Do you speak much Italian then?" Danny asks.

"Course," Isabella says, taking a sweet from Millie's packet. "I've lived there for years."

"Can you say something?" Danny says.

Isabella immediately rattles off a stream of Italian. Why do things always sound so much better in a foreign language? Isabella could be saying she needs to pee really badly but it sounds soooo sexy.

The boys are staring in awe, their tongues practically hanging out.

"It's way cool you can do that. I'm rubbish at languages," Danny says.

"I'm sure you're not that bad," Isabella says. "I could teach you some Italian, if you like?"

Danny pushes his fringe back sheepishly and smiles

the slow smile that makes my tummy flip over. Only it's not directed at me. He's smiling at Isabella.

Wait a minute. Exactly what's going on here? Are they flirting?

"Uh oh. Trouble at twelve o'clock," Jamie mutters. "Don't all look," he says, as we turn around.

When I do, my heart sinks.

It's Jade and Kara.

My nemesis. Or is it nemisi, when there are two of them? I never really understood that cactus, cacti thing. Anyway, earlier this year, Danny and I broke up because of this huge misunderstanding, and Jade and Kara were at the centre of it all. They'd bet each other that Jade could go out with Danny for a month. Although they succeeded in splitting us up, we cottoned on to what they were up to and sorted everything out. Jade and Kara weren't best pleased about the whole thing. And let's say they're not exactly people you want to be on the wrong side of.

Although, now I come to think of it, Isabella would probably get on really well with them. They're much more her type than we are.

As they stalk past, the two girls shoot us dagger-glares that could kill.

"Friends of yours?" Isabella asks.

"Long story," Jamie says.

"It's fair to say they hate us," Millie adds.

"But we don't like them much, either," I say. "They're kind of evil."

My phone bing-bongs with a text, and when I check the message, I see it's from Mum.

Home. Now. Packing.

Ugh, that woman is such a snorefest.

"We need to leave," I say to Isabella. "I promised Mum I'd be home in time to finish my packing."

Isabella huffs.

"I need to go too," Millie says, looking stricken. "Oh, you guys, I can't believe this is the last time we're all going to hang out together for ages."

"Look on the bright side, at least you're getting a holiday," Jamie says, as he sweeps Millie into a huge, enveloping hug.

Danny shuffles his feet awkwardly. He's got a bit of a thing about displaying affection in public. He's loads better than he used to be, but he's still kind of weird about it, especially with someone like Isabella watching him.

"You are coming over to say goodbye tomorrow, aren't you? Millie says. She's clinging to Jamie like he's her lifeboat on a sinking ship.

"Sure," Jamie says. "But you're not going away for that long."

"It's forever," Millie wails dramatically.

"It'll go really quickly, you'll see," Jamie says.

"I suppose you're right," Millie says, cheering up. Typical Millie. She's never down for long.

"Bye, Suze," Danny says. He leans over to give me a gentle kiss. His lips are soft against mine, and he tastes of mint. I realise with a pang how much I'm going to miss him until we get back.

"You will text me while we're away?" I say.

"Course," Danny says. "And I'll email you. Every day. But I'll see you tomorrow."

He gives me a quick hug, and another kiss on the cheek, and I'm trying not to cry, because I don't want Isabella to think I'm pathetic.

"Come on, Suze," Millie says, swinging one arm around my shoulder, and the other around Isabella as we wave goodbye to the boys and they head off out of the other exit. "I guess it's like Jamie said. At least we're getting a holiday. We're going to have a great time."

I'm not convinced. And somehow, I don't think Isabella is, either.

CHAPTER SEVEN

Mum wakes everyone up at 6 a.m. with a cheery, "Holiday time!" bellowed into our bedrooms. Apparently we need to leave early to beat the traffic, and 'make the most of the day'. Everyone's grumpy and bleary-eyed as we head downstairs for breakfast.

"Are we all excited?" Mum says, buttering a huge stack of toast and sliding it into the middle of the table. "We just need to finish packing the car before Clare and Millie get here."

"Where's Amber?" Dad asks.

"Upstairs, with Mark," Mum says. "She'll be down in a minute."

"And where are Millie and Clare?" Dad asks, pacing agitatedly. "They should be here already. We're going to be late."

"Calm down, we've got plenty of time," Mum says,

then clocks Isabella screwing her nose up at the toast. "What's the matter?"

"Do you have anything else I could eat?" she asks. "Like, maybe a croissant, or a pastry?"

"Um, no, sorry, I'm afraid not," Mum says.

"In that case, I think I'll just have an espresso, please," Isabella asks, oblivious to the looks we're all shooting her. "Where's the coffee machine? I haven't seen it yet."

Mum laughs awkwardly. "Sorry, we don't have one. You'll have to have the instant you've been drinking since you got here."

Isabella makes a face like Mum's suggested she drink her own urine.

Mum puts the butter away and adds the cool box to the huge stack of food bags she's packed, which are piled next to the door waiting to go into the caravan.

"Don't they have supermarkets where we're going?" says Dad.

"They do, but the campsite is about twenty minutes from the nearest village," Mum explains, grabbing a jar of jam from the cupboard. She hesitates for a moment before also selecting honey, Marmite, peanut butter and marmalade.

"Is there anything actually left in the cupboards?" Dad asks, pulling open one of the cabinets. It's empty apart from Harry's wand.

"Hey, that's mine," Harry says. "I wondered where that had gone. Did you put it there?" she asks me suspiciously.

I shrug, innocently.

I totally did.

"Just how much have you packed?" Dad asks. "Everything in the kitchen?"

"It's good to be prepared," Mum says. "And there's no point buying things down there when we've got it all here. You're the one always banging on about saving money. Go and put the food in the caravan."

"Clare and Millie have arrived," Dad says, staggering under the weight of the bags. "At last. Only an hour late."

"Sorry. Blimey, how long are we going away for?" Clare laughs, as Dad heaves the multitude of carrier bags down the path.

"Don't ask," Dad calls over his shoulder. "Is Martin not coming to see you off?"

Millie inhales sharply and Clare shakes her head with this weird expression on her face.

"No. We said goodbye at the house. Anything I can do?"

"Give me a hand getting the duvets off the beds and sticking them in the caravan?" Mum says. "Then I think we're pretty much there."

"I packed a whole case of jelly babies," Millie tells me, patting her bag protectively. "I didn't know if you could get them abroad."

"Mills, we're going to *Wales*," I say.

"Abroad," Millie says firmly. "We're crossing a border and the signs are all in foreign. I've seen it on TV. It's best to be on the safe side."

Upstairs comes the sound of a loud wail, followed by sobbing.

"What's that?" Millie asks.

"Mark. Still crying because Amber's going away."

Millie snorts as Mark and Amber walk into the kitchen, holding hands tightly. They're both puffy-eyed and red-cheeked.

"God, I thought we were bad leaving the boys yesterday," I mutter to Millie. "We've got nothing on these two. Hey, speaking of the boys, there they are," I say, spotting them out of the window. They chat with Dad for a moment, then head inside.

It's getting pretty packed in this kitchen, what with all of us and the luggage. There's hardly any room to move.

"Danny, Danny, watch my magic trick I've been practising," Harry says. My sister adores my boyfriend. Given the opportunity, she'd swap me for him in a heartbeat. She produces a pack of cards. "Pick one."

Danny does as he's told.

"Look at it and then put it back," Harry says. "Don't show me. I'll tap the pack with my wand like this, throw them at the fridge, and your card should stick to the door…"

Harry hurls the cards at the fridge and, surprise, surprise, they all fall to the floor.

"Oh," says Harry. "I don't understand why it didn't work. Was this your card?" She picks the top card off the pile and shows it to Danny hopefully.

"'Fraid not," Danny tells her, shaking his head. "Keep practising."

"Nobody told me that damn dog was coming." Dad storms back inside. "Clare, what's Murphy doing in the back of your car? Please tell me you're dropping him off at the kennels."

"That dog's *massive*," Isabella says, peering outside.

She's not wrong. Murphy's the size of a small horse. He's also insane. A giant bundle of crazy mutt. Millie absolutely adores him, but the rest of us? Not so much.

The thought of him, and a tent, and small enclosed spaces… Oh good Lord.

This is never going to end well. They can't be bringing him… Can they?

"He's coming," Clare confirms, and the whole

room groans in unison. "Blame Millie, not me," she says, holding up her hands in protest. "I'd have happily left him at home."

"Dad's working so much and Sophie's at summer school and I couldn't put him in kennels," Millie says, tears brimming in her eyes. "I just couldn't do it to him. He'll be fine with us, he'll behave, I promise. I didn't want him to be left behind and lonely…"

She lets out a huge sniff, and Dad looks alarmed. He doesn't handle crying well at the best of times. Mark and Amber's waterworks already have him on edge.

"Please, Mr Puttock," Millie pleads. "Please. Pretty please. He'll be good. Don't make me leave him behind…"

"All right, all right, he can come," Dad says. Millie jumps with joy, then runs over to give him a huge hug. Dad flushes as he awkwardly pats her shoulder.

"But you'll need to keep him under control. At *all* times. I know he has a tendency to be a little, erm, wild."

"I will," Millie promises. "You'll hardly know he's there, I promise."

"Hmm. I'll believe it when I see it," Dad says. "Right, can we have everyone who's coming on this holiday in the cars, please?"

Everyone apart from Mum troops outside. She's still busy running around, unplugging every electrical item in sight, and checking she's locked all of the windows about eighty times.

"Mark's staying in the house," Dad says in exasperation. "He can keep an eye on all this for us."

"I know," Mum says, "but you know what he's like. He's not exactly..." She peers around to make sure Mark and Amber aren't listening. "... *reliable*."

"I call shotgun!" Harry shouts, running to yank open the front passenger door. "See you, Danny," she calls over her shoulder.

"So..." Danny says to me. "I guess you're going."

"I can't believe you're leaving us behind," Jamie says miserably.

"Yeah, well, that makes two of us," I say.

"Suzy, we're going to have a blast," Millie says.

"I suppose we'll have a laugh, won't we, Isabella?" I say, attempting to be friendly and include her in the conversation. She doesn't even look up.

"You've changed your tune from yesterday," Jamie says.

"You know we're going to miss you," Millie says. "But a holiday will be cool. New things to do, new people to meet..."

"You won't talk to any boys, or anything, will you?" Danny asks nervously.

"Why?" Millie teases. "Worried something will happen?"

"No," Danny says. "It's just... y'know... I..." Then he shrugs and turns red with embarrassment.

"You're going to miss us too, I know," I say.

Danny nods his head as he shoves his hands deep into his pockets and stares at the floor. "Yeah."

"Jen, would you *please* hurry up!" Dad shouts.

"Coming," Mum replies, dashing out with another four carrier bags crammed with food. She carefully locks the door, then immediately reopens it, saying, "I don't think I locked the back door..."

"You did!" everyone says.

"I want to be sure..." And off she disappears again.

Mark pulls Amber close – well, as close as he can in her current state – and then gives her a huge kiss, tongues and everything, which goes on forever. Crystal Fairybelle, squished between them, wriggles and yelps and struggles to get free.

"I'll miss you, Markymoo," Amber says, tears streaming down her cheeks. "I love you. So much."

"I'll miss you too, Ambypamby," Mark says, equally tear-sodden. "And I love you too. And Crystal. And our precious babies. Look after Wolf and Rainbow for me."

"Wolf and Rainbow?" Danny says, incredulously.

"You're not calling the babies that, are you?" Jamie asks.

"Just trying them out," Mark says, pulling a tissue out of his pocket and loudly blowing his nose.

"Look, you two, nobody's dying," Dad says. "Turn off the waterworks, hey? Mark, man up, for God's sake."

"But I'm not going to see my wife for such a long time," Mark replies. "Her, or the bump, or the dog. I'm going to be without my entire family."

"Lucky bugger," Dad mutters. "It's ten days. Ten! It's not long. And those babies aren't going anywhere. Now where's Jen? Jen? Jen! Come on!"

Mum rushes outside. "All fine," she says, then immediately looks worried. "I did shut the bathroom window, didn't I?"

"Yes!" we all shout.

"Maybe I should double-check," Mum says, but Dad grabs her arm.

"Get in the car. The house will be fine. Everyone got everything?"

Dad slams the boot shut, but not before I get a glimpse of Isabella's designer bags nestled next to our battered cases. They look very out of place. In fact, they're probably worth more than the car.

"You won't work too hard, will you, Marky?" Amber says. "And you'll ring me, every day?"

Mark nods. "And you'll ring me too?"

He grabs Amber in another hug and leans his head onto her shoulder. He looks hilarious, leaning over with his bum sticking out to avoid her bump. The two of them stand like that, swaying softly, lost in their own dream world as Dad shakes his head in despair.

"Stop it, Chris, it's sweet," Mum says, swatting at him. "You've forgotten what it's like to be young and in love."

"Hmmm," Dad says. "More like I want to get going. We're going to hit the traffic now."

"Bye, then," Jamie says, pulling Millie close for a cuddle. He gives her a kiss before whispering something that makes her giggle. "Love you. See you soon," he says. "Text me later, yeah?"

"Bye," Danny says. "Have a good time. I'll speak to you later."

"Is that all I get?" I say, teasingly.

Danny clears his throat. "Um, no." He leans forward and gives me the quickest kiss possible, turning scarlet again.

From the car, Harry wolf-whistles, and Danny goes even redder as Dad frowns out of the car window.

Sometimes I can't believe he actually gatecrashed my sister's wedding to dedicate a song to me in front of my entire family.

"For the love of God, we're going on a short break, not

moving to flipping Siberia," Dad says. "Break it up, you lot. Now."

Danny leans in close. "Love you. I'll miss you heaps," he whispers in my ear, sending shivers down my back.

"I'll miss you too," I tell him softly, as he drops a kiss onto my forehead.

Dad hoots the horn impatiently, making us jump.

"Harry, get out of the front seat. Amber's going to sit there," Mum says.

"Aw, that's not fair. I called shotgun," Harry whines.

"Shotgun or not, that bump of Amber's will never fit in the back. She needs all the space she can get."

Harry reluctantly surrenders her front seat, muttering darkly while she transfers to the back, and Clare wanders over.

"How are you feeling about the towing?" Clare asks Dad.

"Absolutely fine. It's going to be a breeze," Dad says, not sounding entirely convinced. He glances nervously at the caravan attached to the back of our aging Volvo, which seems tiny in comparison.

"Fantastic," Clare says. "Right, who's going in front? Have you got satnav?"

"Satnav?" Dad scoffs. "Who needs satnav? I've got an excellent sense of direction. I've studied the maps and know exactly where we're going. Why don't I go in front, because I'll probably be a bit slower than you, and we don't want to lose each other?"

"Sure," says Clare, shrugging. "Whatever you want to do. Who's coming with us? Suzy? Isabella?"

Isabella takes one look at the caravan, registers Dad's apprehensive look, and her sense of survival clearly kicks in. "We'll come with you," she says.

"Do you want the front or the back seat?" I offer, kindly.

"I'll go in the front," Isabella says, hopping into the MPV's passenger seat.

"Okay, I'll get in the back with you, Mills," I say.

Clare peers into the car. "I'm really sorry, but I'd forgotten I dumped all our stuff in the back. We've not got much boot space because of Murphy. I'm not sure there's going to be enough room for both of you..."

"Couldn't we rearrange it a bit?" I ask. "Your car's massive. I'm sure if we jiggle some things around I'll fit."

"Suzy, get in, we need to leave," Dad bellows, revving the engine.

"I'll see you when we get there," Millie says. "Sorry, Suze."

Despondently, I trudge over and get into the car with the rest of my family. I'm squished in the middle between Mum and Harry.

"Ugh. It's raining," Harry says as we wave goodbye to Mark, Jamie and Danny.

Dad drives off nervously, the caravan snaking dangerously behind us.

Something tells me this is going to be one long journey.

CHAPTER EIGHT

"Are you ever going to go at more than twenty miles per hour, Dad?" Harry asks, peering at the speedometer.

"Shhh," Dad says, straining to see out of the windscreen. The rain is lashing down, like someone's chucking a bucket of water at the car over and over again.

"Harry, don't be so distracting," Mum says. "Can't you see Dad's concentrating?"

"But it's going to be dark by the time we get there," Harry says. "And I'm bored. I've been sitting in this car so long the blood's stopped flowing into my bum."

For once, Harry is right. This journey is taking forever. Six hours and counting. We were supposed to be there for lunch. It's now approaching teatime.

Turns out, towing a caravan is not Dad's forte. After we set off, every time we picked up speed the caravan juddered and shook, making Dad turn all kinds of pale, so he immediately slowed down again. When we got onto the motorway, things got even worse. He stayed in the slow lane, but lorries kept overtaking us and every time they did, the caravan weaved and wobbled worryingly, shaking the entire car, and causing Dad to curse violently. I had to put my hands over Harry's ears for a whole minute at one point. Mum had her hands over mine.

Dad's so shaken we've had to stop at every other service station on the way for a cup of tea and a soothing biscuit, and so that Mum can issue words of encouragement to keep him going. Any service station he didn't feel the need to stop at, Amber did, because she needs to pee all of the flipping time. And now we're off the motorway, somewhere in mid-Wales, on the tiniest, windiest roads I've ever seen, and any minute now I think Dad's going to start hyperventilating.

As if all that wasn't bad enough, I suspect we're lost. Amber's a terrible map-reader and Dad's sense of direction abandoned him somewhere off the M5.

Not that he'll admit it, of course. No way.

"Keep that rat on your side," I say to Harry as she lifts a box up to examine Hagrid.

Several hours into the journey, we discovered Harry had snuck Hagrid into the car under her jumper, but has no cage or anything for him. The rat's currently residing in a Tupperware box with one corner of the lid left open so he can breathe.

"Do you think he's all right?" Harry says anxiously.

"He's stuck in a plastic box, what do you think?" Mum says. "Honestly, Harry, I don't know what you were doing, bringing him along. We told you not to. Mark said he was perfectly happy to look after him."

"I'd have missed him," Harry says. "He's happier when he's with me. And how am I meant to do magic without my assistant?"

"I don't know where we're going to keep him," Mum says. "He can't live in that box. We'll have to go and find a pet shop, I suppose, and get him a new cage."

"Will you lot be quiet?" says Dad. "Amber, we're coming up to a crossroads. It seems horribly familiar. Weren't we here earlier?"

Amber doesn't answer.

"Amber, which way do I need to go? Amber? AMBER?"

Amber sniffs loudly. "Hmm? I was thinking about Mark..." Tears start gushing down her cheeks again.

"Oh, for heaven's sake." Dad pulls over and grabs the map book. Good job these lanes are deserted.

"While we're stopped, I'm going to go to the loo," Amber says, inhaling in deep, gulpy breaths. "Look away, everyone, I'm nipping behind that hedge. Pass the brolly, Mum."

Dad's still trying to work out which way to go when Clare appears at our window, her mac pulled tightly around her face.

"Everything okay?" she says, swiping away the rain that's dripping off the end of her nose. "We were here earlier. We seem to have come in a big loop."

"It's Amber," Mum says. "A few minor issues with the map-reading. She's missing Mark so much she's finding it hard to concentrate."

"Well, why don't you let me go in front?" Clare says. "We're nearly there. If you give me the postcode, I'll stick it into the satnav."

Dad's shoulders stiffen. "You've got satnav? Why didn't you say?"

"Because you said you knew where you were going and Jen told me you hated satnavs," Clare says. "Plus, you thought it wouldn't be that much further. But as that was an hour and a half ago, it might be a good idea if you follow us for this last bit."

There's a sharp intake of breath from Mum at this blatant disregard of Dad's ability to get us to our destination.

"I know where I'm going," Dad blusters. "Get back in your car and keep following us."

"Really?" Clare says.

"Yes!" Dad says.

As soon as Amber's safely back in the car, still sobbing, Dad pulls away. But when we arrive back at the crossroads for a third time, Dad admits defeat and gestures for Clare to pass. She gives a cheery toot of the horn, Dad snarls, and then we're on the move again.

Soon Dad's having to drive faster than he's comfortable with to keep Clare in sight, knuckles white as he grips the steering wheel to navigate through the narrow, windy roads.

"I hate this damn caravan," he mutters through gritted teeth as a gust of wind buffets us and we all squeal with fear.

"It'll be worth it when we get there. We'll have a wonderful time," Mum says. "I'm sure it can't be that much further. Look, Clare's indicating. We're here!"

We all sit upright, keen to see the place we're going to be staying. Down some kind of dirt track, and then we've arrived at a wooden hut. I can't see the campsite itself – there's a gateway shielded by overhanging trees blocking the view, but it must be in there.

A man with long hair and wafty grey beard comes out and Clare waves him over to us. He's wearing felt trousers, with a patchwork waistcoat over a white shirt, underneath his raincoat.

"Hello there," he says with a broad smile. "Lovely to meet you. You're a bit later than you said you'd be. Probably down to the wonderful weather, isn't it?" He chuckles, but then sees Dad's stony face. "Ah, not impressed with the rain, I see. Anyway, I'm Devon. You find us okay?"

"Devon?" Harry says. "Like the place?"

"Yeah, no problems," lies Dad, practically limp with relief that we've finally arrived in one piece. He's obviously not feeling his normal self. He's let the mention of Devon's name slide without comment.

"Here's your map. Park your caravan where you can find a space in the field," Devon says, handing over a bundle of papers. "There are plenty of fire pits around, all we ask is that you don't use kindling from the woods. We sell wood – help yourself and put some money in the honesty box," he continues in his gentle Welsh accent. "We also sell fresh bread, milk and eggs in our shop over there. There's information on the nearest shops in that pack I've given you. Mobile reception is a bit patchy, but you can use the payphone in the shop if you need to. We hire bikes, if that takes your fancy. Just come and talk to me and I'll get you set up with wheels and helmets. What else do I need to tell you... Oh yes, we have entertainment some nights in the marquee, so keep an eye on the noticeboard for details of what's going on. Give me a shout if I can help you with anything. Enjoy your stay!"

Hmm. What was that about mobile reception? That didn't sound good.

But the entertainment he mentioned, that'll be the professional musicians. Excellent. Although it's a bit odd they're performing in a tent, isn't it? Anyway, I'm sure it'll be great. Like those exclusive intimate gigs you never hear happened until afterwards. Oooh, I can't wait.

"Where's your internet café?" I ask, leaning forward between the two front seats.

Devon laughs. "We don't have one."

Say *what* now?

"People are usually here because they like to get away from it all," he continues.

Really? Who wants to get away from their email and their internet? Are they mad?

"Thanks very much," Dad says, as Devon goes over to unhook the piece of rope holding the gate shut. As we follow Clare in, I'm eager to see what the campsite's going to be like. But all I can see in front of me is a huge field, rimmed with hedges.

It actually is just a field, with a wooden building in the middle. Scattered around the field are tents and caravans, and at one end there's a big multi-coloured marquee.

"Well, this can't be the right place," I say. "It must be the basic level camping. Where's the bit we're staying in?"

"This is the campsite," Mum says. "What were you expecting?"

"Something better than this," I mutter. "And what's that?" I point with apprehension to the hut in the middle of the field.

"Looks like the toilet and shower block to me," Mum says.

You. Are. Freaking. Kidding. Me.

It's like something from a prison. There's no way on this earth I'm going in there. And just one block? For the WHOLE campsite?

I'd pay a lot of money to see Isabella's face right now.

"If that's the toilet, I'm going in," Amber says. "Let me out, Dad."

"Again?" Dad shakes his head. "You only went five minutes ago."

"You try having two people kicking your bladder and see how you like it," Amber retorts as she slams the car door. She's definitely grumpier with all those hormones sloshing about in her system.

Dad parks the car over in one corner.

"Here looks good to me," he says. "Right, you lot,

macs on and get out. I need to unhook the caravan, then you can all help me move it into position."

Dad wrestles with the tow bar for about half an hour. Eventually he gets the car and caravan separated.

"Right, let's have everyone pushing," Dad says. "Okay, over to the left a bit. On three. One... two... threehhuuuuhhhhhhhh..." With a huge grunt, we all heave at the caravan.

It doesn't move.

"Hmm," Dad says. "Let's try that again..."

I shove as hard as I can, but nothing's happening. Dad's turned purple with exertion and Mum's on the verge of bursting something. Isabella's pushing half-heartedly with one hand, the other clutching her phone again.

"There's no mobile reception," she says.

"What?" Millie and I screech, stopping to grab our phones from our pockets and check the screens. We hold our phones up in the air, waving them around like crazy, twisting and turning, blinking as the rain splashes into our eyes, but there's nothing. Not a single bar.

No. No, no, no. This can't be happening! How am going to keep in contact with Danny if I've got no reception and no email? This is a disaster!

"Mum, we can't use our phones," I say.

"Jen, you have to do something," Isabella pleads.

Mum laughs. "What do you expect me to do? Magic up a phone mast?"

"I'll have a go, if you like," Harry offers.

"Um, I don't think you understand," Isabella says. "I need my mobile. I have to contact my friends. And what if there's an emergency? What if Mum needs to get hold of me?"

Mum shrugs. "Caro knows the name of the campsite. I told her before we left. She can phone and leave a message if she needs us. Don't worry. You're on holiday. It's time to relax. Get away from it all. And that includes mobiles. We never had mobiles when we were growing up and we managed fine."

Ugh. What's she like? She has no idea. Of course she didn't have a mobile when she was growing up, the dinosaurs were still roaming then.

"Anyway, there's a payphone you can use," Mum continues.

A payphone? Nobody's used one of those since the dark ages.

Millie and I exchange stricken glances, while Isabella appears to be about to puke.

"What about you, Clare?" I say in a moment of inspired genius. "What if Martin needs to get hold of you?"

Clare's expression freezes for a moment. "I'm sure

he won't. But if he needs to, he can leave a message."

"You know what, let's leave the caravan here," Dad says, giving up on anyone returning to help him. "It doesn't matter that we're so close to the hedge."

"All right," Mum says. "Oh look, here's Amber. You've been a while. And you're looking very pale."

"I'm feeling a bit funny, to be honest," Amber says.

"What's wrong?" Mum says, rushing forward.

"I think it's because I'm missing Mark so much," Amber says, reaching into her bag for her phone. "I'll give him a ring."

"There's no reception," Mum tells her.

"What?" Amber shrieks, and then bursts into more hysterical tears. "How am I meant to talk to my husband? I want to go home. Right now!"

Mum pulls a face at Dad over her shoulder as she leads Amber over to the car to sit down. "There's a payphone, don't worry," I hear Mum say soothingly.

As Dad bustles about trying to set things up, Millie and Isabella are still trying to get signals. Millie's holding her phone in the air while jumping up and down.

"Nothing," she says eventually, surrendering with a sigh.

"This is like living in the Stone Age or something," I say. "How do my parents expect us to survive in these circumstances?"

Millie laughs. "It'll be fine. There are phones. Retro old-school-type ones. Anyone fancy exploring?"

Isabella shakes her head. "I think I've seen all I need to."

CHAPTER NINE

"Got him," Millie says, breathing heavily as she joins us in the awning. She's soaking wet, and clutching a downcast Murphy by the collar. He ran off about twenty minutes ago, and has been circling the camping field at speed, barking ecstatically and ignoring all shouts to return.

"You said he'd be kept under control," Dad says darkly.

"He'll be good, don't worry," Millie replies. "He just got a bit overexcited after being in the car so long and wanted to stretch his legs. It won't happen again."

"Does it always rain like this?" Isabella says, wrinkling her nose distastefully. "At home I would be sunbathing by the pool. Does this place even *have* a pool?"

"The weather's the fun of a British summer," Mum says. "You never know what you're going to get. You watch, it'll be boiling tomorrow."

"Really?" Isabella says. "And then we can find the pool?"

"I wouldn't hold your breath on either count," I mutter.

114

Isabella frowns in my direction.

"Well, at least the caravan's in place and we're all set up now," Mum says. She's determined to remain optimistic, despite everyone being cold and wet and cross. "Would anyone like a cuppa?"

A few minutes later there's a shout from inside the caravan. "Chris, where's the bag with all the mugs, glasses and plates in?" she asks.

"I put everything you gave me into the caravan," Dad shouts back. "It should be there somewhere."

"I'm sure I gave it to you…" we hear Mum say, then the sound of doors and drawers being opened and closed. Eventually she sticks her head out.

"I can't find the mugs. I think they might have been left behind."

Everyone groans. A vision of Bojangles' steaming hot chocolate pops into my head, and my mouth waters. I would kill for one of those right now.

"I can find teabags, milk, coffee and sugar, but nothing to put them in," Mum continues. "We'll have to go out and get some cheap crockery in the morning, Chris."

"You packed half the house and now we don't even have a spoon to our name?"

"I need a cage for Hagrid, so we have to go out to get that, anyway," Harry reminds them both.

Hagrid's been set up in a cardboard box in the corner of the awning. Isabella's eyes keep flicking in that direction.

"There you are," Mum says. "We can pick up some new crockery at the same time."

"And there was me thinking this was supposed to be a bargain holiday," mutters Dad.

"We can pick up plastic bits and pieces cheaply enough from a supermarket," Mum says.

"Are we seriously not supposed to drink anything until we buy some mugs?" Dad asks.

"Stop being so difficult," Mum says. "Of course you can drink. Just not a hot drink. You've got a water bottle, haven't you? Now, let's get the beds set up. That'll warm us up if we can't have tea."

"Where am I sleeping?" asks Harry.

"Well, Clare's bought a tent, and there's room in the awning, so you four can work it out between you. Dad and I are in the caravan with Clare and Amber," Mum says.

"Goodo," Dad says.

"And don't forget Crystal Fairybelle," Amber adds. "She has to sleep with me, in my bed. She's my only reminder of Mark now."

"He's not dead!" Dad says in exasperation. "Stop talking like he is. We're only away for a few days, not a lifetime."

"Sorry," Amber sniffs. "It's just, I miss him so much.

It feels like forever since I saw him."

"Come on now, love," Mum says. "We'll have a great time, and the days will fly by. You'll see him again soon."

Amber nods bravely.

"We should try to put your tent up before it starts pouring again," Clare says to Millie.

"Can I sleep in the tent with you, Millie?" Isabella asks quickly.

I stare at her. Um, say what now? Millie's *my* best friend. Obviously *I'm* going to be sleeping in the tent with her. What's going on here?

Millie shoots me a glance. "Erm... I kind of thought I'd be with Suze."

"Oh. Right. Never mind," Isabella says. "We had such a laugh in the car on the way down here, I hoped..."

I'd wanted to share with Millie by myself, but don't want to be mean and have Isabella feel pushed out. I can completely understand why she doesn't want to share with Harry. Who would?

"I'm sure we can all fit," I say generously. "We could squish the airbeds together."

"Not with Murphy coming in, too," Millie says.

Isabella looks horrified. Hah. Now she's torn. Risk being stuck in the awning with Harry, or in the tent with Millie and sleep in close proximity to her insane mutt? And Murphy trumps like anything in his sleep. I've spent enough sleepovers at Millie's house to know that canine is seriously toxic.

"I'm very sorry, but I don't think I can share a tent with Suzy," Isabella says. "It's her snoring... I'll never get any sleep."

Ouch. That's harsh.

"That's okay," I shrug. "I'll share with Millie, in the tent out there. You can have the awning, with Harry. You won't hear my snoring from here."

Hah. That's you outsmarted.

Isabella looks around her. "In here? Er, no, I don't think that's going to work. I'm really sorry." She smiles prettily, then forces another sneeze. "But there's no way I can share with that rat. I've got allergies, remember?"

Gnargh! She is *such* a faker! She's totally using this made-up allergy thing to get her own way.

"Murphy's in with Millie," I point out. "Won't that upset your allergies?"

"Nope," Isabella says. "Only small mammals. I'm fine with dogs."

Oh, come *on*. Are people seriously buying this? How can she be allergic to a tiny little rat but not a massive mutt? I'm not convinced she even has an allergy. Seems to me she doesn't want to sleep in this awning.

"I'm sorry, Suzy, but if Isabella can't sleep when you're snoring nearby, and Hagrid's going to make her ill, she's going to have to go in the tent with Millie," Mum says.

"But——" I start.

"Isabella, you go with Millie," Mum says. "We can revisit the situation in a few days, and change around then if we need to. But right now, let's get these tents up, and some food on. The sun's coming out, look."

Isabella and Millie smile at each other and I get a funny pang rippling through my body. Part of me wants to stamp my feet and shout, 'But Millie's *my* friend!'

Why do I have to be stuck in the stupid awning with Harry?

Then I have a brainwave.

"Can't Hagrid go in the caravan with you?" I say. "Then I can share with Millie, and Isabella can share with Harry."

"Nooooo!" wails Harry. "Hagrid has to stay with me. He has to."

"And if you think I'm sleeping in with that damn rat keeping me awake all night you've got another think coming," Dad says. "We've already got the dog in there."

"In that case, I don't think there's anything else we can do," Mum says, apologetically. "Millie and Isabella are in the tent with Murphy, and Harry and Suzy are in the awning. Here are your airbeds, girls. Chris, where did you put the foot pump?"

"Foot pump?" Dad says. "I haven't seen the foot pump."

"You must have done," Mum said. "It was by the door, next to the bag of crockery…" Her voice trails off.

"Aw, Mum, don't tell me we forgot that too," says Harry.

Mum glances at Dad. "I haven't seen the foot pump," he says again.

"Clare? I don't suppose you bought one along, did you?"

"'Fraid not," Clare says. "I assumed you guys would have one. Sorry."

"Right. You lot had better get blowing, then," Dad says.

Inflating the airbeds takes forever, and requires all of us, plus several more lungs than we have access too.

"After all that, I need a beer," Dad says. "At least we remembered those." He grabs a can and pops it open, taking a grateful sip.

"Mum, I'm starving," Harry says.

Actually, now she mentions it, I'm starving too.

"Well, I'd brought pasta for tonight, but that's going to be a bit tricky without plates," Mum says. "So sandwiches it is, I guess. Harry, go and ask Devon if he's got any crockery and cutlery he could let us borrow for the night."

Harry whines for a bit, but then goes off and returns

a short time later clutching a cup, a plate, a fork, a knife and a spoon.

"That's all he could spare?" Dad says. "There are eight of us! What are we meant to do, share?"

"He said he'd leant out all his spares and they never come back," Harry says with a shrug. "This was all he had left. Sorry. Millie, he also said Murphy had to stay on the lead at all times."

"He will, he will," Millie says, patting Murphy's furry head.

If I didn't know better, I'd swear Murphy was smirking.

CHAPTER TEN

Later that evening, Millie and I are piling on macs, wellies and various other waterproofs to trudge across the field and ring the boys.

"It's still pouring," I say, peering out into the gloom.

"It's only a bit of rain, Suze," Millie says.

"Rain that will cause my hair to go into frizz overdrive," I point out. I tug the toggles of my hood together tightly, and make sure every single curl is carefully tucked underneath. "And that's no normal rain. It's like a monsoon or something. None of this would be a problem if we'd actually come to somewhere with flipping mobile reception. I hope Danny and Jamie appreciate this."

"Think of it as an adventure," Millie says. "Are you coming?" she asks Isabella.

"No chance," Isabella says, looking up from her deckchair. She's been engrossed in *Vogue* for the past half hour.

"Don't blame you," Millie says. "We won't be long. And

then I want to have a look at that mag with you."

Ugh. I don't know how anyone can read *Vogue*. It's so freaking dull. Half of it is adverts and the other half is stick insects modelling clothes that nobody can afford.

Well. Having seen a glimpse of Isabella's life from her photos, maybe *she* can.

Holding hands, Millie and I run squealing into the rain. Mills does a quick detour to knock on the window of the car boot and blow Murphy a kiss. He's been banished there after eating both of Dad's trainers.

"Do you even know how to use one of these things?" Millie asks, poking at the payphone in the shop suspiciously with her finger.

I drop some money into the phone and dial Danny's number. It rings a couple of times before he answers.

"Hello?"

"Hi, it's me," I say.

"Who?"

"Me!" I say again.

"Um, I'm sorry, I think you've got the wrong person."

And then I realise. He doesn't know who I am!

Okay, it's not my usual number, but I'm a teeny bit hurt he didn't recognise my voice. I've only been gone since this morning and it's like he's forgotten me already.

"It's Suzy," I say.

"Oh, Suze, hi," Danny says. "I'm sorry. What's up with your mobile? You lost it again?"

"No mobile reception here," I say. "Ringing from a payphone."

"Bummer. So how is it there? Nice campsite?"

"Wet. Very, very wet. How's it going with you? You miss me?"

"Course," Danny says. "Yeah, all right mate, I'm coming," he says to someone in the background.

"You hanging with Jamie?" I ask.

"Yeah. We're in Bojangles."

"Bojangles?" I say, confused. "Isn't it shut?"

"Ha, ha, oh yeah," Danny says hastily. "Um, I meant Tastee Burga."

How on earth did he manage to get those two places confused?

"Suze, I'm really sorry, but my battery's about to die."

All hopes of a long chat evaporate in a flash.

"Oh," I say, trying to hide my disappointment. "Before you go, we're going to have to sort out a time to talk tomorrow, okay? Now we're going to have to use this payphone we'll need to plan a bit better."

"Yeah, sure. I don't really know what I'm going to be up to. So whenever will be fine. I've really got to go. Miss you, okay? Speak tomorrow."

"Bye…" I say, and then the phone line goes dead.

Well, that was all kinds of weird.

Millie rings Jamie, but she's not on the phone to him long, either.

"Did Jamie sound a bit… odd to you?" I ask as we head back to the caravan, passing Amber on the way, who's off to call Mark for the fourth time since we arrived.

"Hmm?" Millie says, dodging a puddle. "Odd how?"

"I dunno. Just not saying much. Danny confused Tastee Burga with Bojangles."

"Um, yeah, I suppose now you mention it, he did sound a bit weird."

"What do you think's going on?"

"Going on?" Millie laughs. "Nothing's going on. How paranoid are you? They're probably in the middle of that stupid dilemma game. You know what they're like."

"I guess," I say, as we duck back into the awning.

The next morning we're woken up at the crack of dawn by the sound of Murphy howling from inside Millie's tent. Seems he's no happier about camping than the rest of us.

"I'm *so* sorry, the noise of the rain on the canvas was freaking him out," Millie says apologetically as we stand around in the caravan, yawning and eating our toast.

Only Amber can have cereal, because there's just the one bowl. And she wins because she's pregnant, and luxury muesli was exactly what she was craving.

Convenient, no?

"Never mind," says Mum, who is still determined that we will enjoy caravanning, even if it kills us. "The morning is the best part of the day. This way we get to make the most of our time here."

There's a dismissive grunt from the bed at the far end of the caravan. Dad's refused to get up and is lying with the duvet over his head.

"Mum, I'm getting pains," Amber says, grabbing her tummy with a scared look on her face.

"Are you all right?" Mum says in alarm.

"I'm not sure," Amber says. "It really hurts."

"We should get her to a hospital," Mum says.

"Hospital?" Dad says, his voice muffled. "What for? I'm sure she's fine. She's had this a lot, and every time they've said there's nothing to worry about. She's got a few growing pains, that's all. You had them during your pregnancies, I remember them well. You worried every time then, too, but everything was always fine."

"But I never carried twins," Mum says. "Twins are different. Riskier. We need to get her to a doctor so she can be examined."

126

"But I'm supposed to be resting on holiday," Dad protests. "I'm still hoping for this lot to clear off so I can get some more sleep."

"Why don't you lie down for a bit and see how you feel in half an hour?" Clare says to Amber. "We'll turn the table back into the bed for you, and go and eat in the awning."

For the next thirty minutes, Mum hovers anxiously by Amber, checking her watch constantly.

"How do you feel now?"

"I've still got the pains," Amber says. "I'm scared, Mum."

"Then we're going to the hospital. Chris, get dressed."

"I don't even know where the hospital is," Dad says.

"We'll ask Devon on the way out," Mum says. "Clare, can we borrow your satnav? No arguments from you," she says firmly to Dad. "Clare will keep an eye on things. We'll get crockery and the other bits while we're out. Once the shops open, that is."

"And a new cage for Hagrid?" Harry says. "And some food and bedding and a water bottle?"

"So now we're having to buy a whole new rat start-up kit?" Dad says, as he clambers out of bed. "You're paying us back, kiddo."

"We'll talk about it later," Mum says, pulling the

curtain across so Dad can get dressed. "Right now, let's get Amber seen to. Hurry *up*, Chris. Ready? Then let's go. If we're a while, sort out some food for lunch, would you, Clare?"

"But how will we know what time you'll be back?" Clare calls.

"We'll text you," Mum calls out of the car window.

"There's no reception," we all call after them. I don't think they hear us.

"I'm going to go read my book," Clare tells us. "If you could try not to disturb me for the next half hour or so that would be great. It's got really exciting and I want to find out what happens at the end."

"Are you going to ring Dad today?" Millie asks. "You haven't called him yet, have you?"

"Um, no, not yet," Clare replies. "I'll speak to him later. Why don't you guys go and have a wander around? Get some fresh air. Just don't go too far."

As she closes the door behind her, Millie, Isabella, Harry and I all stare at each other.

"It's not even nine yet," Isabella says. "I'm never up this early. I'm going back to bed."

It's late afternoon when Mum, Dad and Amber finally get back and we've had the most boring first day imaginable,

128

because of the unending rain. We've passed the time playing a billion hands of Uno, which is the only game Mum appears to have bought with us.

Crazy times, people.

"We were starting to get worried," Clare says, as we go out to greet them. "Everything all right?"

"What, you mean apart from having to do a two and a half hour round trip, then sitting in A & E for an hour, only to be seen by a doctor for ten minutes who told us Amber probably has indigestion but needs monitoring for hours just to be sure?" Dad huffs.

"It could have been anything," Mum says, as Amber hefts herself out of the car. "It's better to be safe than sorry where babies are concerned."

"Not to mention having to look all over town for hours trying to find a flipping pet shop, and somewhere to get plastic cutlery and crockery," Dad continues. He's clearly on a roll. "And finding somewhere Amber would agree to eat."

"I didn't know what I wanted," Amber says. "And actually, now I come to think of it, I'm hungry again. And tired. I think I'm going to go and have something to eat, then a sit down."

"You do what you need to, love," Mum says. "It's important you rest."

"I thought of some new names while we were out," Amber says, grabbing a huge bag of crisps from the cupboard. "What do you think of Cloud and Storm? Or Phoenix and Flame? For boys, obviously."

Flame? Is she planning on giving birth to an American wrestler?

"No?" Amber says, crunching disappointedly when nobody responds. "None of them?"

"Any thoughts on what to have for dinner?" Mum asks, diplomatically changing the subject.

"Not yet," Clare says. "We didn't know what time you'd be back, and we didn't have anything to eat with, or off..."

"Let's build a fire and cook something on it," Dad says. "If we start now, we should have a good blaze going for an hour or so when it's dinner time. Did you bring burgers and sausages?"

"I did," Mum says. "And we've got burger buns, and some salad, and now we've even got plastic plates to eat them off..."

"Pah, salad," Dad scoffs. "Who needs lettuce when we've got meat? Right, now we need to gather some wood. Girls, it's stopped raining, so why don't you go out and get some?"

"Er, we've got a perfectly good gas cooker in the caravan," I point out. "We can do the burgers and sausages under the grill in super quick time. What do we need firewood for?"

"Suzy, Suzy, Suzy," Dad says. "We are *camping*. We can cook on gas at home. But here, under the instruction of your mother, we are getting back to nature, and embracing the elements. Therefore, we will cook on fire. For which we need wood."

"Give us some money, then," I say. "They sell it by the entrance."

"Buy it?" Dad says. "We're surrounded by trees. Why would we pay for wood?"

"Um, because the signs all over the place say you're not to collect firewood?" Isabella says.

"And Devon told us not to?" I add.

"Of course he did," Dad says. "But that's because he's onto a nice little earner, isn't he, getting people to buy sticks from him."

"Actually, I think it's something to do with making sure the wood's safe to burn, and maintaining the local ecosystem," Clare tells him.

Dad waves his hand dismissively. "Where do you think Devon gets his wood from, for goodness sake? Man has been collecting wood since time began. That's what trees are there for. Burning."

We all look at him incredulously.

"Well, that and the oxygenating of the planet, or whatever it is those greenies bang on about," Dad says. "Now look. It's getting cold, and I want a campfire and something to eat later. Off you go, girls."

"I don't think so," says Isabella. "I painted my nails earlier. I'm going to read my magazine."

And with that she disappears into her tent, leaving Millie and me staring after her enviously.

"I was about to paint my nails as well," Millie says quickly.

"Yeah, me too," I add.

"Don't even think about it," Mum says.

"I still reckon we should go and buy the wood," Clare says apprehensively. "I've got some cash in my purse."

"Since when have you been such a goody two-shoes?" Dad grins, knowing that's exactly the thing to rile Clare.

"Just go, please, girls," Mum says, as Clare and Dad continue their bickering. "Take Harry with you. And Murphy."

When we pass the marquee there's a hideous noise coming from inside – a couple of guitars and what sounds like a trumpet, accompanied by a strange wailing sound.

Millie and I make faces at each other as Murphy starts to howl in accompaniment. They must be the warm-up act.

"Come on, Murph," Millie says, tugging him towards

the woods. "I can't believe Isabella got out of this. I don't think she's having much fun, do you?"

"Nuh-uh," I say.

"She's really nice, isn't she?" Millie says, as Murphy stops to pee all over a log I'd been about to pick up.

I'll be leaving that one there, then.

"Yeah," I say, trying to summon up some enthusiasm. I mean, sure, she's okay. But *really nice* is pushing it, in my opinion. She's still hardly talking to me. I just don't think she wants to be here.

"Here's some wood," Harry yells from up ahead.

"She's so generous, isn't she?" Millie continues, as Murphy hauls us off in Harry's direction. "She said she'd lend me her clothes. I can't wait to get my hands on her wardrobe."

"Great," I say, still sounding stupidly unenthusiastic even to my own ears.

Does Millie want someone to talk about fashion with? She loves clothes and style, and all that stuff. She gets out of bed twenty minutes early most days to plan her outfits. Whereas I tumble out of bed at the last possible minute and grab whatever's nearest or clean.

Is Isabella the kind of mate Millie wants?

CHAPTER ELEVEN

We quickly gather up as much wood as we can lift. Even Murphy helps, carrying a mouthful of sticks. We should have brought something to put the logs in because they're damp and disgusting and making us filthy. Millie's seriously unimpressed that she's got a moss skidmark down her top. Plus it's starting to get dark, and the woods are kind of creepy.

We dump the logs into the fire pit by the caravan as Dad comes outside.

"What kept you?" Dad asks.

His only reply is three fierce scowls.

"Well, that'll do for starters. Now let's get this fire going," Dad says, ignoring our glares. He then proceeds to try to light the fire, but fails dismally. "Paper. I need some paper. Has anyone got any?"

"Amber bought tons of magazines with her," Harry says.

"Fantastic," Dad says. "She's in the shower, although

134

Lord knows how she's managed to fit. Go and fetch one, would you, please?"

He enthusiastically rips up the magazine Harry returns with and scrumples it up into balls, then spends forever building a kind of wooden tepee over the pile of paper.

"I'm starving," I say. "Are we going to be eating anytime soon?"

"Shhh," he says, flapping a hand at me. He lights the paper, which flares into life, burns brightly for a few moments, and then goes out again, leaving the wood unscathed.

"Okay. Let's try that again..." Dad says.

He repeats this process over and over again, until eventually the fire starts to burn brightly. "We'll wait for the flames to die down to embers, then we'll put the meat on," Dad says.

"Erm, it's kind of smoky, isn't it?" I say, as plumes of black smoke start billowing upwards.

"It's fine," Dad says. "I was a champion boy scout. Legendary fire-building skills. It'll stop in a minute, you'll see."

But it doesn't. The smoke gets worse, thicker and blacker, and is making us cough. The wind is blowing plumes of smoke all over the campsite.

"Devon seems to be coming this way," Isabella says, pointing at the campsite owner, who's striding across the field towards us.

"Maybe we should put the fire out," Clare says.

"Out?" Dad says. "Don't be ridiculous. It's just getting going. Evening, Devon," he calls cheerily, straightening up.

"I see you've got quite a blaze going there," Devon says, nodding at the flames.

"Absolutely," Dad says. "About to cook supper."

"Can I ask what wood you're using?" Devon asks.

"We collected some from the forest," Dad says.

"One of the camp rules is to only use wood you can buy from our shop," Devon says. "The wood from the trees around us isn't treated, so it's very smoky, as you can see. The dampness doesn't help, either. I'm sure you forgot, but I'd appreciate it if you could extinguish your fire immediately,"

"Extinguish it?" Dad says. "But we haven't eaten yet."

"It's the rules," Devon says firmly. "Please put out the fire, or I'm going to have to ask you to leave."

As he turns and walks away, Dad grabs a saucepan of water and extinguishes the fire, muttering darkly as even more smoke billows up and makes him cough furiously. He stares despondently at the plates of raw meat next to him.

"I'll grill those, then, shall I?" Mum asks.

"Anybody want to see this entertainment?" Dad asks, after we've finished tea and we're lolling around the caravan, being bored and refusing Mum's offer of an ultimate champion Uno match.

Millie and I exchange a glance. "We heard them earlier. They sound terrible," she says. "I think I might go to bed."

"Me too," says Amber, opening her eyes. She's been dozing in her deckchair for the last half hour.

"Ugh, well if you're all going," Isabella says. She glances at her watch. "I don't think I've ever been to bed this early before in my life. Especially not on holiday. Often we stay out all night and don't come home until it's light."

"Wow, that sounds amazing," Millie says.

Millie's asking loads of questions about Isabella's life in Italy, which Isabella's happily answering, while Amber grabs her enormous sponge bag and goes into the tiny toilet cubicle in the caravan first. She's in there for ages. Then in goes Isabella, who takes nearly as long. She's followed by Harry. And Millie. Then it's my turn, at which point Dad gets huffy.

"Enough!" he says. "I'm not going through this every night. I want to get in and brush my teeth but you lot are taking forever. As of now, you can use the toilet block for teeth-cleaning and whatever other nonsense you do before you go to bed. And I'm not having you lot traipsing in and out of here all day and night to use the toilet. The toilet is only to be used at night by residents of the caravan."

"Whaaaat?" I say. "You are kidding, right? The toilet is right there." I point at the cubicle. "Why should we have to walk for miles? And it's raining again now — we'll get soaked."

"I don't want you lot waking me up all night long. It's bad enough with Amber peeing every two minutes," Dad says. "Use the toilet block, all right? You can come in and brush your teeth and whatnot now, but after that, none of you lot can use it again. You're barred."

As Millie and Isabella disappear off to their tent, I watch them enviously. A late night chat with Millie sounds really good fun, like having a week-long sleepover. Plus I bet she's bought good snacks and tons of sweets with her. We could eat those and gossip for hours...

But no. Instead I'm stuck in the awning, with my horrible sister and her flipping rat.

And an hour later, I'm still wide awake.

I'm lying here in the pitch black, listening to the rain hammer down on the awning roof.

Next to me, Harry's making snuffly noises in her sleep.

It's pouring out there. Properly pouring.

And all the rain is really making me want to pee.

Really, really badly.

But I don't really want to have to go all the way across the field to use those disgusting toilets. I'll get soaked.

I could sneak into the caravan, I suppose.

Yeah, I'll do that; even though Dad will go nuts if he catches me.

Oh. He's locked us out. Well, that's charming.

I unzip the awning a smidge and peer outside. Uurrrrgh. It's raining SO hard. And the toilet block is miles away. If I go out there my pyjamas will be drenched in seconds, then getting back into bed will be all kinds of gross. And cold. What to do, what to do...

I'm never going to get back to sleep when I need to go so badly.

I could grab the umbrella and pee round the side of the caravan.

I'm just saying, I *could*. Not that I will.

Because I know that's pretty gross.

And I should go over to the toilet block.

But it's so far. And the rain...

Oooh, I really do need to go. There's no way I'll hold it until morning and this rain is showing no sign of stopping.

It's dark. It's late. Nobody's going to see me. I'm going to do it. I'll pop round the side of the caravan, wee, and be back in bed within two minutes.

I'll use the proper facilities next time. Promise.

I wriggle out of my sleeping bag and unzip the awning as quietly as I can, so as not to disturb Harry. She snorts a bit, rolls onto her back and starts snoring at top volume. Nice.

Mum's umbrella is leaning up against the side of the awning, so I put it up and venture out into the darkness. It's seriously wet out here. More like autumn than summer.

I scuttle round to the side of the caravan, and look around furtively. There's nobody to be seen. Somehow I manage to pull down my pyjama bottoms one-handed, and squat down with the umbrella protecting me from most of the rain.

As I start to pee, the relief is immense.

Ahhhh...

And now I'm done. I feel so much better and am heading straight back to bed.

Although... what's that noise? I can hear a rustling. Oh God. What is it? What if it's a bear? No. That's stupid. We don't have wild bears in this country. Or a wolf? I'm sure I heard something about wolves being introduced back into the wild in the UK... Has it happened yet? And was it Wales... or Scotland? I can't remember.

I jump out of my skin as I see a torch coming towards me. A murderer! It's a murderer!

"Hello?" a voice calls softly.

Eeeeeee! My heart's pounding so hard I'm sure everyone in a mile radius must be able to hear it.

If I stay really still, maybe they won't see me. I creep nearer to the caravan wall, intending to press myself up against it and hope for invisibility... but then the torch beam swings onto me. Busted.

So long, cruel world, it's been a blast. Figures I'd spend my last days at this sucky campsite.

I'm about to scream for help, but as I blink, and my eyes adjust to the light, I suddenly realise it's Devon.

I'm pretty sure he's no axe murderer.

He's almost certainly a vegan, for a start.

"Should you be wandering around at night on your own?" Devon says. "It's very late."

"Um, yeah, I'm going back to bed. I needed to go to the— Erm... I needed to stretch my legs," I improvise.

"But it's pouring," Devon says. "I don't want to be too personal, but you weren't going to the toilet, were you? I've caught several people out over the years doing that, because the toilet block is apparently that little bit too far away."

"Ummm..."

"I thought so. There are very strict regulations concerning toilet use," Devon says. "I'm going to have to talk to your parents about this in the morning. In the meantime, please use the appropriate facilities. Good night."

I stare after him until his weedy grey ponytail disappears into the dark.

I bet Isabella wouldn't be caught dead peeing in a field in the middle of the night.

It's just not a Mulberry girl thing.

Sigh. I'm going back to bed.

CHAPTER TWELVE

I wake up to a deafening scream. As everyone rushes outside to see what's happened, Millie races past us, still in her pyjamas.

"Oh God, Murphy, what are you doing?" I hear her wail as she hurtles by.

"He broke into someone's tent and was trying to get into their sleeping bag," Millie explains, when she returns, covered in dew and dragging a sheepish Murphy behind her. "Scared the living daylights out of them."

"Millie, you really have to keep a closer eye on him," Clare says.

"I was asleep!" Millie protests.

"Which I'd still like to be right now," Isabella says.

"How did he get out, anyway?" Mum asks.

"I'd left the zip open at the top to get some air," Millie explains. "Murphy must have stuck his head through the hole and forced it down. Smarter than he looks, obviously."

Hmm. I remain unconvinced about Murphy's intelligence.

"Can we go back to bed now?" Amber says.

Everyone agrees that's a good idea. After a quick snack – I'm always so hungry when I wake up in the morning – I'm cosying up in my sleeping bag and desperately trying to nod off when I feel something on my head.

Something moving.

Huh? What's that?

Admittedly my hair has been getting madder by the day, but this is new…

I gingerly raise my hand to my head where it touches something wet.

And slimy.

Oh my good God. What the flipping flip is that?

I pluck the thing from my hair, then fling it across the tent with a screech when I see what it is.

SLUG! It's a slug! There has been an *actual slug* in my hair while I was sleeping.

Then I see Harry videoing me from the corner of the tent, absolutely cracking up.

"Gotcha," she sniggers.

I storm over and snatch the phone from her hands, deleting the film.

"Suzy, keep the noise down." Dad's irritated voice comes from inside the caravan.

"But Dad, Harry—"

"I don't want to hear it. Go back to sleep."

Gnargh. This is so unfair! Smirking, Harry pokes out her tongue at me, while I disappear back into my sleeping bag and pull it right over my head.

After such an eventful morning, we're only just getting up when Devon appears at the front of the caravan. "Knock, knock," he says, sticking his head through the door.

Oh God. I hoped he wouldn't come. That he'd forgotten, or something.

"Morning," Mum says.

"Cup of tea?" Clare offers.

"No, I'm fine, thank you. Um, I'm afraid I need to talk to you about a rather, ahem, delicate situation," Devon says.

"Is this about the fire?" Dad says. "I did put it out, like you asked."

"No, it's not about the fire," Devon says.

"Is everything okay?" Mum asks. "Come in, please."

"Um, this is a bit awkward. But I was out and about in the field last night, checking there were no foxes on the site, when I met with your daughter in the field. I believe she'd been going to the bathroom behind your caravan," Devon explains.

Oh good Lord. The humiliation.

I sink down into my seat, my face burning.

"Harry," Mum explodes. "What did you think you were doing? There are perfectly good toilets here. What did you do that for?"

"I didn't," Harry says, looking confused.

"Um, it was that girl, there," Devon says, pointing at me.

"Suzy!" Mum exclaims. "What on earth were you thinking?"

I can feel my cheeks burning as everyone stares at me. Isabella's giving me this look like I'm some dog poo she found on the bottom of her shoe. At least Millie seems to think it's funny; she's chewing on her lip and trying not to laugh. Mustn't catch her eye, then, otherwise we'll end up in fits of giggles and that won't help anything.

"It was raining," I mumble. "I didn't want to get wet traipsing all the way across the field. The toilets are gross. I didn't think it would matter. It's Dad's fault, anyway, for not letting us into the caravan."

"It's very unhygienic to use the field as a latrine," Devon says, seriously. "It will attract rats. And our toilets are not 'gross'. They are eco-compost toilets, which are a better option for the environment. Please don't allow your daughter to foul our field again, or I'm going to have to ask you to leave," Devon tells Mum and Dad.

"She won't," Mum says.

"Sorry," I say.

Devon carries on. "While I'm here I also wanted to talk to you about your dog... Not that one," he says, as Amber hugs Crystal protectively to her chest. "The other one. The big one. We've received a few, erm, comments from the other campers. Please see that you keep your dog under control."

"I will. I'm really sorry about this morning. It won't happen again," Millie says. "He'll be good, I promise."

"Good. Now, you're staying over the weekend, aren't you? Will you be joining us for our Saturday night talent show?"

"Talent show?" Dad says.

"Oh yes," Devon says. "It's a monthly thing. We invite everyone staying with us to come and showcase any talents they might have in our marquee. It's a great evening, tons of fun. We always have a fantastic time. You wouldn't believe the skills some people have. We had a fire-eater win last month, and a saxophonist before that."

"Mum, I could do some of my magic," Harry says, excitedly.

"Ah, a magician. We've not seen any magic yet," Devon says.

"I'll show you," Harry says, running off and returning with a coin, bottle and her wand. "I'm going to magic this coin into this bottle," she announces. "As you can see, the bottle neck is too thin for the coin to fit down..."

She taps the bottle with her wand, covers the bottle with a tea towel, then removes it with a flourish. The coin is still outside the bottle.

"Oh," she says, frowning. "Let's try that again..."

She tries again. And again. But the coin doesn't go in. "I don't understand why it's not working..."

"Keep practising for the big night," Devon says kindly. "What about the rest of you?"

There's deadly silence as we all stare around the caravan, desperately trying not to meet Devon's eye.

"Come on," Devon insists. "You seem a talented bunch to me and we'd love to get you involved. What about you, what can you do?" he asks Isabella.

"Usually, my talent is avoiding holidays like this," Isabella says cuttingly.

Ouch!

"Isabella, that's rude," Mum says.

"There are some fantastic prizes to be won," Devon says temptingly. "Worth hundreds of pounds..."

Mum's face lights up at the mention of prizes. "If there are prizes to be won, that's a whole different ball game. Everyone's going to enter. No arguments," she says, when she sees I'm about to protest, "we need the money."

"I have a talent," Dad says. "Remember, Jen? That bit I used to do at university."

"That? Really?" says Mum, looking alarmed.

"Well, don't leave us in the dark," says Devon. "What is it?"

"Oh, I don't think I can tell you," Dad replies, his eyes twinkling, "but it was cracking. I raised a ton of money for rag week. Although I'm going to need my props."

"Chris, it's been years," Mum says. "You'll do yourself a mischief trying that kind of thing at your age."

"Well, it certainly sounds intriguing," Devon says.

I shudder silently. I hope everyone forgets all about the talent show and it's never spoken of again. I can't think of anything worse. And as for this secret 'talent' of Dad's from about a hundred years ago... well, the mind boggles.

"Don't forget to come and see the musicians tonight at the marquee," Devon adds, as he gets up to leave.

"Is anyone playing that we'd have heard of?" Mum asks.

"Only if you're a regular in Canterbury, where they busk," Devon says. "It's a great duo – a saxophonist accompanied by a singer who performs in Turkish. It's very unusual and rather haunting."

"Buskers?" I say. "I thought the musicians here were professional?"

Devon laughs. "Well, we're not talking chart success here, you know," he says. "But they are professional in terms of earning money for doing what they do."

You are *kidding me*. Any fool can go out and busk on the street. Marcus Fletcher from school was on the high street during the Easter holidays showcasing his Grade One violin skills but that doesn't make him a blimmin' pro.

"So, none of them are professional?" I ask again, to be sure. "The Drifting aren't coming, or anything like that?"

Dad snorts. "Dream on."

Devon's confused. "I don't know who The Drifting are, but the people we showcase are mainly street performers. They're very good, though. Diverse. None of that commercial nonsense. Come and see for yourselves later. Now, remember what I said about the toilet blocks, young lady." He mock sternly wags his finger at me, making me blush all over again.

Yes, yes, all right, all right, I get it. How many times?

"And you keep that dog under control," he says to Millie as he leaves.

"Wait a minute, Devon," Amber calls, hoisting herself up from her seat and ejecting Crystal into an unimpressed Dad's lap. "I'll walk with you. It's time to ring Markymoo again. I miss him so much, Devon, I can't begin to tell you how hard it is for me being here…"

Devon doesn't seem exactly pleased, but there's nothing he can do as he prepares to have his ear bent about Mark all the way back across the site.

"You told me the musicians were professional," I say to Harry, indignantly.

"I lied," she replies. "Sucker."

CHAPTER THIRTEEN

"Ugh, it's so boring here," Isabella moans the next morning as we sit around the awning. "Nothing happens. Every day is the same. Uno. Rain. Yawn, yawn, yawn. There's not even anyone else to hang around with. I really want to meet some boys. It's all right for you, you've got boyfriends, but I seriously need some holiday romance."

Mum pokes her head out of the caravan. "We're going to the beach," she says cheerily.

"Um, it's pouring," Isabella says, looking at Mum like she's a complete imbecile.

"I know, but we should get out," Mum says. "We've all been stuck here too long and I refuse to have another day like yesterday where we all sat around driving each other mad. It'll do us good to have a change of scene."

"I want to ring Mark before we go anywhere," Amber says.

152

"Of course you do," Dad sighs. "Do you know what this place needs? A TV."

"I miss TV," Harry says.

"Stop it, you two," Mum says. "We don't need a TV, I've got a lovely day planned for us when Amber gets back. And even if we don't make it onto the beach itself, I'm sure it'll be clearer down by the coast. There's a lighthouse we can go and look at."

"Oooh, how exciting, a lighthouse," I mutter sarcastically. I've woken up in a very bad mood again. Partly because I was freezing cold in the night. Partly because as I was falling asleep, I could hear Millie and Isabella, talking and laughing away in their tent without me. And partly because my hair has hit new levels of insanity. This weather is doing it no favours, and it's sticking out randomly – a curly, frantic mass of frizz. The longer we stay here, the worse it's getting. I'm spending most of my time smoothing it with my hands, trying to calm it down. My serum isn't working. My leave-in conditioner isn't working. Nothing is working. My hair has an unruly force that's too strong to be tamed.

"What is going on with your hair?" Isabella asks me, her delicately plucked brows furrowing.

"Don't ask," I sigh. "It's the damp. Makes it take on a life of its own."

"And it's always like that?" Isabella says, flicking her smooth, ruler-straight hair over her shoulder.

I seethe with the unfairness of it all. Damn her and her perfect genes.

"Uh huh," I say gloomily.

"Would a hat help?" Isabella asks, a mischievous smile playing around her lips. "Or maybe a balaclava?"

Millie cracks up.

Ouch.

Although I try to smile, I'm kind of hurt Millie's giggling. She knows what a nightmare my hair is.

We pick up Amber by the shop on our way out. Isabella's worked it so she's with Millie again, while I sit in the car with my family and sulk.

"Mum, the fog's not clearing," Harry says, after we've been driving for twenty minutes.

"It'll be better near the coast," Mum says.

But the fog gets thicker. And thicker. And when we pull into the car park, we can hear the sea, but there's nothing to be seen apart from the thick white fog.

"The book says there's a lighthouse around here, somewhere…" Mum says.

We make our way along the coastal path. It's freezing, and everyone's shivering. Even the dogs.

"There it is!" Mum says, pointing at a concrete lump

in the fog. We can't see the top; it's too foggy. We've driven for forty-five minutes to come and see the base of a lighthouse.

"Can we go up it?" Isabella asks.

"Oh no," Mum says. "It's a historic landmark."

"And you wouldn't be able to see anything on a day like today, anyway," Dad says.

"So what was the point in coming?" Isabella asks. I'm not sure if she's being rude or if she's genuinely confused.

Nobody answers.

"I know, let's go to the café and have a nice cuppa," Mum says. "Back along the path, everyone. Mind yourselves, it's very slippery."

As we make our way back, I hear Mum talking to Clare.

"Have you heard from Martin since you've been here? How are things going at work?"

"I'm leaving him to it," Clare replies.

Behind me, I hear Millie sigh heavily. I turn to look at her, but she's gazing off out to sea.

Or at least, where the sea would be if it was visible.

"What do we think about Pocahontas and Mulan for the babies?" Amber asks, looking up from her celebrity magazine.

"No!" everyone choruses together.

We're squished into the awning eating crisps and rejecting Mum's attempts to play some more Uno.

Déjà vu, much?

"You lot are so hard to please," Amber says, getting up to put the kettle on.

"Suggest something normal, then," Harry says.

"I've been thinking about that talent show Devon mentioned," Clare says, diplomatically changing the subject.

"We're all entering," Mum says.

"It could be fun," Clare encourages us. "And it'll give us something to do, especially if this rain continues."

"We could always go home early instead?" I offer hopefully.

"I'm happy to enter," Amber says. "I'm going to sing."

"You're singing?" Mum bursts out before she can stop herself. She and Dad exchange panicked looks. Amber's singing is appalling.

"Well, I can't do much else, can I?" Amber says, rubbing her tummy with one hand and stroking Crystal Fairybelle with the other. The dog gives her chin a sympathetic lick. "I'd love to do my street dance routine, but I'm way too big. I'm going to sing a ballad and dedicate it to Mark, so he knows how much I miss him."

"But he won't be here, will he?" Dad says, looking confused.

"No," Amber says, her eyes brimming with tears. "But he'll feel it in his heart. I know he will. Our love knows no boundaries."

"Right. Well, we'll look forward to hearing that," Mum says. "What about you lot?"

"Street magic!" Harry says, pulling a ten pence piece out from behind her ear with a flourish.

"Hey, very good," says Clare. "You're getting better."

I wonder if I should tell Clare that I saw Harry stick the coin there earlier using a piece of chewing gum.

"And what about you girls?" Mum asks, looking over at us.

We've totally avoided discussing the subject. I think we're all hoping that if we don't mention it, it'll go away.

"We're undecided," I say.

"Well, I'd like you to decide," Mum says.

"We'll think about it," I mutter. There's got to be a way to get out of this.

"Everyone needs to enter," Mum reiterates. "You heard Devon, there are prizes up for grabs that are worth hundreds of pounds, and we need all the chances we can get to win them."

"But you don't know what the prizes are," I say.

"It doesn't matter," Mum says. "We're winning them."

"And we're Puttocks," Dad chips in. "Puttocks do not fail when they put their minds to something. A Puttock always succeeds!"

"I'm not a Puttock," Millie says.

"Or me," Isabella adds.

"And I just wish I wasn't," I mutter.

"You're honorary Puttocks," Dad says.

"You're busy nagging us, Mum, but what about you?" I say. "What's going to be your contribution to this?"

Clare and Mum look at each other and start to laugh. "We thought it might be fun to do something together... We're considering doing a routine with the dogs."

"With the *dogs*?" I ask in amazement. "As in Crystal and Murphy? What kind of routine? Are you *mad*?"

"You know how you see those dancing dogs, who move around with their handlers?" Clare says. "That kind of thing. It can't be that hard, can it?"

"Not if you've got a properly trained dog in the first place," I say.

"Hey!" Millie says indignantly. "Murphy *is* well trained. He just forgets himself sometimes. He's very excitable. And he'd love to perform with you."

"Are you honestly expecting Murphy to dance?" Isabella asks Clare, as Murphy buries his head in his paws and lets out a whimper.

Clare snorts with laughter. "Well, no. Not properly. But we can have a go, can't we?"

"So we've got singing, dog dancing and magic, plus as-yet-to-be-decided acts from the girls," Mum says. "That sounds pretty good to me."

"Let's not forget about me," Dad says.

"Chris, you're not going to do that thing you did at university," Mum says. "You were twenty years younger then. Besides, you haven't got your—"

"Shhhh!" Dad says, holding up his hand. "Don't give the game away and tell them what it is. I don't have my props, but that's okay. I know exactly where they are in the loft at home. I'll go back and get them."

"You're going to drive all the way home to get your—"

"Sssshhh!" Dad says again. "My *props*. Yes."

"You're out of your mind," Mum says. "It's a six-hour round trip. At least. And this isn't a proper talent show. Not like on the TV or anything like that. You do know that, right?"

"Of course I do," Dad says. "But six hours of peace in the car sounds like heaven right now. Besides, I've never shown the girls what I can do. I'm sure they'd love to see it, wouldn't you?"

"I think you're going to be great," Harry says. "I can't wait to see your act."

159

"You see?" Dad says, proudly. "It'll be the experience of a lifetime."

I very much doubt that, but no matter. If I think too much about it I'll only start to freak out as to what he could be up to.

"Shall we go and hang out in your tent for a bit?" I ask Millie.

"Good thinking," Millie says.

As we scramble into the tent, Murphy follows after us, and settles himself lying horizontally across the two airbeds, taking up all of the room.

"How do you put up with this dog?" Isabella asks, wrinkling her nose. "He stinks."

"It's only because it's wet," Millie protests, reaching over to give Murphy a hug. "He's gorgeous, and doesn't normally smell, does he, Suze?"

"Um, no," I lie. Because Murphy honks. Permanently. He's usually been off rolling in fox poo, or some other horrific substance, and his breath is terrible too. But Millie will never forgive me if I say that.

Isabella fiddles with her phone and soon music's filling the tent. It's not stuff I've heard before, the lyrics are in a foreign language.

"What band is this?" I ask, as I grab a magazine, and shake my head at Millie's offer of a jelly baby.

"Ezra. They're Italian," Isabella says.

"Got any English stuff on there?" I ask. "We love The Drifting, don't we, Mills?"

Isabella sniffs dismissively. "I prefer more unusual stuff. Give this a while. You'll get into it."

I doubt that. I don't have a blinking idea what this singer's on about. He could be singing about cat poo, for all I know.

"So what are we going to do for this talent show?" Millie asks.

"Nothing," Isabella says, pulling out a mirror and checking her reflection. She carefully starts to touch up her eyeliner.

"Aw, come on," Millie wheedles. "Mrs P says we have to. And it could be fun, you know."

That's so Millie. Only she could think this ridiculous camping talent show could be fun.

"Besides, it'll be something to do," Millie continues. "It's not like we've got much else on, stuck here in the rain."

"Maybe," I say, dubiously.

"I'm not doing it," Isabella says. "No way. Nuh-uh."

"Okay, then," Millie sighs. "Suzy, you'll do something with me, won't you? You mentioning The Drifting made me think about our old routines..."

She stares at me, all wide-eyed and hopeful, and my heart sinks into my shoes.

When we were really little (like, about nine, practically babies) we were obsessed with making up dance routines to songs. And when I say obsessed, I mean ob. Sessed. We'd dance every break and lunch, and spend hours after school making up new moves and practising over and over again. Millie was always loads better than I was, obviously, because I've got two left feet and fell over a lot. I used to do a lot of standing still while hip-wiggling and clapping as she did the complicated stuff around me.

But to do it all again, now? In public? We're teenagers. This could be mortification to the max.

And that's coming from me, no stranger to embarrasmentitis.

"It's going to be so lame," I protest, although I know there's no point arguing with Millie once she's got an idea into her head. If she wants us to do this, I know it's going to happen.

"C'mon, it's not like anyone knows us here," Millie says. "Please? Pretty please?"

"Oh, okay," I agree reluctantly. "But don't make it too complicated."

"I'll be your choreographer," Isabella says. "I've got loads of dance experience. I was the under-fifteens freestyle champion last year."

Of *course* she was.

"Fantastic," Millie squeals. "You'll be able to make it really good."

Brilliant, that's all I need. Isabella bossing me around and telling me how rubbish I am at dancing.

Millie flings one arm around me and another around Isabella, pulling us closer for a group hug. I notice that Isabella seems to be going out of her way to avoid any contact with me.

It's then that Murphy releases a deafening fart. In seconds the tent is filled with stinking, toxic gas that leaves us coughing and flapping our hands in front of our faces in disgust.

"Oh God, oh God, I'm going to die," Isabella chokes, scrambling past me with one hand clamped over her nose, and the other wrestling with the tent zipper. "I need to get out, I need to get out..."

I follow and soon we're all standing outside the tent, gasping in huge breaths of fresh air.

"That dog is disgusting," Isabella says.

"He's..." Millie begins to protest, but then starts giggling. "Yeah, who am I kidding? When he does things like that he is totally rank. Hey, it's stopped raining out here. We could go and start practising."

"Let's do that," Isabella says. She glances at me. "Something tells me we're going to need all the time we can get."

CHAPTER FOURTEEN

"I bet the boys would love to be a fly on the wall to see this," I say to Millie as we look for somewhere to practise.

"I know, right?" says Millie. "They'd think it was hilarious."

"Can you stop going on about your boyfriends all the time?" Isabella asks. "It's getting kind of boring."

All right, all right, just because you're too much of a diva for a boyfriend, I think, meanly.

Millie just laughs, obviously thinking Isabella's joking. "Where are we going to go? We need somewhere with enough space for us to dance in."

"Um, the table tennis shed?" I ask. It's the only place I can think of with a roof.

"No way," Isabella says. "That place has an open wall, anyone could pass by. We want to surprise everyone; we don't want them seeing you beforehand."

I'm getting the impression that Isabella is more than a smidge competitive. Sure, she doesn't care enough about the talent show to risk humiliating herself by entering it, but wants us to enter and win it for her. That way she gets all of the kudos with none of the shame. Not daft, is she?

We head down one of the tracks into the wood, dodging around the mud as we do so. Murphy, who's with us, stops to take a long drink from a puddle.

"Look, there's a clearing," Millie says. In the woods there's a circular grassy area, surrounded by tree stumps. It must be a teaching area or something of Devon's.

"This is perfect," Isabella says, leading us over. Millie ties Murphy to an alarmingly flimsy tree.

"We haven't got any music, have we?" I ask.

"I brought this," Isabella says, waving her phone around. "What do you want to dance to?"

"Definitely something by The Drifting," Millie says, and I nod in agreement. We love, love, love The Drifting. My friends all went to see them in concert earlier this year, without me. Long story. I'm still a teeny bit bitter about it, although hopefully they'll be touring again soon and we can figure out a way to go and see them again.

"I don't know why you guys like them so much," Isabella says, as she scrolls through her phone. "They're so *mainstream*."

"Oi, don't be rude about The Drifting," Millie says. "We won't hear a bad word said against them, will we, Suze?"

"Nuh-uh," I say, shaking my head fiercely.

"Whatever," Isabella says. "Right, I've only got a couple of their songs. Of course if we were anywhere near civilisation I could download whatever you wanted, but as we're stuck in the butt end of nowhere there's not a lot I can do, sorry. I've got 'Break Up, Make Up' or 'One Special Love'."

"*One Special Love!*" Millie and I chorus. It's The Drifting's newest and it's *so good*. We've played it over and over and over again. We had it on repeat one day after school so many times Clare threatened to throw Millie's docking station out of the window.

"Okay, so what do you remember from your last routine?" Isabella asks, folding her arms authoritatively.

"Um, there was a kind of shimmy," Millie says, wiggling around with her hands in the air.

"And some heel kicks," I say, demonstrating.

"And a twirl, then a kind of leapy thing," Millie says, grabbing me. "Followed by a little hand action..."

We clap hands together enthusiastically.

"Oooh, and then there was that sort of squat jump we did at the end..." I squat down to the ground, wincing at the stretch in my thigh muscles. I was a lot more limber when I was nine. Then I wobble, and have to put my hands out to stop myself toppling over backwards.

Gross. Now I'm all dirty.

Millie and I are giggling like crazy, remembering the hours we spent dancing around the playground. We used to have a lot of fun, doing this. I catch Isabella looking at us weirdly, and for a moment I wonder if see a flash of jealousy cross her face.

I'm probably imagining things. What does she need to be jealous of?

"Do you remember when we put on the show?" Millie says.

"Yeah, for our families? And we made tickets, and charged them to come in? Wow, we were lame."

"Hey," Millie protests. "We were cool."

"Terrible dancers, though," I say.

"I'm not going to argue with you there," Isabella says. "Well, you're not too bad, Millie."

Oof. Isabella's snarky comments are getting harder and harder to ignore. I've tried and tried with this girl, but I'm just getting nowhere. How is Millie not seeing what she's really like?

"Those moves might have been okay when you were younger, but they aren't going to work now," Isabella says.

"Especially if we want to win this thing. You're going to need some serious training."

"We've only got a few days," I say.

"I want those prizes," Isabella says. "And let's face it, it's something to do."

"You probably have to participate to get the prizes," I say grumpily.

"I am participating," Isabella says. "I'm choreographer. Now, can either of you do back flips?"

Millie and I stare at her.

"Cartwheels?"

"I used to be able to..." Millie says.

"I stopped after I cartwheeled into a canal," I mutter. "Gymnastics is not my strong point."

"Then this is going to be tougher than I thought it would be. Okay, give me a moment."

"I brought my pompoms along, if they're any use," Millie offers.

Isabella shakes her head. "Let me hear the song again."

Isabella walks around as The Drifting plays out of her phone, scrutinising us, before she stops and says, "Right, I've got it. I'm going to adapt one of my routines for you both. I danced with a boy, so we'll have to change it around, but it should be fine. Suzy, you'll obviously be the boy, and——"

"Hang on," I interrupt. "What do you mean, obviously I'll be the boy?"

"Don't be silly. It's just, you know, Millie's a bit more... girly."

Ouch.

"I don't mind playing the boy's part," Millie interjects.

"The boy's part is easier," Isabella says.

"Oh," Millie says. "In that case..."

"Yeah, yeah," I say, defeated.

Isabella starts demonstrating what she wants us to do. And she's seriously, seriously impressive.

"Are you sure you don't want to enter the competition?" Millie asks, in awe. "You're amazing."

"I'm not going from performing to a crowd of thousands at professional competitions to a crowd of ten in a marquee in a field. It's humiliating," she says.

I guess it would indeed be one hell of a come-down.

"Okay, let's get going," Isabella says. "What I want you to do is walk forward for four, swinging your arm like this, then..."

And after that I'm totally lost. She's reeled off a ton of instructions that sound like she's speaking Dutch. I've no idea what she wants me to do past the arm swinging.

"Got that?" Isabella says.

"Think so," Millie says.

"Suzy?"

"Yep," I lie, not wanting to admit I don't have a clue. Isabella will only think I'm even more stupid.

"Try it and see how you get on," Isabella says. "I'm turning on the music in three, two, one."

As the opening bars of The Drifting tinnily spill out of the phone, I rack my brains, trying to remember what we had to do first. Marching in a line with arm swinging. I scamper after Millie, who's already several steps ahead.

"Stop!" Isabella calls, pausing the music. "Suzy, you should be starting on the beat."

"I know," I say.

Millie smiles at me sympathetically, and while her back's turned away from Isabella, she rolls her eyes, which makes me laugh.

"Let's try again!" Isabella calls.

But I just can't get it.

I'm late on the beat. I'm not 'sashaying' enough. I'm not swinging my arms the right way.

According to Isabella, I'm wrong, wrong, wrong.

"You're not taking this seriously," Isabella complains.

"I am," I say. "Well, no, maybe I'm not. But how serious do I have to be?"

"Do you want to do it one more time?" Isabella asks.

"Not really," I say.

"We need to have a think about costumes, too," Isabella says. "You do realise that on the night you're going to have to do this in heels, don't you?"

"What?" I say, horrified. I can hardly dance in flats, never mind heels. "I, um, didn't bring any with me," I say.

"Well, you're going to have to find some. You have to do this kind of dancing in heels. And you need matching outfits."

"Come on," I say. "Aren't you taking this a bit far?"

"Look, if we're doing this, we're doing it to win, okay?" Isabella says.

"We don't exactly have much that matches," I say.

"Hmm," says Isabella, scrutinising us. "Yes... I can believe that. You've got very different styles. Millie, you're so individual and eclectic, and Suzy, you're more, um, high street."

Hmph. She may as well have called me boring.

I'm about to protest, but Isabella's not paying any attention.

"Look at that," she says, a slow smile crossing her face as she points towards the campsite. It's easy to see what she's spotted. Across the field, a minibus has just pulled to a stop. And emerging from it, behind a younger boy about Harry's age, are five older lads.

172

Oh my sweet Lord.

With the exception of one, who's a bit scrawny, the others are seriously buff, and *seriously* sexy.

Millie grabs onto my arm and squeezes. "Oh, wow."

"Suddenly things have got a lot more interesting," Isabella says. "I think it's time we got to have some fun. Come on, Millie, let's take some plates over to the sinks so we can pretend to do the washing-up and get a better look."

"Okay!" Millie says.

Although I'm pretty sure Millie wouldn't do anything, especially after she saw what happened with the whole me, Danny and Zach disaster, there's something about the way she's staring at the boys and giggling with Isabella that's making me nervous.

"Um, I think I'm going to go and ring Danny," I say.

"Say hi from me," Millie says distractedly.

"Do you want to come and speak to Jamie?" I ask.

"Don't you dare," Isabella threatens. "You have to come with *me*. It'll look too obvious if I'm by myself."

As Isabella drags Millie away, my mate doesn't even look back.

I'm almost at the shop when I see Clare walking ahead. I haven't managed to catch her up by the time she enters and makes her way over to the payphone. Oh yeah, that's right, she told Millie she was going to call Martin today.

I'm about to say something, to let her know I'm here, but as her hand reaches out for the phone, she pauses for a moment and then it drops back down to her side. She stands in front of the booth, leaning her forehead against the wall for the longest time and then turns and walks back out.

I duck down behind a shelf, and she doesn't spot me.

Something tells me she wouldn't have wanted to be seen.

CHAPTER FIFTEEN

Later that night, we've finished our dinner – Dad finally got his fire-charred burgers and sausages tonight, after using the Devon-approved wood in his fire pit – and are all sitting around the campfire. Mainly because it's the only place that's warm, although it's actually stopped raining, which is some kind of miracle. Millie and Isabella have been on full alert for the boys, who've all pitched their tents around a fire pit not too far away. Right now their camp is empty. They left a while ago, carrying maps and wearing hiking boots.

"Hey, Mum, did you speak to Dad?" Millie asks.

"Um, yep," Clare says. "He sends his love."

Huh? That's weird. She didn't ring him. Unless she went back later, after I'd seen her. I guess that's what must've happened.

"A sing-song, anyone?" Clare asks. "It's traditional to sing around a campfire. What do people want to sing?"

Singing? Nuh-uh, I don't think so. We're not that sort of family. Not for the first time, I wish I was at home, hanging out in the dry, cosy Bojangles with Danny.

"How about 'Kill Me Now'?" Isabella suggests.

"I don't think I know that one," Clare replies, completely missing Isabella's sarcasm. "What about 'Kookaburra'?"

There's a deafening silence as only Millie and Amber look even half-interested. Isabella shakes her head and returns to fiddling with her phone. I think she's playing some kind of game.

Dad clears his throat awkwardly. "Um, I don't think my voice is up to singing. Throat's a bit sore. But it's nearly seven. Do you lot want to see tonight's entertainment?"

Isabella shoots a look at Millie. I know what she's thinking. She's thinking those boys might turn up there.

"That sounds like a great idea," Isabella says sincerely, smiling winningly at Dad.

"Good," Dad says.

"I need to put some make-up on..." Isabella says. "Won't be a tick. Millie, will you give me a hand?"

As they dart off into their tent, giggling together, I'm suddenly feeling really left out. Why didn't she ask me to go, too? I head into the awning to fix my own make-up and try to sort out my hair. Ten minutes later I give up in despair, change into a nicer pair of jeans plus a snuggly sweatshirt (I'm *freezing*), then grab the book I'm reading and return to my wobbly log seat by the fire. I bury my head in my book, trying to ignore the shrieks and laughter coming through the canvas.

Half an hour later, Dad's starting to lose patience.

"Look, we'll go over and meet you there," he says in exasperation, pacing around the fire pit.

"Almost ready," Millie calls from the tent.

"I don't understand how you women always take so long," he says, just as Isabella and Millie emerge from their tent.

Dad's eyes almost pop out of his head.

Millie's wearing pretty standard Millie attire — a turquoise T-shirt that matches the front of her hair with a silver heart on the front, purple skinnies and red pumps. She's wearing more make-up than usual, and her eyes are all dark and smoky. But it's not Millie that's getting Dad stressed. It's Isabella. She's wearing a very short red miniskirt, strappy black and white top and possibly the entire contents of her make-up bag. Her hair's been swept back on one side, but the rest of it tumbles around her shoulders. She looks about eighteen.

I'm so envious I could pop. And I'm feeling seriously underdressed. I'm wearing a sweatshirt and trainers, for goodness sake. I dressed for warmth and comfort. I can't go looking like *this* if they're looking like *that*.

"You're not coming in those clothes, you'll freeze to death," Dad says.

"Um, could you be any more of a cliché?" Isabella says.

"We're responsible for you at the moment," Mum says. "That outfit seems more appropriate for a nightclub, not a campsite."

"My parents let me go out like this all the time," Isabella replies. "Who do you think paid for these clothes?"

"Even so, I'm not sure…" Mum dithers.

"Well, if you really want me to go and get changed again…" Isabella says. "It might take a while to choose a new outfit, though."

"Oh, let's go," Dad says. "If she freezes, that's her lookout."

"I might go and put on something else," I say, jumping to my feet.

"*No!*" says Dad. "There will be no more outfit changes. None!"

Amber hauls herself to her feet. "I think I'm going to give it a miss and go to bed. I'm missing Mark too much to have a good time, anyway."

"Uh oh, Devon's heading this way," Dad says. "What did you lot do now?" He eyeballs us all suspiciously.

I rack my brains. Nothing comes to mind. It can't be me, not this time.

"Evening," Dad says.

"Evening," Devon says, his voice sounding tense.

"You seem to be spending a lot of time visiting us," Dad says, with a fake-sounding laugh.

"Don't I just," says Devon. He shakes the rain off his ponytail. "I've come over for two things. Firstly, Mr Puttock, um, this is a little awkward, but there's something I need to speak to you about. I'm afraid we had a complaint about you peering in the window of the Gilberts' caravan."

"Chris! What were you thinking?" Mum says.

"I wasn't doing anything bad," Dad protests. "They had their TV on and I only wanted to watch five minutes. It was the athletics!"

"They thought you were a peeping Tom," Devon says. "Mrs Gilbert was very upset."

"It *was* unfortunate she took her dressing gown off," Dad concedes. "And even more unfortunate she didn't have anything on underneath."

There's a sharp intake of breath from Mum while the rest of us try not to laugh.

We fail.

"I assure you this is no joke," Devon says. "Next time,

bring your own TV if you want to watch one so badly."

"I would have brought one this time if I could," Dad says, shooting a look at Mum.

"Now, the other reason I'm here is because I've been getting calls from Mark—" Devon continues.

"Mark?" Amber interrupts. "Is something wrong? What's happened?"

"Nothing, as far as I can tell," Devon says. "But he's called six times in the last half hour, wondering where you are."

"Didn't you speak to him before supper?" Mum says.

"I did," Amber wails. "But we're missing each other sooooooo much. How did he sound, Devon? Like he'd been eating okay? Like he was missing me?"

"I really couldn't say," Devon says. "But if you could call him back so he stops distracting me from my stocktake, it would be wonderful. He also wanted to know what you thought about the names Mufasa and Simba for the babies."

"Aw, he's been watching *The Lion King* again," Amber says. "I'll give him a call, and then I'm going to go to bed to read my baby books. After I've read Conni G's pregnancy update in my magazine. You all go to entertainment without me. I'll see you in the morning."

As Amber dons her waterproofs and waddles off behind Devon, the rest of us look at each other.

"To the entertainment?" Isabella says hopefully.

"To the music," Dad says, leading the way.

We duck our way into the marquee and our ears are immediately assaulted by a terrible noise.

"What is *that*?" Millie asks.

"It's very loud, whatever it is," Mum says.

Inside the marquee, it's dimly-lit and there's an overwhelming scent of incense. There are about four people sitting watching a middle-aged couple. The woman's singing something in a foreign language, and the man is playing something like an oboe or a clarinet. It doesn't sound like either. It sounds kind of... alarming.

The song comes to an end and there's some half-hearted applause from the people watching, none of whom are the boys Isabella and Millie were hoping for.

"Thank you, ladies and gents," the man says. "It's a joy to hear your appreciation of my wife's glorious voice and my shenai. Now for our next song, a number we composed ourselves..."

As the woman's voice starts warbling again, harsh and shrill, we all gaze apprehensively at each other.

"Shall we sit down?" Harry says. "I like them. I think they sound awesome."

"Um, okay," I say. Next to me, Isabella and Millie are frantically whispering.

"They might come later," Isabella hisses.

We sit through four more songs, each one worse than the last and increasingly ear-assaulting.

Mum stands up. "I'm going back to check on Amber," she says.

"I'll come with you," Dad says, jumping to his feet.

Clearly it's not just me that wants to get outta here.

"Harry, it's bedtime," Mum says.

"Awwwww," Harry whines. "Can't I stay a bit longer?"

"Well... I suppose you can stay for a bit, as long as Suzy keeps an eye on you," Mum says.

Up on the stage, the performers, who we've learned go by the name of Laka and Shan, are giving us evils as the man gives a long, detailed and exceptionally dull history of the shenai.

"Make sure you girls are back by eleven," Mum says. "I won't go to sleep until I know you're back safely, so don't think about breaking curfew unless you want me to appear in my pyjamas to retrieve you."

She would too. She has no sense of shame.

"They're not coming, are they?" Isabella whispers.

"Doesn't look like it," Millie replies.

"Want to go back?" Isabella says, disappointment written all over her face.

"Might as well," Millie replies, and I silently sigh with relief.

"Night then, have fun," Mum says.

"It's all right, we'll come back with you," Millie says, standing up.

"Awwww," Harry whines. "Does that mean I can't stay?"

"'Fraid so, kiddo," Dad says.

I follow everyone out of the marquee, watching as Millie and Isabella continue to whisper non-stop to each other. Seeing them gives me a hollow feeling I can't quite place.

For some reason I can't get to sleep. I'm counting my eighty-eighth sheep when I hear a load of people walking past the tent, chattering and laughing as they go.

"Keep it down, lads, people are sleeping," a man's voice says.

I sit up to peep out of the curtains, and although it's dark, I can just about make out from the light of their torches the group of boys returning to their tents. And it's then that I hear something else.

A strange rustling noise, coming from the food area. Because Mum bought so much stuff along with us, half the food has had to be stored out in the awning.

The rustling's coming from bag of vegetables on the floor. And then I hear a squeak.

Oh God. It's Hagrid. He's escaped.

"Harry," I hiss. "Harry, wake up."

But Harry doesn't stir.

I'm not going to get back to sleep knowing that stupid rat's on the loose in here. And besides, Harry will be devastated if anything happens to him.

Honestly, the things I do for a sister who torments me and a rat I don't even like.

Sighing heavily, I haul myself out of my sleeping bag and walk over to where the cereal boxes, crisp packets and spare tins have been stored.

"Hagrid," I say softly. "Hagrid... come here..."

Another squeak and more rustling. This time coming from my rucksack. Uh oh. He'd better not have found my secret chocolate stash, otherwise I'm actually going to kill him.

I start moving things aside, trying to see in the semi-darkness, and then scream as my foot brushes something soft before the most awful pain shoots up my foot.

I've been bitten!

I grab at my big toe, hopping up and down, trying not to cry with the pain, as I see the shape of a rat disappearing off into the night.

"Whass going on?" Harry says blearily.

The caravan door flies open and Dad jumps out, waving

184

a rolled-up pregnancy magazine threateningly.

"What is it? What happened?"

"Hagrid bit me," I say. "Ow, ow, ow, it really hurts. . ."

"Hagrid wouldn't bite you!" Harry says.

"Want to see the teeth marks?" I shout.

Dad lets the magazine drop. "Am I ever going to get any sleep in this damn place? How did he get at your foot, anyway?"

"Thanks for the sympathy," I say. "I was trying to catch him. He's escaped."

"He's escaped?" Harry says, leaping out of bed. "Where is he? Where did he go? Hagrid? Hagrid!"

"What's the matter, girls?" Mum says, emerging behind Dad in her pyjamas, hair tousled.

"Hagrid's gone," Harry says.

"Er, hello, can we focus on my toe, here? I'm still in a lot of pain, people," I say.

"He's here," Harry says, peering into Hagrid's cage. "It can't have been Hagrid that bit you."

"It was definitely a rat, I saw it," I say.

And then I realise.

If it wasn't Hagrid that bit me, it must have been a wild rat.

My mother realises at exactly the same time as me and immediately lets out a scream of horror.

"You were bitten by a rat? Oh God. Oh God, Chris, can't you catch diseases from wild rats?"

"Diseases? What kind of diseases?" I ask. "Am I going to die?"

"Weil's disease. You can get that from them, can't you?" Mum says.

"What's that?" I ask, feeling increasingly alarmed.

"She's not going to get Weil's disease," Dad says.

"How do you know?" Mum asks. "She should go to a doctor. She needs to get that toe looked at..."

"What *is* Weil's disease?" I ask again.

"I think you can die from it," Clare says, as she joins us in the awning. "I was a first-aider for a while."

"You what?" I shriek.

"Do we need to suck the poison out or something?" Amber suggests, finally having dragged herself out of bed.

"It was a rat, not a snake," Dad says through gritted teeth.

"What if Suzy gets seriously ill?" Mum asks.

"She's not going to get ill," Dad says. "It's only a little bite..."

"Are you a doctor? Do you have medical training?"

"No," Dad sighs.

"Then how do you know? If anything bad happens to her it'll all be your fault, and then you'll be sorry..."

"Suzy, come over here," Dad says. "Let's look at it in the light. Look, it's a tiny nibble. It's not even bleeding much."

"Let's clean it off and put some antiseptic cream on," Clare says. "I've got a first-aid kit in the car."

Murphy starts frantically barking as she goes to the car.

Clare cleans up my foot and slathers it in cream. Ouch. Stingy.

"So what do you want to do?" Clare asks. "I think it looks all right, but it's not up to me."

"I think we should all go back to bed," Dad says. "We can look at Suzy's toe in the morning and decide what to do then."

Er, hello, I could be totally dead by then! Easy for him to say we can decide in the morning, when it's not his foot that could have this Weil's disease they're all banging on about. Plus it really hurts. It's properly throbbing. Does that mean I've got it?

It feels like I've literally only just dropped off when I wake to see Mum's face looming over me, as she unzips my sleeping bag and grabs my foot. Outside it's light, and I can hear the sounds of the small kids running around screaming. Which is obviously the cue for Murphy to start howling at the top of his doggy voice.

"Whaaa are you doing? Gerroff," I say.

"Let me look at that bite," she says.

That wakes me up in a flash. Oh yes. The bite. They're lucky I didn't cark it in the night, if you ask me.

My toe still throbs like crazy. It's kind of pink and red, but doesn't look too bad this morning. The rat didn't bite that hard, you can hardly see the teeth marks now, but I don't find that hugely reassuring.

Dad appears in the doorway of the caravan, still in his pyjamas. He yawns widely as he ruffles his hair. "I'm so tired," he says. "Amber woke me up about eight times again last night with her constant peeing."

"She's pregnant, what do you expect the poor girl to do?" Mum says. "Now, we need to discuss Suzy's foot."

"I don't want to die," I whimper pathetically.

"You're not going to die," Dad says.

"I think she needs to get checked at the hospital," Mum says.

"Well, I can't take her. I'm supposed to be driving back today, to get my equipment for the talent show."

Thanks for nothing, Dad. Heard of compassion?

"That can wait," Mum says. She holds my foot up for Dad to examine. "Look, it's swollen. All round there. And it's red by the bite marks."

188

"What bite marks?" Dad says, squinting. "I can't see anything. And it doesn't look swollen to me. Are you sure she hasn't just got a funny-shaped toe?"

A funny-shaped toe? How flipping rude!

"I'd be happier if we got it looked at," Mum says.

"Oh, all right," Dad says, realising that giving in is the only way he's going to get some peace. "Let me have my breakfast and a cup of coffee first, then we'll go back to the hospital."

"Thank you," Mum says. "We'll get you seen to, don't worry, Suzy. And with luck, we'll have caught it in time and they won't have to amputate."

Amputate? Say *what* now?

Am I seriously about to lose a toe because of a stupid rodent?

CHAPTER SIXTEEN

My toe doesn't need amputating.

But it does take a really long time to sort out.

It's hours before we get back to the campsite. Dad got lost on the way to the hospital, refusing to take Clare's satnav as he'd driven there before and of course he could remember the way, what did we take him for, an idiot?

Turns out, he is indeed an idiot. He totally couldn't remember the way.

Then when we signed in at A & E, the receptionist looked like she was trying not to laugh as she squinted at my toe. I'd limped for dramatic effect and everything, but it made no difference – she just told us to take a seat, and warned we could be a while.

A while was right. Over three hours, in fact.

We eventually got seen by a doctor Dad called 'a young upstart', who said she thought it would be fine as my tetanus was up to date. It was only when Mum started freaking and

190

shrieking about Weil's disease that she sighed heavily and wrote out a prescription for antibiotics to be taken as a precautionary measure.

This was after she'd explained that Weil's disease comes from rat wee, so unless the rat bit me then peed on my foot before scarpering, it was extremely unlikely that I had it.

In all honesty, I think she just wanted Mum to shut up and go away.

The only good thing about the whole experience was that I discovered I had mobile reception again. Hurrah, and indeed, huzzah.

Lagging behind the parentals as we return to the car, I excitedly dial Danny's number. The phone rings and rings.

Come on, Danny, pick up, pick up...

Just when I think it's about to go to voicemail, Danny answers. I can hear a weird noise in the background, like drilling or something, then a 'shhhhhh' noise, and everything goes quiet.

"Danny?"

"Hey, you," Danny says. His voice, so familiar and reassuring, immediately makes me feel better. "How's it going? I didn't think you could get a signal."

I'm about to explain when I hear a huge crash on the end of the line. "What was that?" I ask.

191

"Erm, nothing. Walking around outside and there are some roadworks," Danny says. "Having a good time?"

"I'm calling you from the hospital car park," I say. "I got bitten by a rat."

"You what? Hagrid?"

"No. It's a long story. I can't flipping wait to come home. It's not stopped raining, we're bored stiff and to top it all off, we've been forced into entering some ridiculous talent show."

Danny starts to laugh. "A talent show? What are you going to do? Recreate some of your more spectacular accidents?"

"Oh, ha ha. No, Millie and I are doing a routine to The Drifting," I say.

Danny laughs harder. "What, one of those routines you used to do when we were little? Seriously? That's hilarious. I might get my dad to drive me across so I can watch."

"Don't you dare," I warn him, although I'd give anything to see Danny right now. "Millie talked me into it." I hear another crash and some muffled swearing.

"What's going on?" I ask. It doesn't sound like Danny's outside.

"Um, that's still the roadworks," Danny says.

Really? One of the voices sound awfully female to me... but I must be imagining things.

"Look, I really need to talk to you. Millie's acting

really strangely, and these boys have turned up on the campsite. Isabella's really into them, and I—"

"I'm sorry, Suze, but I've got to go," Danny says, sounding distracted. I'm not sure he's heard a word of what I've said. "Can't wait to see you again."

"But—"

"Bye!" And then Danny's gone, leaving me staring at my phone in disbelief.

Pfff. Boys. I seriously need some cheering up.

"Can we go and have a wander around town?" I ask. "Mum and I could go shopping while you sit and have a coffee and read the paper?" I say to Dad.

He's tempted. I know he is. I can tell by the way he's jangling the car keys thoughtfully.

"Come on, Mum, it'll be nice to have a mooch around," I say, silently adding in my head, *and it's something to do other than hang around the utterly boring campsite.* Plus I reckon I could convince Mum to buy me some stuff...

Civilisation! We're so very close to civilisation!

"What do you think, Jen? We could grab an hour or so before we go back, couldn't we?" Dad says.

Mum's torn. "It does sound lovely, but no, I don't think so, I'm sorry. We should really get back to the others. I don't want to leave Amber too long, in case she needs anything."

Dad and I exchange a forlorn look, but know better than to argue with Mum when it's something to do with Amber's babies.

Pfff. It was worth a try.

"Where's Millie?" I ask Clare. There's no sign of her or Isabella when we get back. In fact, the whole campsite's pretty much deserted. Clare's busy wrestling with Murphy. She's wielding a hairbrush, trying to groom him, but Murphy's having none of it.

"Murphy, come on, you stupid dog, I need to get these burrs out of your fur," Clare says, as Murphy flips onto his back, waving his legs in the air. She should know better than to try to make him do something he doesn't want to do. He's more stubborn than Harry.

"Will you give me a hand?" Clare asks.

"Um, I was looking for Millie?" I say.

Clare makes a frustrated noise and releases her hold on Murphy's collar. Murphy gives a triumphant shake and darts into the caravan.

"I give up," she says. "I was trying to get him vaguely presentable before your mum and I start practising with him."

I still have *no* idea how she thinks that's going to work.

"Devon was around again while you were away.

194

Apparently more people have been complaining about all the noise he's making. He's going to get us chucked off the campsite at this rate," Clare sighs. "Devon said we were on our last warning. I don't know why Martin couldn't look after him. Murphy's his pet."

"Um, Millie?" I ask again.

"Oh, yes. I think she's gone somewhere to practise the routine with Isabella," Clare says.

"Thanks," I say. I grab a couple of biscuits and then head off to the clearing to see what Millie and Isabella have come up with while I've been away.

When I finally catch up with them, I stand from a distance, watching in horror.

Isabella is demonstrating the most complicated move as Millie copies her. While she looks amazing, people would think I was having a seizure if I attempted something like that. Millie looks great too. But then Millie always was a million times more coordinated than me.

I swallow. Hard.

"Hi!" Millie says, catching sight of me and giving a huge wave. "How's the foot? Didn't they bandage it?" She peers at my toe in its sandal. "Gosh, you can't even really see the bite any more. What did they do to it in the hospital to make it disappear? That's amazing."

I don't want to tell her all they did was clean it again

and whack on more antiseptic cream.

"Oh you know, some tests and stuff," I say vaguely.

"And have you got that disease?"

"I've got some antibiotics, so it should all be fine."

"Thank goodness for that. I was properly worried about you. We've been working on the routine loads while you've been gone, did you see?"

"Yeah," I say. "It seems very, um… complicated."

"It's looking great," Isabella says. "We'll show you. Obviously you'll be doing my part."

"Isabella made me spend the whole afternoon spying on those boys," Millie whispers as Isabella walks a short distance away to her starting position and fiddles with the phone to get the music started.

"Nightmare," I whisper back.

"It was actually quite funny," Millie replies, with a giggle. "We were listening to them outside the bathroom block. They're here on an adventure sports week or something. They were wandering around in these small towels, you should have seen their abs, Suze! Anyway, Isabella's come up with a plan to get them to notice us," Millie smiles mischievously. "We're going mountain biking tomorrow."

"Ready?" Isabella calls.

"I was telling Suzy about your idea for tomorrow," Millie says.

"Oh, right. We're going to hire some bikes from Devon," Isabella says. "The boys are mountain biking, which means we are too. We're just going to happen to be on the same paths as them."

"Um, okay, sounds fun," I say dubiously, while I'm actually thinking that me on a mountain bike sounds like a disaster waiting to happen. "Speaking of boys, I spoke to Danny earlier. There was mobile reception at the hospital."

"Aw, cool, how is he? How's Jamie?" Millie asks.

"Are we going to do this, Millie?" Isabella asks.

I really want to talk to Millie properly, but it's impossible with Isabella butting in.

I swallow down my disappointment at not being able to dissect the conversation I had with Danny, and get ready to watch the routine. Never mind. I'll talk to Millie later.

I try not to seem too freaked out as I watch Millie and Isabella strut their stuff. I mean, they look great. It's just I can't see myself doing what Isabella's doing. It's never going to happen. Not in a million, trillion years.

"So what do you think?" Millie asks eagerly, after they've finished.

"Yeah, fantastic," I say, trying my best to seem enthusiastic.

"Should be simple enough for you," Isabella says. "We'll start practising tomorrow, when Millie and I get back from mountain biking."

"You're coming too, aren't you, Suze?" Millie says.

"Course," I say, trying to ignore the fact Isabella's just made it pretty clear she doesn't want me there.

"I'm really looking forward to getting off this campsite," Millie says. "If I have to spend another day hanging around with Mum I'm going to scream."

Huh? That's not like Millie. She and Clare have always got on well, and Millie doesn't put her down often. Millie's acting... kind of different, I suppose. Not in any way I can put my finger on, but there's definitely something off.

"Tomorrow's going to be a laugh," Millie says. "I've never been mountain biking before. You haven't either, have you, Suze?"

"No, but it sounds good," I lie. "I haven't ridden a bike in forever."

"We used to have matching pink bikes when we were younger," Millie tells Isabella. "They had these streamers on the handles and baskets on the front. We used to put our dolls in them. Talk about lame."

Lame? Is that what she really thinks about our childhood stuff? I always thought it was kind of sweet that we'd insisted on having all our possessions matching for about

198

three years. It showed what good friends we were.

"Jelly baby?" Millie offers Isabella. "There's no point asking Suzy, she thinks they're evil."

"You're terrible, you've got me totally addicted to these things," Isabella says as she takes a handful.

As I watch Millie with Isabella, I feel all kinds of confused.

Maybe she and I aren't the friends I always thought we were.

CHAPTER SEVENTEEN

I'm wobbling my way across the campsite on a hired bike, and it would be the understatement of the century to say I'm not exactly happy about it. However, I need to prove to Isabella I'm up for a laugh and not utterly rubbish at absolutely everything.

Mum was a bit disappointed we didn't want to go to the stately home she'd found nearby, but delighted that Isabella's finally taking an interest in something, so she gave us some money to hire bikes from Devon. Her only condition was that Harry had to come. And Murphy, of course. He's running around barking his head off.

We hired our bikes from an equally excitable Devon this morning. I think he was thrilled to see us partaking in something he deemed worthwhile and outdoorsy, plus we're all vacating the campsite. As far as he's concerned, it's a win-win. We got a big lecture about sticking to the cycle paths in the woods – the bikes he's lent us aren't suitable for going off-road – and following the coloured arrows so we don't get lost.

Isabella, Harry and Millie immediately zoomed off in front, while I'm following behind at about two miles per hour, doing my best not to fall off.

"We'll ride past their pitch all casual," Isabella's saying when I finally catch up. "We'll stop and get talking to them and drop it into the conversation that we're going for a ride too, so why don't we all go together. I'll do most of the talking, so act natural, okay? Especially you, Suzy. Harry, don't you dare give the game away."

Huh? What does she mean, especially me? And Harry's being surprisingly good about the whole thing. Usually this is just the kind of thing she likes to ruin for everyone.

"If anyone asks, the three of us are sixteen, okay?" Isabella adds.

"We're lying about our ages?" I ask.

"They're not going to want to hang around with babies," Isabella says, loftily. "So we're sixteen."

I don't look sixteen. Nowhere near. They're never going to believe it. But I can't stuff this up. Isabella and Millie will never forgive me.

"Okay, let's go," Isabella says.

I set off again, wobbling crazily, following behind

everyone else. This ground is too bumpy. And why are my pedals so hard to turn? I must be in the wrong gear or something. I fiddle around with the levers, but the pedals get even stiffer. There's no way I'm revealing my ignorance to Isabella, so I decide to push through the pain. It'll probably be easier going once we hit the cycle paths.

Over by their pitch, the boys are wheeling out their bikes and poking at their front tyres.

"Hi," Isabella says, skidding to a stop and leaning over the handlebars.

The boys look up and give Isabella huge grins, staring at her in awe. To be fair, she does look amazing, in these teeny shorts which make her brown legs appear a mile long, with a couple of vests layered over the top showing off her impressive cleavage, and wedge sandals. She must be freezing. I'm still bundled up in my jeans and sweatshirt. I only wish I bought that thermal vest Mum got me last winter which I refused point-blank to wear at the time.

"Hi," one of them says. He's tall and muscly, with cropped blond hair and a stud through his eyebrow. He's absolutely gorgeous. I'd kill for Isabella's confidence. Imagine being able to just go up and talk to boys like that!

"You heading into the woods for a ride?" Isabella asks.

"Yeah," the boy replies.

"Us too. Maybe we could all go together?" Isabella says,

flipping her hair over one shoulder and beaming a megawatt smile.

The older man accompanying the boys emerges from a tent and eyes us with suspicion.

"These girls were asking if they could cycle with us today, Dave," the blond boy says.

Dave starts pumping up a tyre. "'Fraid not. Sorry, girls. Our insurance doesn't cover you."

"Hmm," says Isabella. "But there's no law against biking in the woods, is there?"

"Not that I'm aware of," Dave says.

"Well, that's where we're going. You'll just happen to be there at the same time," Isabella says.

Dave rubs his hand along his goatee and frowns. "We're going off-road. You haven't got the bikes to keep up."

"Why don't you let us worry about that?" Isabella says.

Dave decides that ignoring her is the best option, and instead of replying, calls, "Come on, Ant, we're leaving."

A boy of about Harry's age emerges from the tent absorbed in a massive book, reading as he walks along.

"How come you've got a kid with you?" Isabella asks.

"My brother," one of the other boys replies. He's taller and skinnier than Blond Boy with jaw-length light-brown hair flecked thorough with natural auburn highlights. There's a stud through his lip and a beanie on his head. Like Blond Boy, he's completely gorgeous.

"Come on," Dave says to Ant again. "Put that down if you're coming with us."

"Okay, Dad, I'm coming, I'm coming," Ant says distractedly, as he turns the page. "I need to finish this chapter... okay. Done. Cool dog, by the way. Is he friendly?"

He carefully sticks a bookmark between the pages, and, as he puts the book down on the table and starts making a fuss of Murphy, I see it's the penultimate Harry Potter book.

"Hey, Harry, another Potter fan," I say.

"You're actually called Harry? You're so lucky," Ant says.

Harry doesn't answer, although out of the corner of my eye I think I can see her turning slightly pink.

"You've read them all, haven't you?" I say.

"Uh-huh," Harry replies, staring down at her pedals.

"They're good, aren't they?" Ant says. "Which is your favourite?"

"Um, I don't know," Harry says.

"You never shut up about how your favourite is book three," I say. What is going on with my sister? "Harry even does magic, don't you?" I persevere.

Harry shrugs.

"Wow, magic. That's pretty cool," Ant says. "Can you show me some?"

"Um, maybe," Harry says. "I haven't got any of my stuff with me at the moment, though."

"Maybe when we get back?"

"Yeah, I guess that should be fine," Harry mumbles.

How weird. Under most circumstances Harry would kill for a captive audience to show off her magic skills to.

"Right, lads, that tyre's sorted. Let's go," Dave calls. "Follow me."

We follow the group of boys into the wood. The tracks are wide enough to ride two abreast. Isabella's with Blond Boy, whose name turns out to be Tom. He says the other lads are Joe, Matt and Tim. Son-of-Dave-and-brother-of-Ant is Ben, who immediately starts talking to Millie. Ant's riding alongside Harry and the rest of the boys are riding up front with Dave.

I'm left by myself, right at the back, struggling to join the conversations the others are having.

"So are you guys here on holiday?" I hear Isabella ask, like she doesn't know.

"Yeah, we're doing adventure sports for Ben's birthday," Tom replies. "Dave agreed to take a bunch of us away for a few days. So far we've done night orienteering, abseiling, coasteering and hung out.

It's been a right laugh."

"We are going to stay on the path, aren't we?" I say nervously, as up ahead Dave veers into the forest.

I'd only intended Millie to hear, but Isabella replies. "Don't be so boring. We'll be fine. The boys aren't going to take us anywhere too dangerous, are you?"

Tom laughs. "I'm not making any promises."

Before long I'm falling even further back, wrestling with my pedals. It seriously feels like I'm pedalling through sand. Is my bike broken? I keep fiddling with the gears, but apart from making a few scary clanking noises, nothing seems to be happening. And my bum is so sore. Every bump I go over, pain shoots up both bum cheeks and down my thighs.

Murphy's having a fantastic time, sniffing every tree, stick and stump. Tom, Ben, Isabella, Millie, and even Harry and Ant, are chattering away and I'm feeling seriously left out. Everyone's having fun, apart from me. Well, and the skinny boy who looks like he's hating his bike as much as I am.

As we're cycling through the wood, bumping over tree roots and rocks, we pass a series of cave openings. Most of them are covered with railings, but one of them is open, a dark mouth in the hillside.

"What's that?" Isabella asks.

"A cave from when they used to do mining around here," Tom says. "We checked it out on our walk the first

206

night we were here. It's huge. Would be a great place for a party."

"Talking of parties, are you guys doing anything for the talent show?" I call. Yeah, okay, so it's a tenuous link, but I need to get in on this conversation.

The boys snort. "As if," Ben says. "That's all kinds of lame. Oh… wait. You're not, are you?"

"Um, well…" I mumble, wondering if I've said the wrong thing, then Isabella jumps in.

"I'm choreographing these two an amazing routine to a Drifting song," she says. "You should come along and watch. They're going to be amazing."

"Well, if you're going to be there, maybe it'll be laugh," Tom says.

"It will be," Isabella says. "Millie's doing really well, but Suzy's having a few problems. If she doesn't improve by Saturday, it'll be hilarious."

Fantastic. Thanks so much, Isabella.

I'm about to open my mouth to protest when Dave calls, "This way," and shoots off the path, down a sloping bank.

"Woohoo!" yell Ben and Tom. Even Millie's squealing with delight.

I want to yell too. Something with four letters, preferably.

I'm going way faster than I'm comfortable with and I hate this. Hate it, hate it. I could kill Isabella, with her stupid ideas. And now we're schlepping up the other side of the bank, onto a massive hill that's going on forever and my legs are burning with pain and——

"Look, don't take this personally, but you're kind of holding us back," I hear Tom say. "We'll go on ahead and catch up with you later on, yeah?"

"Oh. Okay. Bye, then..." Isabella calls as the boys pedal off, Ant trailing after them. She's obviously disappointed. "I bet that was because of you," Isabella hisses at me crossly as I catch up with them. "You came down that hill at the speed of some old granny."

I'm saved by the sound of Isabella's phone chiming.

"Mobile reception!" Isabella screeches.

I grab my phone from my pocket and wait impatiently for it to come on. Three bars! I've got three whole bars!

The bing-bong text receipts from Isabella's phone go on and on.

"How many messages have you got?" Millie asks enviously. Her phone's only gone a couple of times.

Isabella's scrolling through her messages at about ninety miles an hour, wincing and laughing and tapping back answers at top speed.

"Um, a hundred and three," she says. "I need to reply

to some of these. You guys are going to have to wait a bit."

I stare down at my phone. Still no messages. Not one... oh wait. A message! It's from Danny!

How RU? Hope ur havin fun. Sorry cldnt tlk y'day. Miss u x

Really? I've been away for days and all I get is one message. And that's what it says?

I'll try to give him a ring. I haven't spoken to him in ages and I really want to hear his voice. I press the green call button, but the phone just rings. There's no answer.

I try again. Still nothing.

Sighing, I stick my phone back in my pocket. Isabella's still got her head bowed over the phone, her thumb moving in a speedy blur as she types out texts.

"How much longer are you going to be?" Harry whines.

"I've missed loads," Isabella mutters. "I think my friends were on the verge of putting out a missing person announcement for me. I've never been without my phone for so long. Never!"

"Even when you were a baby?" Harry asks.

Isabella rolls her eyes and doesn't reply. I'm smirking, but don't let her see.

"Okay, we can go," Isabella eventually says.

We set off again, legs pumping hard as we struggle to make it up the hill. I'm on the point of thinking I'm going to either pass out or die because my lungs have exploded when we finally reach the top of the slope.

"Tyre tracks," Isabella says, pointing to the ground. "They went this way."

Now we're on a downhill strip of path again. Ah, this is much better. My bum's still painful, but I'm not feeling like I want to keel over any more. We're freewheeling pretty fast, but actually, it's kind of okay seeing the scenery whizz past. Downhill is good.

"Hole!" Millie calls, veering around a big dip in the ground. But I've been so busy daydreaming I don't register what she's said until it's too late. I slam on the brakes, but my front tyre has dipped. Before I know it, the bike's flipped forwards and I'm flying through the air.

I put my hands out to brace myself against the impact and my wrist buckles underneath me.

Oh, oh, oh, it hurts, it hurts so bad!

There are spots in front of my eyes and I think I'm going to pass out...

CHAPTER EIGHTEEN

I don't pass out.

I almost do, then Murphy runs up and slobbers all over my face. I pull myself back from the brink to shove him and his gross doggy breath away from me with my non-hurty hand. Not before his tongue actually went into my mouth, though.

Gagfest.

As if French kissing the stinky mutt wasn't bad enough, my arm is killing. I have to bite the inside of my cheek to stop myself crying. It's embarrassing enough to fall off my bike, without boohooing and making everything worse.

"Harry, Isabella, stop! Suzy's fallen off! Ohmigod, Suze, are you okay?" Millie flings her bike to the ground and rushes over.

"No," I whimper. "I think I've done something really bad to my wrist."

"Now we're never going to catch up with the boys," Isabella moans as she skids to a halt nearby.

Millie gently helps me to stand and puts her arm around me protectively. "Can you move it?"

"Careful," Isabella says. "I damaged my wrist once, during a tournament. We need to make you some kind of sling. Harry, chuck us your jumper."

Isabella busies herself fashioning a sling and soon my wrist is nestled up against my chest. It feels weird having Isabella so close to me, literally breathing down my neck.

"Thanks," I say, weakly, but she doesn't respond.

"Are you feeling strong enough to go back?" Millie asks. "You've gone a really weird colour."

"I'm not sure I'll be able to cycle," I say. I try to flex my hand and yelp with pain. Oh, oh, oh, it really huuuurttts. The pain is throbbing up all the way to my shoulder.

I attempt to pick up my bike, but can't manage it. It's just too painful.

"We need to get you back to the campsite," Millie says, sounding concerned. "If you can walk, we'll take turns to push your bike."

Isabella's clearly not happy about this plan, but she's got no choice but to pitch in.

It's not easy manoeuvring these slopes and bumpy ground pushing two bikes, so whoever's pushing mine

212

really struggles. I'm walking gingerly behind as any kind of sudden movement or jarring sends pain shooting up my arm again.

Mum comes racing over when she sees us.

"What on earth's happened?"

"I fell off my bike and I've done something to my hand," I say, in so much pain I don't even mind her fussing.

"Let me see. Can you move it? No? In that case, we need to get you to the hospital to get that looked at. Chris! Get your car keys!"

As we sign in at the reception, one of the nurses recognises us, and makes a dumb joke asking if we'd like a loyalty card.

Nobody laughs.

Why do these things *always* happen to me? There's probably nobody else on the planet who could end up in hospital twice in one week because of a rat bite on their toe and a horrible injury to their hand.

We're eventually seen by the same doctor I saw last time. She pokes and prods me, before announcing I could have fractured it, so they need to send me for an X-ray.

I keep trying to ring Danny, but he's not answering his phone.

213

I want to cry. Where's he gone? Has he forgotten about me, just because I've gone on holiday?

"I'm going to get another cup of tea," Mum says. "Want one, Chris?"

Dad rustles his paper. "Might as well, can't see we're getting out of here anytime soon."

Mum's on her way out of the cubicle when rat-bite doctor comes in.

"Right," she says. "Your X-rays showed us you've got a minor fracture in your wrist. We'll put a soft cast on it now to let the swelling go down, then you'll need to go to the fracture clinic and get it put in a proper cast. We'll give you a letter so you can sort that out at your local hospital when you get home."

"Is she going to suffer any kind of permanent damage?" Mum asks. "She is going to be able to use her hand properly when it's better?"

"Absolutely," the doctor says. "It's not a severe break. We'll give her a sling to help support the arm. And it's not your dominant hand, is it?"

I shake my head.

"You're one of the unluckiest people I've ever met," the doctor says. "A rat bite and a fracture – some holiday, eh?"

I do my best to smile at her. But I don't feel much like laughing about it yet.

214

"You'll need to keep the hand as still as possible," the doctor tells me. "We'll get you bandaged up as soon as we can."

"Well, that's you out of the talent competition, then," Mum says.

Oh yeah. Ah well. I suppose every cloud has a silver lining. I hope Millie won't be too gutted. I think she was kind of looking forward to it. She's weird like that.

And now at least Isabella won't be winning any prizes. Hah. Serves her right.

Millie and Isabella are wandering out of the awning when we pull up in the car. Millie rushes over and yanks open the door.

"Are you okay?" Millie asks. "Oh my God, you're all bandaged up – and you've got a cast! It was broken, then?"

"Yeah, my wrist is fractured," I say, shuffling myself out of the car with difficulty. Turns out it's harder to do things one-handed than you'd think. Don't get me started on how hard it was to get my jeans back up after I went for a pee earlier.

I'm so focused on trying to get out of the car without falling flat on my face that it's a while before I see Millie and Isabella are wearing matching outfits.

215

"Um, what's with the clothes?" I ask, trying to give a relaxed, I-don't-care giggle, but it comes out sounding like someone's strangling a cat.

"I figured you wouldn't be able to dance," Isabella says. "You went down with such a crash. Millie's put so much effort in, I decided to take your place. I wanted to get the right clothes for our first practice. You don't mind, do you?"

"Course not," I say, trying to force a smile.

"Are you sure?" Millie asks, and I can tell she's genuinely concerned, which makes me feel a bit better. I don't know why I care so much. I didn't want to do the stupid dance, anyway.

"Sure," I say, still trying to force that smile.

"Suzy needs to sit down," Mum says, fussing around me.

"Have you got a plaster cast?" Harry says, running up, Ant following close behind. "Oooh, you have!"

"We should keep practising," Isabella says to Millie.

"Do we have to?" Millie says. "I haven't seen Suzy all afternoon and I want to make sure she's okay. Besides, we've practised loads."

"I know, but I'd be happier if we could go and do a bit more. It's not long until the talent show, you know."

"But..."

Isabella pouts. "Can you imagine the humiliation if a dancer of my status didn't win this stupid thing? It would be mortifying. Mort. If. Fying. I would literally die. Please, Millie."

"You looked pretty good to me," Millie says, but I can tell she's weakening.

"Pleeeease," Isabella pleads.

"Oh, all right," Millie says, admitting defeat. "But not for long, okay? I want to come back and see Suzy."

"I could always come and watch," I say.

"Nope, you're staying here where I can keep an eye on you," Mum says.

Protesting does no good. Mum's determined that I rest.

Isabella links her arm through Millie's before they run off together.

As I watch them go, I realise that anyone watching would think they were best friends.

CHAPTER NINETEEN

"So who's coming over to the entertainment later?" Mum asks breezily as we clear away the plates from supper. "Tonight they've got a Romanian pan-piper. It should be good."

"Actually, we thought we'd go and hang out with some friends we've made," Isabella says casually.

Huh? That's the first I've heard of it.

"That's great," Clare says. "I haven't seen many teenagers around. Whereabouts is their plot?"

"Just over there," Isabella says, waving her arm vaguely.

"So tell us more," Mum says. "You said friends. Sisters? Or girls here with friends, like you?"

"Nope, it's that group of boys," Isabella says, smiling brightly.

Mum and Clare exchange a look. Dad looks up from his paper and raises his eyebrows.

"We're just going to sit around their campfire for a bit,"

Isabella elaborates, seeing the not-entirely-pleased faces of the parentals.

"I'm not sure about this," Mum says.

"I'm with Jen," Clare says. "Those boys are definitely older than you."

"So?" Isabella says. "Who cares?"

"Mum, we're not babies," Millie chips in. "All we're going to do is sit and talk. We do it at home with Jamie and Danny all the time."

"Yes, but we know Jamie and Danny," Mum says. "And Isabella, we're supposed to be responsible for you. I'm not sure what your mum would say about this."

"She'd let me go. She wouldn't care," Isabella says. "Seriously. She wouldn't be bothered."

"We're going to be right over there," Millie says. "What do you think's going to happen?"

"I'm not sure..." Mum says.

Part of me is relieved they're saying no. I don't want to go and hang out with those guys. I don't want to have to pretend to be sixteen, watching my friends flirting while I get ignored. But something tells me Isabella and Millie aren't going to give in easily.

"Jen, nothing's going to happen," Isabella says, smiling sweetly. She's clearly on a charm offensive, determined to get her own way.

"What do you think, Chris?" Mum asks.

Dad sighs heavily. "I know about teenage boys. They're trouble. But as long as they're just going to sit around a campfire, in full view of everyone, I fail to see how they can get into that much mischief. Their chaperone's going to be there as well, isn't he? Dave, his name is. Good bloke. I got chatting to him at the shop."

Isabella and Millie nod their heads furiously.

"Clare?" says Mum.

"Do you promise you'll stay with the group? And not wander off? And you'll be back by ten-thirty?" Clare says.

"Ten-thirty?" Isabella howls in outrage. "It's hardly worth going out."

"Ten-thirty," Clare says. "Those are the conditions. Take them or leave them. What do you think, Jen?"

"Sounds reasonable to me," Mum says.

"That's so unfair," Isabella mutters.

"Take it or leave it," Mum says.

Millie shoots me an excited glance.

"Um, am I coming too?" I ask Millie quietly once we're out in the awning.

"Course you are!" Millie says.

"It's just you didn't say anything, so I didn't know…"

"Don't be daft. Sorry I didn't tell you. We arranged it with them earlier today while you were at the hospital.

220

I'm just going to get ready. See you in a minute."

"Your parents are really strict, aren't they?" I hear Isabella say as they disappear off to their tent. "My mum wouldn't care what I was doing. Or what time I'd be back."

I'm not going to make the same mistake as last time, when I looked a wreck while they got all glammed up, so I take my time choosing an outfit. Skinny jeans, long pretty blue top and a thin cardi that I get Amber to help me put on. It's not exactly the warmest, but it looks nice, and we're going to be sitting near a fire – it can't be that cold.

Hair, hair, hair… what am I going to do about my hair? It's a hopeless case. Beyond rescue. I could spend all night grooming it and it still wouldn't behave. I'm limited in what I can do to it with one hand, so in the end I put some serum through the front, and get Mum to put the rest of it back into a loose ponytail. I'll just have to hope it doesn't start raining. Now for my make-up, and I'm good to go.

From Millie and Isabella's tent I can hear the sound of helpless giggling.

Once again I get that pang of left-outness. I try to tell myself I'm just being silly, that I'm imagining things, that Millie's my best friend and nothing – and nobody –

is going to change that, but it's becoming harder to convince myself.

"What's so funny?" I ask, unzipping their tent.

"Long story," Millie says. She and Isabella catch each other's eyes, then crack up again. Meanwhile I'm left hovering like a lemon outside the tent.

"Um, are you guys ready?" I ask, when it becomes apparent they're not going to share the joke.

"Yeah, sorry, we're just coming," Millie says, adjusting the streak in her hair and quickly giving her eyes a flick of black eyeliner at each corner. She looks fantastic, and blows a kiss with her cherry-red lips at the mirror. "Ready, Isabella?"

Yet again, Isabella looks absolutely stunning. She's wearing a floaty dress with these big boots and a gorgeous navy coat to keep her warm. Her face might as well have been airbrushed, it's so flawless.

I felt all right a moment ago, but now, compared to these two, I'm suddenly not so sure. Now I feel like the frumpy one.

"Let's go," Millie says, ducking out of the tent and linking her arm into mine. "You look great, Suze. Love your top. Although won't you be cold?"

"Nope," I lie, doing my best to control my teeth, which are already starting to chatter.

Harry's following us, but doesn't come near the fire. Instead she does a detour round to one of the tents. "Going to hang out with Ant. See you later," she calls.

The boys are milling around, sitting on logs arranged in a circle around the fire. I can't see Dave there. When we approach, Ben and Tom jump to their feet.

They're even better-looking than I remember.

Am I seriously going to be expected to talk to these guys? This isn't like on a bike ride when there's something else to concentrate on. This is just us and them. My mouth's so dry I don't feel like I'm ever going to be able to speak again in my life and I'm sure people must be able to hear my heart drumming away in my chest. Oh God, I need to think of things to say that are cool and funny. Millie and Isabella will never forgive me if I stuff this up.

"Don't forget we're sixteen," Isabella says in a low voice.

Aagh! I *had* forgotten we were supposed to be sixteen. What do sixteen-year-olds talk about? Won't they be able to tell straightaway that I'm not as old as I'm pretending to be?

"All right?" Tom says, as he leaps over a log to join us.

"Hi," chorus Millie and Isabella. I open my mouth to speak, but still can't form any words, and make a weird strangled noise instead. I cover it up with a cough.

"What happened to your arm?" Tom says, indicating my cast.

"Fell off my bike. Idiot, right?" I say, trying to sound flippant and breezy. I attempt a flirty smile, but I suspect it comes out as a grimace, because Tom frowns slightly before turning his attention to Millie and Isabella.

"Coming to sit down?"

I follow the others nearer the fire, where they join Tom and Ben on their log. I hover awkwardly until they're settled, and then realise there's no room for me. I'm going to have to go and sit somewhere else.

"Hi," I say nervously, as I plant myself next to the guy who was struggling with his bike on the cycle ride. A kindred spirit. I rack my brains for what his name was. "Joe, right?"

"Yup," he says. "And you're, um... I really sorry, I can't remember your name."

"Suzy," I remind him.

"What happened to your arm?"

"Flipped over my handlebars and fractured it," I say. "Spent all day in A & E."

"That sucks."

"Yeah. Adventure sports really aren't my thing."

"Me neither," Joe says, staring into the fire. Sneaking

a peek out of the corner of my eye, I can see he doesn't seem the adventure sports type. In fact, he looks kind of... weedy. Really skinny, with pale skin and more than a few spots smattering his jawline. His dark hair is jaw-length and hanging loosely around his face.

"How come you're here, then?" I ask, genuinely curious.

"Dad thought it would be good for me," Joe tells me. "He said I was spending too much time playing video games and needed to get out and experience the world, or something equally lame. He loves this stuff. So do my brothers, Ben and Ant."

"Ben's your brother?" I ask, incredulous. They look nothing like each other. I don't mean to be rude or anything, but Ben is seriously hot. Joe... well, he really isn't.

"Yup," Joe says. "Big brother."

"So how old are you?"

"Fourteen."

"Oh, same as us," I say without thinking.

Then I wince as an icy horror trickles through my veins. Nice going, Suze! You've been here less than ten minutes and you've already blown it.

Isabella and Millie are going to *kill* me.

"I thought you were older," Joe says.

"Ha ha, yes, I meant I'm fourteen. Millie and Isabella are the same age as Ben," I say, backtracking hastily. I'm on the spot, and there's no other lie I can think of that won't give the game away about the others.

"So, um, you like video games?" I ask, trying to change the subject.

"Yeah," Joe says and starts telling me all about what level he's up to on this shoot-'em-up, and how he's formulated a master plan to get past some big enemy and can't wait to get home to try it out... or something. I'm not really listening.

As Joe's speaking, I'm keeping half an eye on Millie and Isabella. Tom's definitely into Isabella. And the more I watch, it looks horribly like Ben thinks he's in with Millie.

To my dismay, Millie doesn't seem to be acting like a person with a boyfriend.

Unless I'm very much mistaken, she's flirting like mad, flicking her hair around the place and laughing like a lunatic. What's going on? Has she forgotten all about Jamie? She's talking non-stop and... oh, God... now she's got her hand on his arm.

What's she *doing*?

I feel sick. Does Millie want something to happen with this guy? What if she gets off with him and doesn't tell Jamie? Will I have to keep secrets for her?

Stop it, Suze, I tell myself firmly. *Nothing's even happened yet.*

On the other side of the fire, I realise the boys are passing around a cola bottle. But given the way they're all swigging from it, I'm going to say it's a pretty safe bet it's not cola in there.

Uh oh. What if I get offered that? I can't not drink it, I'll look a total baby. Maybe I could pretend... but would anyone be convinced? Gah, I'm rubbish at being mature and sophisticated. I want to go back to our caravan, and I never in a million years thought I'd be saying *that*.

Even Uno's sounding appealing right now.

As I look to see if Millie and Isabella have noticed what's going on, Tom places his hand on Isabella's waist, and lowers his head down to hers. In a matter of seconds, they're kissing passionately.

Lordy, she doesn't waste time, does she? Some of the other boys start clapping and cheering so Tom pulls away.

"Come on," he says, a smile dancing around his lips as he takes Isabella's hand and pulls her to her feet. She looks like the cat that got the cream as she allows herself to be walked away from the circle and into the woods.

"Um, should we do something?" I say to Millie, who's mucking around with Ben.

227

"About what?"

"That!" I say, indicating to where Isabella's gone. If anything happens to her, Mum's going to kill me.

"She'll be fine," Ben says. "Tom's sound."

"I don't fancy your chances if you go after her," Millie says. "I'd leave them to it, if I were you."

"Fancy some of this?" Ben asks, pulling his toasting fork out from the fire and blowing on the melty marshmallow. He pulls off the charred piece and blows it, then drops it into Millie's mouth, getting sticky strands all over her chin.

"Millie, can I have a word?" I say.

"Sure," Millie replies. "What's up?"

"Not here," I say. "Um… somewhere a bit more private?"

Millie doesn't look overly impressed to leave her warm spot next to the fire, but follows.

"What are you doing?" I ask, trying not to shiver. It's *so* cold out here.

"What do you mean?"

"You. And Ben. What's going on?"

"Nothing," Millie says. "Just having a laugh, that's all."

"It's just… it sort of looks like more than that, that's all. And I'm worried about Isabella, too."

"Would you just chill?" Millie says. "Don't worry so much. Just have a good time, okay?"

"But what about Jamie?"

"What about Jamie?" Millie says, her eyes sparkling. "He's not here. I'm just having fun. Like you should be doing. Why don't you go and talk to that boy again? I think he likes you."

And with that, she returns to Ben, who immediately starts feeding her more marshmallow.

I slump back next to Joe, who looks delighted to see me. "You're back."

"Yeah," I say, distractedly looking for Isabella. There's still no sign of her. What the heck is she up to in that forest?

Joe inches nearer. And then nearer still. And then I cotton on to what he's doing.

Oh good grief, does he think he's got a chance with me?

"Um, where's Dave?" I ask nervously.

"Gone to the entertainment," Joe says.

He gets nearer still, and now I can feel his leg pressed up against mine.

Irk! What do I do now?

"I've got a boyfriend," I say quickly.

"Blown out! That told you, Joey-baby," hoots Matt. He's sitting on the other side of Joe.

Joe immediately gets up and disappears into one of the tents without saying another word.

I have never wanted to leave anywhere more in my life.

And then, to my relief, Isabella and Tom join us in the circle. To say Isabella looks smug would be the understatement of the century.

"Um, it's ten-thirty," I say, checking my watch.

Isabella rolls her eyes. "So?"

"So that's curfew and we need to get back?" I say awkwardly, aware of what a saddo I sound.

"It's fine. They've all gone to bed. The lights are off in the caravan, look," Isabella says.

I shake my head. "Mum won't be sleeping. So unless you want her to actually come and get us in her pyjamas, which she will, let me assure you, we'd better go."

Isabella huffs. "Honestly, it's like we're babies. I'm not going yet."

"Great," Tom says, grabbing hold of Isabella's hand.

Gah. Am I going to get into more trouble for going back late, or going back by myself and leaving Isabella?

What do I doooooo?

I'm still trying to figure out what the answer is when I see Dave approaching. He doesn't look happy.

Ben clears his throat. "Dad's coming, mate…"

Isabella and Tom hastily pull apart.

"What's going on?" Dave asks, standing at the edge of our circle.

"Nothing," Tom says. "Just toasting marshmallows. Want one?"

"I meant these girls," Dave says, frowning.

"We were just passing and really fancied a marshmallow," Isabella says, smiling sweetly. "I'm sorry, we didn't mean to get anyone into trouble. We were just leaving."

Dave's expression suggests he's unconvinced, but his stance softens. "Well, as long as you're not staying. I'm responsible for this lot – can't have any funny business going on!"

"Of course. Come on, Millie, Suzy. Let's go," Isabella says. "Night," she says, as she wafts past Dave.

Finally. We're outta here.

I make a short detour to collect Harry from Ant's tent as Ben and Tom follow Millie and Isabella.

"You guys around tomorrow?" Isabella asks.

"No. We're canoeing all day," Tom says. "But we're around tomorrow night. Come and hang out with us again?"

"Sure," Isabella says. She gives a quick check to make sure Dave's not looking, then stands on tiptoes to give Tom a kiss goodbye.

Ben looks expectantly at Millie.

She grins cheekily and blows him a kiss. "See you."

Isabella and Millie are clearly on a high as Isabella gives Millie the low-down of what she and Tom got up to in the wood. Long, romantic kisses under the stars, apparently, with no detail left undiscussed.

I don't say a word all the way back.

I'm not sure anyone notices.

CHAPTER TWENTY

I don't get a lot of sleep. My wrist is still throbbing despite the painkillers, and every time I turn over I wake up because it hurts so much. Next morning I'm sleep-deprived and cranky.

My mood isn't helped by the fact it's raining incessantly again, and showing no signs of letting up. Is this flipping summer ever going to actually arrive?

"I can't spend another day on this campsite in the rain," Amber says. "Mum, what can we do?"

"I'm going home to get my bits and pieces for the talent show," Dad says. "And I *am* going today. There will be no more trips to hospital on this holiday, you hear?"

"I still can't believe you're doing a round trip all for a tr—"

"Ah, ah, Jen!" Dad interrupts. "Don't give anything away. And yes, it'll be a long journey, but to be honest,

I'm looking forward to it. Time to myself in the car? Sounds blissful."

"You're being so mysterious about this whole talent show thing," I say. "You can't have that many skills we don't know about."

"Ah, you'll see," Mum says.

"I thought Dad's only talents were watching telly and eating a whole tube of Pringles in one go," I say.

"Oh, ha ha," Dad says. "You wait, young lady. You'll eat your words when you see what your old dad's been hiding up his sleeve."

Yeah, yeah, I won't hold my breath. I bet Dad's talent turns out to be a talking hand puppet, or something equally lame that he's totally hyping.

"Dad, can I come?" Amber asks. "Only for the day. I really, really want to see Mark. I miss him so much..."

"Won't Mark be at work?" Dad says. "I'm sorry, Amber, but I need to get there and back quickly. It'll take much longer if I have to stop at every service station en route for you to pee. I'll take Harry, if Harry wants a road trip, but not the rest of you. What do you say, kiddo?"

"Erm, do you know what, Dad, I think I'm going to stay here," Harry says, shuffling her feet and looking sheepish. That's weird. She never turns down opportunities for Dad time, and the chance to do a road trip where she'll get control of the radio and sit in the front seat – plus Dad will feed her all sorts of sugary and salty snacks – is not one she'd give up easily.

"Why don't you want to go?" I ask.

"Um, I'm meeting Ant when they get back from canoeing," Harry says, fidgeting in her chair. "He's got the Harry Potter board game I really want to play and he said we could do it today."

"I want to go home," Amber says, her bottom lip wobbling dangerously. Honestly, since she got pregnant this girl leaks more water than a tap. "I really, really, want to see my Markymoo…"

"Well, we'll have to think of something fun to do," Mum says, hurriedly. "Don't cry, love, you know stress isn't good for the babies. Why don't we drive into town? I know it's a bit of a way away but we've nothing else to do and we can buy some things for the babies."

"We can? So far we need… well, everything, I suppose." Amber suddenly starts to freak out. "We don't have anything. Nothing at all. Oh God, what if the babies come early and we don't have any clothes for them? And they don't have anywhere to sleep? We'd be the worst parents in the world! They'd take the babies away!" Amber's voice has risen into a banshee-like wail.

"Calm down. We will buy what you need ready for

when these little ones make their appearance." Mum gives Amber a squeeze.

"Really?" Amber says, between gasping, shuddery breaths. "Phew."

Dad goes pale. "You're spending more money?" he asks.

Mum pats his arm. "Don't worry, it won't be much. We'll get a few essentials – a few baby clothes and whatnot to cheer Amber up and make her less worried. She can get the rest of the things when we get home."

"Well, make sure that's all it is," Dad says. "Budgeting rules still apply on holiday, you know. A couple of Babygros and maybe a rattle or a nice teddy or something, but that's it, all right? Amber and Mark are living rent-free in our house; they can afford to buy their own things for *their own children.*"

Dad stresses the last part meaningfully.

"Absolutely," Mum says, nodding her head. Dad doesn't see the wink she sends in Amber's direction.

Just then, the minibus containing the boys drives past and trundles across the field out of the gate. Isabella stares after it longingly.

"If we're all going to town, you're going to have to take Murphy," Mum says to Dad.

"What?" Dad says.

"Well, we can't take him shopping."

"Would you mind?" Clare says. "We'd be ever so grateful. We can't leave him by himself."

Crystal Fairybelle is staying in the caravan – all that dog does is sleep, anyway. Murphy's different, though, shut him in the caravan for more than half an hour and by the time you come back there'll be no caravan left.

Dad grumbles, but Clare eventually sweet-talks him, and soon Murphy's in the back of our Volvo, panting happily as he stares out of the window.

Then we're off, crammed into Clare's car. There's loads of room now the dog grill's taken down and Murphy's not hogging all the space. Admittedly it takes hours to drive to a town with a shopping centre, but no matter. We're out!

"Right, I'm going to start at the bookshop," Clare says when we pull into a parking space. "I'll meet you back at the car later, okay?"

"Don't forget to ring Dad," Millie calls after her.

Clare doesn't look like she's heard.

Isabella eyes the high street with undisguised delight. "Let's shop! Where first, Mills?"

"We'll meet you back here at about midday, girls," Mum says. "Does that sound okay? That should be enough time to look around and get a few things, then we can have some lunch and head back."

"Suze, you're coming with us, aren't you?" Amber says.

"Um, I was actually planning on going with these guys…"

No way do I venture into the unmitigated hell of baby shops. Hitting the bridal boutiques earlier in the year was bad enough.

"Please, Suzypoos," Amber says, making puppy dog eyes. "Please, please. You're going to be auntie to the babies. Your opinion really matters."

I can't really argue with that, can I?

"But…" I say, turning towards Millie and Isabella. Isabella's already pulling Millie away, clearly eager to start spending.

"Bye," Millie says apologetically.

"Yeah, bye," I mutter.

Left out. Again.

"Right then," says Mum. "To the baby shops!"

"Wow, look at you, Mum-to-be," a shop assistant gushes, coming over as we enter. "When are you due? Looks like any day now."

"I've still got over a month to go," Amber says.

"Really?" the assistant says. "But you're massive!"

"It's twins," Mum interjects before Amber gets too offended.

"Twins!" the lady exclaims, clapping with delight. "How wonderful. Double the trouble, double the joy, or so they say. Have you chosen your names?"

"I'm thinking about Lemon and Lyme," Amber says. "Lyme with a y, though, obviously."

"Obviously," the shop assistant says, her smile wavering. "What unusual choices. Now, what do you already have, and what do you need?"

"Um, well, I have some baby books," Amber says.

"Excellent," says the shop assistant. "And what else?"

"Er, nothing," Amber tells her.

"Nothing?" the shop assistant looks horrified.

"No," Amber says, and her breathing gets all quick and panicky again.

"We were just hoping to get a few bits and pieces today," Mum interjects, rubbing a hand over Amber's back. "Not much. Maybe a couple of Babygros and a blanket, or something like that."

"But you do know twins can come early, don't you?" says the sales assistant.

"Well, we're hoping that won't happen," Mum says, laughing nervously. "We're planning on buying most of the bits when we get back home. We're only here on holiday, you see. Only popped in to get an idea of the things we might need."

"But we've got a wonderful sale on at the moment," the woman presses. "And if you're buying two of everything, saving money is going to be important, am I right?"

 239

"She is," whispers Amber. "And what if the babies do come soon?"

"It *would* be awful if they came early and we had nothing for them," Mum agrees, weakening.

The assistant clearly has no intention of letting this sale go, especially when the pound signs are clanging in her eyes at the thought of all the commission she stands to make selling double of everything. "Let me show you some products you'll need…"

An hour later Harry and I are collapsed in the corner of the shop, while the pile of stuff Amber and Mum have picked out grows higher and higher. Baby bottles, monitors, changing mats, sterilisers, baby baths, clothes in neutral colours, bedding, even something called a wipe-warmer. Who knew that such tiny people needed so much?

All I can think about is the fun Millie and Isabella are probably having somewhere. Without me.

Amber's asked Harry and my opinion on everything little thing. And really, it's sweet that she cares, but we have nothing useful to offer. We know nada about babies, or baby things.

I get up and, out of sheer boredom, wander over to the prams. Yeowch. Prams are seriously expensive!

"Can I help you, madam?" a slimy-looking male assistant comes over. "When are you due?"

"What?" I splutter as Harry starts giggling. "It's not for me. It's for my sister."

The sales assistant raises an eyebrow dubiously, and I vow never to wear this outfit ever again if it makes me look flipping pregnant. How blimmin' rude!

I sit down again and refuse to look anyone in the eye, busying myself fiddling with my phone. I try Danny's number again, but surprise surprise, there's no answer.

I'm starting to think he's avoiding me.

The shop doesn't only sell baby stuff, it sells children's clothes too, and Harry's wandered off and started browsing. She emerges with a denim skirt.

"Um, what do you think of this?" she asks me, a little sheepishly.

What's she picking up that for? Harry's the biggest tomboy on the planet. I didn't think she even knew what a skirt was.

"What are you getting a skirt for?"

"No reason," Harry says, but her cheeks are flaming. "I, um… just like it, that's all. I'd like to wear it at the talent show. I'm going to add it to the pile of stuff on the counter. Mum'll never notice."

Half an hour later, we're all struggling out of the shop, laden down under the weight of tons of bags.

Dad is going to flip when he sees them. Mum and

Amber got totally carried away, and we haven't even got it all with us — Mum's arranged to have half of it posted on. As she tries to force bags into the boot, she turns and eyeballs us fiercely.

"Nobody say a word to your father about this, you understand?" she instructs. "I'm going to have to hide all this stuff somewhere in the caravan to get it back home."

"What's it worth?" Harry says, never one to miss an opportunity. "There's that magic set I've been wanting for ages, and a toy shop over there…"

"That's blackmail, young lady," Mum says. "And we've spent more than enough money today."

"Okay then," Harry says, shrugging. "Although I can't promise something won't slip out when Dad asks what we've been up to today."

Mum extracts her purse from her handbag, passing Harry twenty pounds. "I suppose I can't really treat Amber without getting things for the rest of you too," she says. "Off you go. But make sure you come straight back, okay?"

"Brilliant! Thanks, Mum, you're the best," Harry says, dashing off towards the toy shop.

"Dad's going to go nuts when he sees this," I say. "There's no way you're going to be able to hide it from him."

"Shhh," Mum says. "Of course we'll be able to. We'll tell him… someone gave it to us. Or something. It'll be fine.

Now help put this into the boot, would you, please?"

And then I see it. Hanging on a nearby market stall.

A Mulberry bag. It's beautiful.

I wonder how much it is? I know they're dead expensive.

I go for a closer look, and do a double take at the price tag. Far from being the hundreds of pounds I expected, it's actually pretty reasonable. Because it's not actually a Mulberry bag at all. Although you'd never know unless you looked really, really closely.

Oh. I love it. I love it, I love it.

And nobody would know it's not an authentic one. It looks exactly the same.

I disappear off into a wonderful daydream where everything's different with the bag. I'm glossy, I'm groomed, I'm swishing around in a confident swirl. Everything about me would be better if I had that bag. I'm sure of it.

"You buying that, love?" says the market trader.

"Um... let me go and talk to my mum a minute," I say, running back to the car.

Harry's sprawled across the back seat, pulling apart her magic set with glee.

"Mum, you know how Amber got all this baby stuff, and Harry's got her magic kit?"

"Hmm," Mum says distractedly, still wrestling with all the baby clothes.

"Could I get a bag?"

"Well, I can't get something for both of your sisters and not for you," Mum says. She opens her purse again, and passes me another twenty.

"Uh, it's a bit more than that," I say.

"I haven't got any more," Mum says.

"Please?" I beg. "Please, please, pretty please with a cherry on the top? It's not much more, and you can give it to me as part of my birthday present if you like?"

"It's not your birthday for months," Mum says.

"I know," I say, "but I really love it. Please? Please, please, please..."

"Oh, all right," Mum says wearily. She passes a pack of nappies to Harry. "Try to fit these somewhere while I nip to the cashpoint, would you?"

"Thanks, Mum, you're the best!" I say, bouncing up and down, then giving her a big one-armed hug.

"Hi." Mum waves, seeing Clare walking towards us. "Did you manage to track down Martin?"

"No," Clare says vaguely. "He was in a meeting. Crikey, you've been busy, haven't you?"

"All essentials," Mum says. "I'm just popping to the cashpoint. Keep an eye on this lot until I get back, would you?"

As soon as Mum returns with the cash, I head over to the market stall and buy my bag. The trader puts it into a carrier bag for me and I grin broadly at him.

I know it's just a bag. I know it's not going to change anything dramatically. But everything feels that bit better and a touch more sparkly with my almost-Mulberry packed up and ready to go.

I'm swinging my carrier bag happily when I spot Millie and Isabella emerging from one of the little side alleys. Their arms are linked, and their heads are close together as they chat away non-stop.

My happiness disappears in a flash.

They look more and more like best friends every day.

And check out the bags Isabella's carrying. She's given her credit cards a serious workout. And they're not the cheapy plastic carrier bags she's got, either. They're the proper ones, made of cardboard, with ribbons for handles. Designer bags, from expensive shops.

Millie's got one too, a funky turquoise one with hot pink ribbons. How did she get the money to shop there?

All of a sudden I feel cheap and silly, with my plastic bag full of fake Mulberry from the market.

"Hi!" Millie says, running over.

"Hi," I say, forcing a smile.

"How did you get on at the baby shop?" Millie asks.

Without waiting for my answer, she continues, "Isabella and I had such a great time. She spent so much money, it was insane. She's brought us these amazing new matching outfits for the talent show." Millie holds the shopping bag aloft, bubbling away. I can't remember the last time I saw her so happy.

"It wasn't a big deal," Isabella says, dismissively. "This was nothing compared to how much I usually spend. The shops are rubbish here."

"And you got something too," Millie says. "What did you get?"

"Um, just a new bag," I say, trying to hide it behind my back, but Millie grabs it and peers inside.

"Ooooh, a Mulberry," she squeals. "It's gorgeous."

Isabella peers in. "Fake."

"Well, yeah," I say. "But you can hardly tell it's not the real thing…"

"You really can't," Millie says, loyally.

"If you don't know what the real thing looks like, maybe," Isabella says. "But the stitching's all wrong, and the clasp is different…"

I snatch the bag back.

Why does Isabella always have to do that? And why doesn't Millie ever notice?

CHAPTER TWENTY-ONE

I'm dreading hanging out with the boys tonight.

I just don't want to. I don't want to get stuck with Joe again, although he'll probably avoid coming anywhere near me, after last time. I don't want to watch my best friend conveniently ignoring the fact she's got a boyfriend. I don't want to feel left out and miserable.

But Isabella's not stopped going on about Tom. And Millie's going where Isabella is. Which means I'm stuck.

As soon as supper's finished, Millie and Isabella are racing out of the caravan to get changed. Then we're traipsing across the field to where the bonfire's burning. Ant's waiting for Harry, and they immediately disappear off to his tent. If I didn't know my tomboy sister better, I'd think something was going on with those two. Isabella nestles in close to Tom, while Millie finds a spare seat on the log next to Ben. There's enough room for me, too, so I squeeze in next to her. Matt's on my other side. That should be safe enough.

"Dad doesn't know you're here, so if you see him coming, make yourselves scarce, okay?" Ben says.

"Will do," Isabella says, putting her hand onto Tom's thigh.

"So, what have you guys been up to today?" Millie asks. "Was it the canoeing? How did it go?"

"Mind if we join you?"

We look up to see two girls standing at the edge of our circle. Gorgeous girls. Older girls. Ridiculously tall girls. One blonde, one brunette, with swishy hair, amazing figures and an easy confidence. Girls who wouldn't have to pretend to be sixteen.

"Sure," Matt says, the biggest grin in the world on his face.

Isabella's expression is the polar opposite. She's giving the girls the fiercest death stare I've ever seen in my life.

"I'm Jem," the brunette says as they collapse down onto the logs. "And this is Cat."

Isabella scoots possessively closer to Tom.

"When did you get here?" Matt asks.

"This afternoon," Cat says. "With my parents. It's dead round here, isn't it? Thank God we found you."

"You not got any parents with you?" Cat asks.

"Yeah, my dad's around somewhere," Ben says. "I think he's in the entertainment tent or something."

"Oh God, the entertainment, what's that about?" Jem says. "It's actually painful to listen to."

"Keeps the olds out of the way, though," Tom says, hefting another log onto the fire.

"So what are you lot doing here?" Cat asks. "Family holiday?"

"Adventure sports," Matt replies. He's clearly thinking his luck's in.

"We're going white-water rafting tomorrow," Cat says. "You done that yet?"

"Not yet, we're going tomorrow too. It's Ben's birthday."

"Fantastic," Cat replies, flashing Matt a flirty smile. "Maybe we'll see you down at the centre."

"So what else are you doing to celebrate your birthday?" Jem says, twisting a strand of hair around her finger and raising an eyebrow quizzically. "Something fun, I hope?"

"Erm, yeah, we were thinking about going to hang out at this cave we found out in the woods tomorrow night," Matt says.

"You are?" Isabella says, looking put out. "You didn't ask us."

"Didn't think you'd be able to come," Tom says.

"We're going late. After Dave's gone to bed. He'll never let us, so we're sneaking out."

"Sounds fun," Cat says. "We'd be up for that, wouldn't we, Jem?"

"Absolutely," Jem says.

"Us too," Isabella says hurriedly. I stare in horror. My parents will kill us if we get caught. Like, properly dead and grounded for all eternity. And I don't want to be grounded when I get home. Or dead. I want to see my boyfriend!

"What do you say, Millie?" Isabella asks.

"If you're going, I'm going," Millie says. "I don't want to miss the fun. And you'll come too, won't you, Suze?"

"Sure," I say weakly.

"Has anyone got any speakers?" Isabella asks. "We could rig the cave up like a club."

"Couldn't bring mine," Tom says. "Not enough space. Had to leave them at home."

"I'd kill to go to a club right now," Isabella says.

Isabella's actually been clubbing? I suppose she could easily pass for eighteen. Unless, of course, she's lying.

"Where do you go out?" Ben asks.

"Places in Italy, mainly. That's where I used to live," Isabella says. She's clearly relishing playing the sophisticated European card.

"There are some great places in London, you'll love it

when you get there," Millie says, and I turn to her in astonishment.

What does Millie know about London nightclubs? Only what she's read in magazines. Same as me. But no, she's now chattering away with Isabella and Tom, talking like she's a regular at half the places in London. She's lying her head off!

"Is anyone up for a game of spin the bottle?" Jem suggests, smiling wolfishly.

My heart sinks into my shoes.

The boys laugh. "I am if you are," Tom shrugs. "Isabella?"

Isabella quickly rearranges her features into something resembling a smile. She's obviously realised that she can't lose face in front of these girls. "Sure," she says. "Sounds fun."

No, no, no! I don't want to play this game! Only Joe, who's sitting opposite me, looks equally horrified. Oh God, what if I have to kiss him? Or anyone else, for that matter? How am I going to get out of this without looking like a complete baby and incurring the wrath of Isabella forevermore? I have a boyfriend! A boyfriend I came perilously close to blowing it with not that long ago, so I can't go around kissing random boys.

I look over to Millie for help, wondering how we're

going to get out of this one, since we're clearly the only ones who are attached. I'm stunned to see her grab a discarded bottle and place it down on the ground next to the fire.

"Who's first?" she asks.

"Me," Matt says. He spins the bottle and it lands on Joe.

"No offence, mate, but I'm not kissing you," Matt says.

"Spin again," Jem says.

Matt spins the bottle and I hold my breath as the bottle slows down... but it comes to a stop pointing at Cat.

Matt couldn't look more chuffed if he tried. He crosses over to where Cat's sitting, and they share a long, lingering kiss.

Oooh, this is horrible. This is proper making out!

Now it's Cat's turn. She spins the bottle and it lands on Tom. She stands in front of him for slightly longer than necessary. He's sitting down, so he's staring right up at her boobs, and something tells me she knows exactly what she's doing. Then she reaches down to take his face in her hands and pulls his lips to hers.

Isabella looks ready to maim and kill.

"Tom, your turn!" she says shrilly.

Cat pulls away, smirking.

The bottle spins around again. It gets closer and closer to me, and once again I hold my breath. It wobbles its way past me... and lands on Isabella.

252

Isabella is thrilled, and doesn't release Tom for ages, clearly trying her hardest to erase the kiss with Cat from his mind.

Then Isabella kisses Joe, but very quickly. Joe spins the bottle and it lands on Jem.

How much longer can I keep getting away with this? It's going to be me soon. It's got to be.

Jem kisses Ben, and then Ben gets Millie.

Oh God. She's not... is she?

"Mills! You're up!" hoots Tom as Ben grins at Millie.

I can't watch this.

What am I supposed to say to Jamie when we get back? Do I tell him what Millie's been up to? Or is Millie expecting me to lie to him? I thought she loved him. I thought she loved our group of mates and hanging out in Bojangles... but maybe I was wrong. All kinds of wrong. Maybe she wants to be like Isabella, wearing expensive clothes, kissing boys that she hardly knows, pretending to be sixteen, and lying about nightclubs she's been to.

I can't watch this. I just can't.

I don't care if it makes Isabella dislike me more than she already does, I'm not staying.

"I'm not feeling well. I'm going to go to bed," I say.

Nobody pays attention as I stand up. I don't think

anyone's even registered I've spoken, because they're all watching Ben and Millie.

Ben reaches for Millie and leans in slowly, their lips getting closer and closer.

And that's when I turn and leave.

CHAPTER
TWENTY-TWO

I'm heading over to brush my teeth the next morning when I hear footsteps slapping in the wet grass and then Millie's alongside me.

"Hey! Where did you go last night? I looked up and you were gone."

"Went to bed," I say, shrugging like it's no big deal.

When actually, it *is* a big deal.

A huge deal.

A deal so massive I want to grab Millie by the shoulders and scream, "WHY WERE YOU KISSING SOMEONE WHO ISN'T YOUR BOYFRIEND?"

But I don't. I just keep on walking like everything's normal.

"Isabella was *not* happy about Jem and Cat rocking up," Millie says. "Jem was giving Tom the serious come-on after you left, so there's no way Isabella's not going to this party later. We're waiting for the parents to go to sleep after the talent show, then we're heading out. I can't wait, can you?"

"I guess."

"Oh, come on, live a little. We're on holiday, Suze. We never do this kind of thing, so let's enjoy ourselves."

I don't reply.

"What's up?" Millie asks. "You're acting kind of weird."

"I'm fine," I mumble.

"So you'll come?"

"We're going to get into a whole heap of trouble if we get caught," I say.

"So we don't get caught," Millie says, like it's obvious.

"I'm just not sure..."

"Weren't you having fun last night?" Millie asks.

I wrinkle my nose. "Not really," I admit.

I want to tell her how I felt awkward and uncomfortable and babyish compared to everyone else. How I felt ignored and left out. How I felt majorly boring for not wanting to play spin the bottle because I have a boyfriend.

"Um, are you going to break up with Jamie?" I say instead. I hate not knowing what's going on.

Millie looks at me like I'm insane. "What? No! Why'd you say that?"

"Because of last night. You kissed Ben."

"It wasn't a proper kiss," Millie says.

"Looked that way to me," I say.

"It was only on the cheek," Millie says, frowning. "Did you really think I'd do that to Jamie?"

"I dunno," I say. "It looked pretty bad."

"After everything that happened with you and Zach, I can't believe you thought I'd do the same thing to Jamie," Millie says. She seems really miffed.

Oof. That was kind of out of order, bringing Zach into things.

"You know what, let's just forget it," I say.

"Let's," Millie says, forcing a smile. "I've got to get back. Isabella wants us to nail this routine for tonight. The boys are coming so she wants it to be perfect. I'll see you later, okay?"

The rest of the day is spent sulking by myself as everyone busies themselves with last minute practising for the talent show.

Considering nobody apart from Mum was all that bothered about it, all of a sudden, people seem very keen to win.

Finally it's the evening, and we're getting ready to head over to the entertainment tent.

"Everyone ready?" Mum asks, walking out of the

caravan, Clare following close behind. "Dad'll be with us in a minute."

She and Clare are dressed in matching jeans and white T-shirts. They did their best to make Murphy look presentable, but he ran away before supper and rolled in a cow pat, requiring a hasty wash-down in the showers. He's still whiffing of eau du bovine, and his curly fur is sticking out at all angles. Maybe Murphy and I have more in common than I knew.

Harry stands up. She's dressed as a wizard, with a bin liner cape that's been covered in tin foil stars. She's fashioned herself a wizard's hat that doesn't stay on properly, so she's holding it with one hand, and clasping Hagrid with the other. The most surprising thing of all is that she's wearing the skirt she chose the other day. To the best of my knowledge, Harry's never worn a skirt in her life. Who's she trying to impress?

"I can't wait to go and perform my magic in front of a proper audience," she says, tugging at the hem of her skirt.

"What, to all three people coming?" I ask.

"Oh, you're just grumpy because you're not taking part any more," Harry retorts.

"Relieved, more like," I say.

"Go on, Amber, out you get," Dad says from inside. "I need to get dressed."

"Oof," Amber says, her hand clutching her ever-expanding bump as she joins us in the awning.

"Seat?" I offer my sister.

"No thanks," she says, wincing. "Oooh, these weird pains. I think if I sit down I'll never get up again. Mum, can you get me some salt water to gargle with? I need to warm up my vocal cords."

"Of course," Mum says. "You're going to catch your death in that," I hear her say to Dad as she returns with the water and passes the glass to Amber.

"Thanks," Amber says. She tips her head back and gargles enthusiastically, before spitting the water into the glass. "La la la la la la la…" she trills. "I can sing, I can sing, I can sing," she says, getting higher and more out of tune. "This is what Conni G does before a performance, I saw it on YouTube," she explains, seeing the funny looks we're giving her.

"Yeah, and look how well Conni's singing career went," I say. Conni released a terrible single earlier in the year, that, despite a string of media appearances featuring her pregnant body in a skintight lemon-yellow lycra catsuit, only managed to scrape into the charts at number sixty. Amber bought about eight copies, 'to be supportive'.

"Her song was great," Amber says loyally. "It didn't get enough radio airplay, that's all."

I'm pondering getting into a debate with Amber over the merits of Conni G's musical talents when a shout comes from inside the caravan.

"Are you lot ready?" yells Dad. "Brace yourselves. I'm coming out."

Oh dear Lord. Oh no, no no no no.

Dad's squeezed himself into tiny gold hot pants, gold boots and absolutely *nothing else*.

There isn't enough brain bleach on the planet to recover from this.

His beer gut, hairy chest and pasty chicken legs are on display for the whole world to see. Plus, it's so cold, he's covered in goosebumps and is turning a rather nasty shade of purple.

"These trunks fitted better when I was a student," Dad says, tugging the side of his shorts and wincing as he pulls some leg hair.

"That's because you were about two stone lighter back then," Mum says.

"Oh, ha ha," Dad replies. "I admit, I've put on a few pounds, but they still fit, don't they?"

He bends down to grab two large, battered, rectangular cases.

"What's in there?" Harry asks.

"Just wait," Dad says with a grin. "I don't want anything

to take away from the surprise. You're going to be blown away. Now, let's go. I hope there's heating in that marquee, I'm freezing." For the first time he properly clocks Harry's outfit.

"Harry, what are you wearing? Oh God... it's happening. You're becoming just like the rest of them!"

Dad stops his moaning as Millie and Isabella duck into the awning. They take one look at Dad and stop dead. Millie's mouth flaps open and shut, her eyes blinking at twice the normal speed. Isabella on the other hand, is clearly horrified.

"I'm so sorry, we'll let you finish getting dressed."

Dad laughs. "No, you're fine, I'm ready. This is my costume. Right, now we're all here, let's go."

I don't want to think what we look like as we traipse across the field. I'm trying to catch up with Millie, who's ahead, speaking to Clare. Millie's voice is raised.

"Why won't you do it?" Millie says.

"It's not that easy," Clare says. "I'm doing my best but there are problems on both sides, okay?"

"But if you ring..."

Clare sighs heavily and rubs her hand across her head. "Please drop it, okay? Let's not do this here. There's a lot you don't understand and you're really not helping."

"But—"

"But nothing. I said, not now."

What are they talking about? Their voices sound so tense.

There are stifled titters when we enter the marquee and people catch sight of Dad. He takes it all in good humour, laughing and slapping his beer belly enthusiastically, getting the crowd on side as they whoop and applaud him.

Millie and Isabella clock the boys sitting on the far side of the tent and immediately distance themselves from the rest of us, waving at them.

There are plastic chairs set up around the horribly precarious looking 'stage' in the middle of the tent, and quite a lot of people here. I guess they were bored and had nothing better to do tonight. All the boys have come, plus Dave. And just behind us, Cat and Jem have walked in with some people I presume must be their parents.

As we settle into our seats, I notice Millie's got a weird expression on her face and keeps staring off into the distance. The marquee is filled with the sound of chattering, which dies down when Devon walks in and heaves himself up onto the stage, smiling.

"Welcome, everyone," Devon says, with a quick glance at his clipboard. "Thank you so much for coming to our exciting event! Tonight we've got nineteen acts to watch – it's a brilliant turnout. I'm sure you're all going to have

262

a wonderful time, and don't forget, there are some fantastic prizes to be won, worth hundreds of pounds!"

There's an intake of breath and Devon laughs. "Oh yes. I can tell you're excited. Right, let's get cracking. I did a random draw earlier and the first act is... Clare and Jen with Murphy and Crystal Fairybelle!"

A few boos ring out as Mum, Clare and the two dogs take to the stage.

Murphy's not made many friends here.

"I'm not sure about this," Millie mutters in my ear. "Murphy's got that look in his eye – that one he gets when he's about to do something wild."

"Let me know when you want me to start your music," Devon calls, hovering with his hand over the play button on the stereo.

Mum and Clare take their places on stage, Mum holding Crystal and Murphy trotting between them.

Clare unclips the lead and Millie grabs my hand in alarm. "This isn't going to end well," she hisses. "Mum," she calls. "Be careful with Murphy!"

But Clare doesn't hear.

"We're ready," Mum calls to Devon, who hits the play button.

Mum and Clare fix smiles onto their faces, and start walking jauntily across the stage. You can see Mum's lips moving as she counts the number of steps she needs to take.

But Murphy doesn't go anywhere. In fact, he sits down, watches for a moment, and starts to howl. He howls so loudly you can hardly hear the music, then he lies down, flips onto his back, and yowls some more, waving his legs in the air.

"Stop it, Murphy!" Clare says, tugging at his collar. Behind her, Mum looks unsure, but carries on strutting.

Crystal Fairybelle's actually doing pretty well, trotting prettily and looking adorable. But Murphy howls again, then jumps to his feet, barks like he's gone mad, takes a flying leap off the stage, barges through the chairs and starts running laps of the marquee. He runs faster and faster, head down, ears flapping, moving so fast he's just a blur.

I have to admit, it's pretty funny. And lots of other people agree too, especially when Clare starts to chase him. Up on the stage, Mum stops dancing. "I've forgotten what to do," she mouths.

"Well, that was entertaining," Devon announces, after Murphy has been reclaimed and Mum and Clare have sat down, the panting Murphy between them, lead clipped firmly back on.

We sit through a couple more acts – a small boy with a screechy recorder, followed by a young gymnast who's actually really good, but the stage is a little too small.

Then Devon announces it's Amber's turn.

"I'm going to sing a love song," Amber announces. Her eyes are already glistening with tears. "This is for my husband, who's not with us. He's the father of my babies, and I miss him so much..."

"He's not dead," Devon interjects quickly, seeing several members of the audience showing signs of alarm. "He's fine. Rings me all the time."

Amber sniffs loudly and takes a deep breath. "Okay. You can play the music now. I'm ready."

As the high notes of the ballad ring out, Amber starts to sing. "*I miss you daily, nightly...*" She's getting more upset and more out of tune as the song goes on. She makes it as far as the chorus before she cracks. "I can't do this. I'm sorry, everyone. I miss him too much." She sits down, burying her head in her hands as she weeps loud, snorty sobs.

Harry's up next. She climbs up onto the stage where she places her bag down onto a chair. Ant applauds her enthusiastically. As Harry opens the bag to retrieve her playing cards, Hagrid pokes out his nose and sniffs the air.

"It's a rat!" someone screams. A lady jumps to her feet and pushes her chair back.

"Rat! Rat!"

Squeals ring out around the tent.

"He's friendly," Harry calls, but she can hardly be heard over the noise.

"Would it help if I put him down?" Harry asks, placing Hagrid on the floor by her feet.

Another lady stands up, knocking her chair over backwards, and sprints out of the tent.

"I think you need to go back to your seat," Devon says kindly, patting Harry's shoulder as the screams intensify. "And I'd put the rat away if I were you. Quickly."

"But I've not done any of my tricks," Harry says, looking gutted. "There's a really good one where I make Hagrid disappear under a cup and reappear on my shoulder."

"I'm sorry," Devon says. "Another time."

After Harry there's a woman called Mimi who performs a deeply inappropriate dance dressed as a French maid, complete with garter and low-cut top revealing way more cleavage than is fitting for a family show. She doesn't do much apart from trot around the stage, bending provocatively as she pouts and dusts the front row, but most of the men in the audience seem to enjoy it. Dad gets a firm jab in the ribs from Mum as he gives Mimi some very hearty applause.

"And now we've got Millie and Isabella, who are performing a dance routine," Devon says.

266

The boys roar their approval as Millie and Isabella take to the stage. Cat and Jem don't clap, and do their best to look bored.

The Drifting music rings out in the tent... and they're brilliant. They look great, in their matching costumes and sky-high heels and they've not got a foot out of place. As much as part of me is willing Isabella to fall over, or slip on her bum, or something equally mean and uncharitable, another part is really impressed. After they've finished, they give each other triumphant smiles, and Isabella looks extremely smug. I can tell she thinks they've got it in the bag.

More acts pass, and then Devon's back on the stage again.

"Now we have our final act of the evening," Devon says. "It's a very mysterious one... we have Chris, doing 'entertainment', so let's see what he's got in store for us."

I sink into my chair, trying to hide my face as Dad squeezes past. He kneels down on the stage and pulls some juggling batons out of one of the cases. All that hype, for some juggling?

Then Dad also pulls out a trombone.

Say what now? Dad plays the trombone?

And then he unclips the other case.

From which he pulls out a unicycle.

Dad clambers onto the unicycle, trombone balanced on one arm, and starts to cycle around the stage, before playing the song that accompanies every circus performance I've ever seen. I hate to admit it, but he's actually pretty good. Yeah, sure, there are a few duff notes, but the man's wearing next to nothing and balancing on one wheel, for goodness sake.

"More!" the crowd screams, thoroughly overexcited. "More!"

Dad jumps off the unicycle to grab the batons and a match, and sets fire to them. The ends ignite with a *WHOOOPHF!* and then he's holding three canes of ferocious flames.

Devon goes pale. "Health and safety!" he shouts, grabbing a bucket of water from beside the marquee.

He throws the water all over Dad, who looks utterly put out.

In more ways than one.

The crowd seems to think it's part of the act, and goes bananas.

"That's all we've got time for," Devon says crossly, ignoring the boos from the crowd, who clearly want to see Dad set fire to himself. "Now it's time to vote. We'll divide the contenders into pairs, and cheer for each person.

The one in each pair that gets the loudest cheer will go through, and we'll whittle down to the final two that way. Okay?"

Devon's convoluted voting system takes a while. Mum, Clare and the dogs don't get anywhere, and nor does Amber, who's still crying to herself and hasn't really noticed anything else going on. Harry also gets knocked out in the first round. Ant rushes up to the side of the stage to greet her.

"You were robbed," Ant says loyally. "I'd love to see the trick with Hagrid and the cup if you still want to show me."

"Sure," Harry says, beaming.

Up on stage, the French maid has been eliminated and only leaves after giving Devon a thorough dusting.

Now the two acts left are Millie and Isabella, and Dad. Yes. My father in his scary tight pants could be about to win this thing.

Mum's jumping around like crazy, clapping her hands above her head.

"Right then, ladies and gents," Devon says, clearly relishing his role as MC. "Our last two acts. We've got our lovely dancers and our unicycling, trombone playing, fire-starter here. Let's start with applause for the dancers."

There are pretty loud cheers, especially from Ben and Tom. But they get louder still when Devon announces Dad.

"I think it's obvious we have our winner. Well done, Chris!"

Millie congratulates Dad, and I can tell that she means it, but Isabella hasn't moved. I stifle a snigger at her expression. She was so sure she had the prize in the bag.

Ah well. I guess nobody expected a half-naked, middle-aged man tromboning on a unicycle. It's hard to compete against that.

"And now the prizes," Devon announces.

"For you two in second place, you win a bundle of firewood each! A great prize, I'm sure you'll agree. Should keep you going for a good few nights."

Snort. This is getting funnier by the minute. Isabella now looks like someone's kicked her in the face, she's so horrified. All that effort, and she's won some sticks?

"Thanks," Millie says, taking her voucher. She's trying not to smirk, I can tell. At least she can see the funny side.

"And now our star prize," Devon says, grimacing slightly. "It's a fantastic treat. We'd like to award our winner tonight one week's free camping next year, here at this site!"

Devon doesn't look exactly overjoyed at the thought of us returning, but that's nothing compared to Dad's expression. His face falls as Devon thrusts a bottle of elderflower champagne into his hands.

As does mine.

That's the prize worth hundreds of pounds?

All of a sudden I'm not laughing any more. We're going to have to come back?

Oh. Please. No.

CHAPTER TWENTY-THREE

Back at the caravan, Mum's popped the champagne and is handing it around. I take a sip from the plastic glass and wince. Devon's home brew is *disgusting*.

"I still can't believe it was such a ridiculous prize," Dad grumbles for the eighty-eighth time.

"Oh, stop being such a grouch," Mum tells him. "You won, enjoy it!"

"We were misled," Dad insists. "Devon said the prizes were worth hundreds. He deliberately gave the wrong impression about what they were. I spent a fortune in petrol going back to get my props."

"Well, you didn't have to," Mum points out. "And anyway, it *is* a prize worth hundreds. In August, the rates are very high to stay here."

"That's not the point," Dad says.

"Well, I'm pleased," Mum says. "Now we've got a good reason to keep the caravan. Another free holiday next year – brilliant!"

Hmmm. Brilliant is not the adjective I'd use.

"Um, I think we're going to go to bed," Isabella says, shooting a meaningful glance at Millie.

"Yeah, I'm really tired," Millie says, faking a yawn and stretching.

"Are you sure, girls?" Clare asks. "It's still early."

"Need some beauty sleep," Isabella says. "We'll see you in the morning."

My insides twist into a tense knot. I know they're going to their tent to get ready to sneak out later.

"I'm tired, too," Amber says. "I'd like to go to bed."

"Well, I'm not ready to sleep yet," Dad says. "Let's talk about my act some more. It's a shame you didn't get to see my fire juggling, that was the best part, but did you like the bit where——"

"I can't sleep if the lights are still on," Amber interrupts.

"It won't hurt for us all to get an early night if Amber needs some rest," Mum says.

From the gleeful glances they're exchanging, Millie and Isabella clearly can't believe their luck. Everyone downs their champagne (or chucks it outside, like I do) and gets into their pyjamas.

I lie awake, nervously waiting for Millie and Isabella to come and get me. Are we really going to be able to sneak off without getting caught?

I'm rigid as a plank in my sleeping bag, checking my watch obsessively. Soon it's 1 a.m. What time is this party starting, anyway? Surely we're leaving soon.

And then I hear the sound of someone shouting outside.

"Who's that?" Harry sits up in bed, yawning.

"What's going on out there?" Dad says, opening the caravan door.

"It sounds like Dave," I say, suddenly worried. Because he's shouting the names of the boys. Which means he must have discovered they're missing.

"Excuse me," Dave says, outside the caravan. It sounds like he's knocking on the windows. "I need your help."

Groaning, Dad heads outside.

"Have you seen my lads?" Dave asks furiously. "They've gone. Snuck off somewhere."

"All right, let's just calm down," I hear Dad say. "It's very late."

"I'm sorry to wake you," Dave says, "but I know that your girls have been hanging around them and thought they might know something."

I stare over at Millie and Isabella's tent. It's silent. But I refuse to believe that with all the commotion going

274

on they wouldn't have woken up.

They can't have gone already. They wouldn't do that to me.

Would they?

"I assume you've heard that?" Dad says, sticking his head into the awning. "Any idea where the boys are?"

"Er, no," I lie, blinking rapidly.

"You sure?"

"Sure," I lie again.

I do *not* feel good about this.

"What about your mates?" Dave asks. "Tom seems pretty keen on that Isabella girl. Do you think he's said anything to her?"

"I'll go and see if she knows anything," I say.

"I'll go!" Harry says, starting to dart off. I grab the back of her pyjama top and yank her back.

"No, don't!" I say, panicked. "I just mean, they're not going to be happy to be woken up. I'll do it."

I walk over to the tent. It's dark and silent.

I undo the zip for Millie and Isabella's tent and poke my head inside.

Just as I thought.

They're not there.

They went to the party without me.

Doing my best to ignore the hurt I'm feeling, I try to

figure out what to do. What am I supposed to tell Dad and Dave now? As much as I'd like to tell the parents where they've gone, I can't drop Isabella and Millie in it, even after what they've done.

"They were both still asleep," I say to Dad. "They haven't seen the boys. No idea where they might be."

"Right. Then we're going out looking," Dave says. Dad goes to wake Devon, then the three men head off in the direction of the woods.

I feel sick. If they find Millie and Isabella out there, they're going to kill them. And me, for lying.

Just over an hour later, there's commotion across the field, and it quickly becomes apparent that the boys have been found.

I scour the group. Cat and Jem are with them, following sheepishly, but there's no sign of Millie and Isabella.

"I'll deal with you all in the morning," I hear Dave hiss, followed by the sounds of tent zippers.

But... but that means Millie and Isabella haven't come back.

Which begs the question – where the flipping heck are they?

"They were hanging out in a cave in the woods," Dad says wearily as he joins us. "Excitement over. Let's go back to bed."

276

He turns off the caravan lights, and Harry curls up in her sleeping bag. In a matter of minutes, she's fast asleep.

I lie, wide awake, listening out for the zip that'll tell me Millie and Isabella have returned. But there's nothing. Nothing apart from an owl hooting.

Millie and Isabella are still out in the woods somewhere.

And nobody else knows they're missing.

CHAPTER TWENTY-FOUR

The minutes tick by and I still don't hear Millie and Isabella come back.

Where *are* they?

They'll be back soon, I reassure myself, over and over.

But they aren't.

What if they went out looking for the boys and got lost in the woods? What if they're stranded out there, all by themselves?

It's been too long. I'm going to have to go and look for them. They were definitely going to meet up with the boys, I'm certain of it, especially after what Millie said this morning about Isabella not wanting to leave Tom and Jem together.

I throw on a hoodie and some jeans over my PJs, and then my trainers.

278

I wobble into the food shelves as I'm trying to tie my laces with one hand, and a tin falls to the floor.

Eep! I freeze, but nobody in the caravan seems to have heard me. Harry, however, rolls over and half opens her eyes. "Whatchoo doin'?" she mumbles.

"Nothing. Go back to sleep. Just going to the loo," I whisper as I grab a torch and venture out into the night.

My first port of call is the girls' tent, just in case they've come back and I haven't heard them, but they're still not there. Their sleeping bags lie flat and unopened.

I suppose next I need to find out if they were definitely with the boys.

Am I really going to wake them up to ask if they've seen my friends?

I guess so. I don't seem to have any other choice. I can't abandon Millie. Even if she hasn't acted much like a mate this evening.

Or all holiday, come to that.

I sneak over to the tent I'm pretty sure is Tom's. I'm going to be in so much trouble if I get caught, and do I have a good explanation as to why I'm sneaking into a boy's tent in the middle of the night?

No. No, I do not.

Please don't be awake, Dave, I think, over and over.

I grab the zipper and sneak it up as quietly as I can.

To me, it sounds like it's deafeningly loud. I freeze, but nobody else seems to have heard it.

I shine my torch inside.

It's not Tom. It's Joe and Ant.

"Who's that?" Joe says, sitting bolt upright as the light shines onto his face.

"Shhhh!" I hiss, pressing my finger to my lips.

"Suzy? What are you doing?" Joe says, in a low voice.

"Were Millie and Isabella with you tonight?" I say. "At the cave?"

"Yeah," Joe says, squinting against the light. "Would you stop shining that torch in my face?"

"Did they come back with you?" I hiss urgently.

"No," Joe says, as Ant continues to sleep next to him. "They'd already gone by the time Dad busted us. Why?"

"Because they're not in their tent," I say. "They haven't come back."

"They definitely weren't there when we left," Joe insists.

"I'm going to have to go and look," I say.

"You can't go wandering around the woods on your own," Joe says. "You could get lost. You need to get proper help, tell someone what's going on."

I know I should. This is the point I should do that. But I can't bring myself to. Things seem weird enough between Clare and Millie at the moment as it is, and this won't help anything. My friends would never forgive me if I said something, and my parents and Clare would be mad I didn't say anything sooner.

Basically, if I tell now, everyone will hate me.

"I can't," I say. "You were in that cave off the track, right? I'll start there. Sorry to wake you."

"Suzy, you can't go wandering around on your own," Joe repeats.

"Haven't got much of a choice," I say. "Thanks for your help."

Joe sighs heavily and reaches for his trainers. "I'll come with you. You'll never find the way by yourself."

It's weird being in the woods at night. They're all kinds of creepy. Branches crack. Leaves rustle. I try not to imagine a mad axe man hiding behind trees, about to attack me. I'd never admit it, but I'm glad Joe's with me.

"The cave was empty when we left," Joe says, his voice sounding unnaturally loud in the quiet.

"Well, we need to start somewhere," I say.

"If they're not there, or anywhere obvious, we're going to have to get proper help," Joe says firmly. "Watch out for that puddle." He grabs my good arm and steers me round it.

Maybe I had Joe wrong. He's not that bad after all.

"I'm sorry about the other night," I say, awkwardly,

as we pick our way through the mud. "I didn't mean to embarrass you."

"Me too," Joe says. "It's just, you know, Ben and Tom were all over your friends and I thought..."

His voice trails off, but I know what he's saying. He was trying to keep up with his mates. Boy, can I empathise with *that*.

"I get it," I say. "And thanks so much for coming out here with me. I'd have been terrified by myself."

"I just hope we find them. The cave's up there," Joe says.

We clamber over rocks and roots, until we're standing at the large black mouth of the cave. They'd better be here. Because I don't want to think about what might have happened to them if they're not.

Ooh, this cave is seriously creepy. It's huge and so dark I can't see anything at all inside. Don't think about the moths, Suze. Don't think about the moths that live in this cave... or the bats. Or ghosts or anything else horrible.

And then I hear the sound of familiar voices, echoing around the cave.

Oh thank the Lord and all that is holy.

We've found them.

The relief is immense, and I'm about to call out when I tune into what they're saying.

"I really don't want to go home," Millie's saying.

I freeze, and put my hand on Joe's arm to prevent him moving.

What's Millie talking about?

I can't wait to get back to Danny and Jamie and Bojangles and away from this campsite. I thought Millie felt the same.

"I get it," Isabella says. "It's so difficult to be stuck in the middle of everything."

"I just don't know what to do," Millie says miserably.

Do about what?

"It's such a flipping nightmare," Millie continues. "She's making everything so complicated."

She? Who's she talking about?

As the realisation sinks in, my heart starts pounding. It's me.

There's no other reason why Millie wouldn't have said something. We don't keep secrets from each other. We never have.

She doesn't want us to be best friends any more, because she wants to hang out with people like Isabella, and doesn't know how to tell me. Breaking up our friendship group really would be complicated, especially with Danny and Jamie being best friends.

It all makes sense.

"Aren't you going in?" Joe says, swinging his torch into the cave. "That's them, right?"

There's a deafening shriek.

I lift my torch, and eventually it settles on two figures, arms wrapped around each other, huddled together on a large rock at the back of the cave.

"It's me," I say.

"Suzy?" Millie and Isabella jump to their feet.

"Thank God!" Millie runs over, Isabella following close behind. They stumble over the stones underfoot, and then Millie collapses onto my shoulder to give me an enormous hug.

I want to hug her back, but can't bring myself to do it.

You ditched me, I want to say. *You went off without me. And now you're sharing secrets with your new best friend and telling her you don't want to go home.*

Isabella's stopped a short distance away, looking like she doesn't quite know what to do with herself. A thank you would be a good place to start. Seriously, I risk life and limb to rescue her in the middle of the night, and she can't even bring herself to do that?

"What are you doing here?" Joe asks. "We thought you'd left."

"We needed to pee," Millie says, shamefaced. "So we left the cave. And then we heard shouting, and Dave's voice, so we hid. We were going to follow you back from a distance. But we didn't have a torch and you guys were further ahead than we thought. We figured we'd hide in the cave until it got light and then head back. But that cave is seriously, seriously spooky. I'm so glad you guys found us. Are we in tons of trouble?"

"Nobody knows you're gone," I say. "I told them you were in your tent. So if we get back without everyone waking up, we should be fine."

"Phew," Millie says, gratefully. "Thanks, Suze, you're such a good mate."

Unlike you, I think to myself.

"You didn't tell anyone?" Isabella says.

"Nope. Didn't want to land the pair of you in it," I say.

I can't read Isabella's expression as she stares at me. She looks almost... astonished?

"Thanks for your help," I say to Joe, once we're back. I'm so relieved that everything's turned out okay, I give him a one-armed hug. I feel his body stiffen against mine, then he relaxes and hugs me back.

"No worries," he says. "At least we found them, yeah?"

"Night," Millie says to me, as we approach the awning. "See you in the morning. Thanks again, for everything."

"Uh huh," I say, as coldly as I can manage, and go back to bed.

I don't sleep much. I spend most of what's left of the night staring up at the canvas above my head, waiting for morning to come and wondering what I should do.

CHAPTER TWENTY-FIVE

I still feel like poo when I wake up a few hours later. Lack of sleep hasn't helped, but it's mainly because I'm upset about the Millie stuff. Everyone else is up at stupid o'clock too, thanks to Murphy's howling. For once, it doesn't bother me.

I feel like howling too.

I'm avoiding Millie and Isabella as much as I can, which isn't exactly easy, given our cramped living space. And now to top things off, Devon's coming across the field towards us.

This can't be about last night, can it? I thought we'd got away with it.

"Uh oh. What've we done now?" Dad asks.

Devon shakes his umbrella and ducks inside. "Nothing I'm aware of."

Phew. Big relief.

"I've had a call from the Meadow Park Nursing home," Devon continues.

Mum gasps and her hand flies up to her mouth. "Aunt Lou! Is everything all right?"

"They asked if you could give them a call," Devon says. "They did say not to worry, but she's had a fall. It wasn't anything too serious..."

"Not too serious!" Mum says. "What does that mean? Thank you for coming, Devon, I'll ring them right now."

"I'm sure it's fine, that woman's immortal," Dad mutters, as Mum puts her mac on over her nightie, pulls on her wellies and tramples off at speed across the field.

"Everything all right?" Dad asks, when she returns.

"I'm not sure," Mum says. "The doctor's checked her over, but she's a bit shaken, and apparently she's asking for us."

"Well, we'll be home tomorrow," Dad says. "We can see her after we get back."

Mum grimaces. "The nursing home said she was being a bit difficult."

"Nothing new there," Dad says.

"Chris!" Mum says. "They said she's gone on some sort of hunger strike and is refusing to eat until we visit. I think she's forgotten we're away on holiday."

"She hasn't forgotten," Dad says. "You know full well Aunt Lou has a memory like an elephant. Don't be sucked into her mind games. She's blackmailing you to get her own way."

"Well, she might be," Mum says, "but what if she's not? I'm wondering about going back early, then we can see her tomorrow. I'd really like her to eat something, there's so little to her as it is... What do you think?"

Dad pauses. He's torn. Giving in to Aunt Loon versus getting the hell out of this caravan.

"I want to go home," Amber says. "I really, really want to see Mark. I've—"

"Missed him so much," everyone choruses.

"I don't want to leave," Harry protests. "I'm having a great time! And I'm supposed to be seeing Ant today to show him how to do magic."

"I think we should leave," Mum says.

"Fine," Dad says. "We'll go back. Although the thought of towing the caravan doesn't fill me with much joy."

We're going home.

At last.

Home where I can sleep in a bed. Where the toilet is across the landing, rather than the other side of a soggy field. There is phone reception. There's food that isn't charred on the outside but raw in the middle.

I have my own space away from my family and can escape with my boyfriend and my mates.

Although, I'm not so sure about that last one. I have no idea how things are going to be when we get back. I thought I'd be happier to leave, but now everything feels all messed-up.

I start chucking things into my suitcase. Outside, Millie and Isabella are dismantling their tent.

"We should go and say goodbye," I hear Isabella say.

"Sure," Millie says, and then appears in the awning.

"We're going to say goodbye to the boys," she says. "They're packing up too. Dave must be taking them back early, after what happened last night. Want to come?"

"Nope," I say, keeping my eyes firmly on what I'm doing. I'll say goodbye to Joe by myself later. And thank him again for his help. I'd have been in a whole world of trouble without him.

"Um, Suze, are you okay?" Millie asks.

"Yup," I reply.

"Okay, then. If you're sure you don't want to come. Won't be long."

Hello! I want to shout at the top of my voice. Isn't it obvious? Of *course* I'm not okay.

Jeez, it's like she doesn't care about me at all any more. Just because she's got a new, glamorous bezzie who buys her expensive presents.

"I'll come," says Harry, pushing past.

"Hey," I object. "You're supposed to be helping me deflate the airbeds and sort the bedding."

"She said we wouldn't be long. I want to say goodbye to Ant," Harry says.

I wallow in self-pity until they return.

"Harry got kissed by Ant," Millie sing-songs.

For a moment I forget I'm in a strop. "You did?" I say, staring at my little sister in amazement. I was right all along – she does have a crush on him!

She refuses to meet my gaze, shuffling her trainers and fiddling with her belt.

"Shut up," she mumbles.

Oh, this is good. This is too, too good.

Revenge is mine at last. I can dine out on this for weeks.

But then I spot that Harry's eyes look a little wetter than usual. And I realise that saying goodbye to your first love is probably a pretty big deal.

Aw, rats. Why did I have to notice the tears?

I can't take the mick out of her when she's hurting so badly.

"Did you get his email address?" I say.

Harry nods. "Yeah. We're going to compare notes on Pottermore."

"And there's always Skype," I reassure her. I put my arm around her shoulder and Harry leans into me for a fraction of a second. Then she sniffs loudly and pushes me away.

"Get off me, you loser," she says.

"I need to get hold of Martin, tell him we're coming back early," Clare says to Mum, as they head over to do some washing up.

Millie stares after her. It looks like her bottom lip's wobbling, and I want to ask her what's wrong. But then I remember last night and what she did, and bury my head in the suitcase again, concentrating on making sure everything fits.

"Suze, can I talk to you?" Millie says, a short time later, after everything's pretty much packed. Mum's crammed the contraband shopping bags into the caravan bathroom, oven, our suitcases and any other space she can find.

"Sure," I shrug, although I won't meet her eyes.

"Somewhere a bit more private?"

I huff heavily, but don't object, instead following Millie a short distance away and watching Dad attempt to manoeuvre the car onto the caravan.

"Um, is something wrong?" Millie asks.

I shrug.

"You've been in a weird mood all morning," Millie says.

"Oh," I say, fighting to keep my expression blank.

"*And* acting really strangely since last night," she presses.

I shrug, dismissively. I don't know what else to do.

"Are you annoyed you had to come and get us? I'm really sorry. You were such a star last night."

"Are you really not getting this?"

"No!" Millie says. "Tell me what's the matter."

"I was supposed to come with you," I say. "How did you think I'd feel being left behind?"

Millie seems genuinely baffled. "But you didn't want to come. When I talked to you yesterday you said you didn't want to risk it."

"So you thought you'd just go without me?"

"I thought I was doing you a favour," Millie says. "And... Isabella told me it would be a bad idea."

"She *what*?"

"It was so late she said you were probably asleep and there was more chance of us getting busted if we came for you. Mum would have gone mental if she'd caught us, so it kind of made sense. I knew you weren't that bothered, so——"

"So you just went?" I say furiously. "Leaving me out, yet again? Just like you've been doing all holiday."

"What?" Millie looks baffled. "No, I haven't."

"Yes, you have. You've been off with Isabella all the

time, with your in-jokes and everything…"

"We haven't!" Millie protests.

"You have! And apparently I'm not even a good enough friend for you to tell your secrets to any more." All my anger and upset is bubbling over. "Even though you'll talk to Isabella, who you've known for five minutes. I heard you last night before we found you."

Millie's face falls.

"Yeah, that's right. Anything you'd like to say to my face?"

Millie doesn't respond.

"Nope, didn't think so." I glare at Millie fiercely, hoping it doesn't give away the churning, sick feeling I'm experiencing. She still doesn't say anything, so I stalk off towards the car, where Dad's muttering about all the stuff he's trying to cram in.

I angrily grab my new bag from the floor, to throw it into the back, but as I do so, the handle snaps off. It's broken.

Flipping brilliant.

CHAPTER TWENTY-SIX

It's typical that, after more than a week of rain and grey skies, the sun finally comes out as our car pulls onto the main road, the caravan clattering behind us.

The journey home doesn't take as long as the one here, although Dad's still not got the confidence to drive at road speed. He's convinced the caravan is going to flip and we're all going to die horribly.

This time, though, he does make it to forty miles per hour.

When we pull up at the house, Mark rushes out to greet us. His reunion with Amber is tear-filled and snotty. Love is a beautiful thing.

I thought I'd be happier to be home. All I've wanted to do since we left is come back. But I'm just miserable.

I feel terrible about the fight with Millie.

We're properly, properly not talking for the first time in our lives.

And I absolutely hate it.

I could try to speak to Danny about everything, but I don't really know what to say, plus he's been acting so weirdly since we've been gone. I need some time to myself, some head space, to try to figure everything out.

Because I have no idea if Millie's ever going to talk to me again.

No more Suzy and Millie.

The end of our amazing foursome.

This is all such a big fat mess.

Although I'm still über-miserable at bedtime, I have to admit it's so good to be sleeping in a proper bed again. I'm rejoicing in the feel of a mattress, rather than a lumpy airbed under my back, although Isabella's not so lucky. She's still on the floor on the camp bed. Her suitcases are packed and ready to go, lined up on the landing outside my bedroom door.

We've not said a word to each other since we got home.

I've given up. She clearly doesn't like me. She wants my best friend, not me. And she leaves in the morning, so what's the point making an effort now?

"Night, girls," Mum says, peering around the edge of the door. "Sleep well. Especially you, Isabella. You must be excited about seeing your mum and your new house."

Isabella doesn't answer, but gives a dismissive grunt before rolling onto her side, pulling the duvet over her shoulders.

"Night, Mum," I say, then lie stiff and rigid, staring up at the ceiling in the dark. I don't think Isabella's sleeping yet; her breathing's still really shallow.

And then she makes a funny noise. Kind of like a choked snort.

Then there's a strangled, shuddering sniff, and I realise what's happening.

She's crying.

Isabella's actually crying. She's trying really hard to hide it, but I'm sure that's what's going on.

Oh help. Do I say something, even though I'm pretty sure she wouldn't want to talk to me? Or do I fake sleep?

As she snuffles again, I realise I can't pretend I'm not hearing her.

"Um, are you okay?"

Isabella doesn't answer.

"You don't have to talk to me if you don't want to," I say.

Nobody else wants to, I add, silently and self-pityingly.

Isabella still doesn't answer.

This makes no sense. What's she so miserable about? After spending almost a fortnight with us, I'd have thought she'd be dancing a joyous jig about returning to her luxurious lifestyle.

There's a super long pause. I'm about to give up on her, when Isabella speaks.

"Everything's so messed up."

I've got absolutely no idea what's she's talking about.

"What's messed up?" I ask.

"*Everything.* My whole entire life, to be exact."

What's she on about? Isabella has the perfect life. She's rich. She's beautiful. She has rich, beautiful friends.

I snort. "Yeah, well, try being me, then you'd know what messed up was," I say. The words are out before I can stop them.

There's a pause. "You don't get it, do you?" Isabella says bitterly. "How lucky you are. My mum talks about your family all the time. She never stops going on about your parents, and how in love they are. That they've been that way since university. That they've got three kids that they adore and blah blah blah."

"But—" I try to interrupt, but Isabella continues like she's not heard me.

"You have a best friend. A boyfriend. Friends you've

known forever. Your family. A house that you've always lived in."

"Well, yeah," I say, still not really understanding. "My friends are cool. But my family's bonkers. And my house isn't all that. Especially not compared to the amazing places you've lived. And you've got loads of mates. You're always texting them."

"They're in a completely different country and I have no idea if I'm going to see them again. And it's not like I have a proper best friend. Not like you have with Millie."

Like I *had* with Millie.

"I've got to start over," Isabella says. "Nobody will know me in London. Nobody will want to be my friend because they'll already have friends. Nobody wants to know the new girl. You end up feeling like you don't fit in anywhere."

Oh.

"And this keeps happening," Isabella says, hardly pausing for breath. "Mum gets married and then a few years later she gets divorced and then it all gets repeated. I really liked Luca, and thought she might actually keep him around. But nuh-uh. It sucks. I had a huge fight with Mum before I left when I said I wanted to keep in touch with him. She went mad."

I bite my lip. That *does* sound rubbish. And here I was

thinking Isabella had it all, because she had designer clothes and big houses and lots of money.

"I didn't realise..." I say feebly.

"Yeah, well, why would you?" Isabella replies. "You, with your perfect family and your perfect friends."

I don't reply.

"Do you realise Millie's the first person I've talked to that's properly understood how it all feels?"

"I *tried* to talk to you," I say indignantly. "You didn't want to know."

"That's because you'd made it obvious you didn't like me," Isabella says.

"Huh?" I prop myself up on my elbow to peer down at her. "What made you think that?"

"You didn't want me around," says Isabella. "I heard you in the kitchen the morning after I arrived. You tried to ditch me with your mum. Just like my mum did, because she didn't want me hanging about either."

I'm mortified. Absolutely mortified.

"Oh, no. I'm so sorry you heard that," I say hastily. "I totally didn't mean it the way it came out. It was only because Millie and me and Jamie and Danny... we're a foursome, you know? And it was our last day together, just us, before the holidays. You have to believe me, it was nothing against you. I promise."

"It felt like nobody wanted me around," Isabella mutters.

"It wasn't meant that way, honest," I say. "I feel awful now. But you weren't exactly friendly, you know, even before then. When you arrived it was obvious you didn't want to be here."

"I didn't," Isabella says, matter-of-factly. "But I was also trying not to cry. I'd had that huge fight with Mum, almost got on the wrong train, didn't know any of you, and got dumped here all by myself."

"I thought it was because you didn't like me," I say. "You seemed really annoyed when I threw that bra on your head. Jeez, I can't believe this turned into such a big mess. I really am sorry about it all."

"I believe you," Isabella says, and at last she seems to be softening. "And I'm terrible for holding grudges, Mum always tells me that. I'm sorry too."

We lie in silence for a while until Isabella speaks again. "Suzy, can I ask you something? Did you and Millie have a fight?"

"Yeah," I say.

"Thought so," Isabella says. "Millie was miserable all the way home. It was obvious something was going on. And you weren't talking to each other at any of the service stations on the way back. Was it because of me?"

"Um..."

"I'm really sorry if it was. I like Millie so much, and wanted a friend, you know? You didn't want me around. My mum didn't want me around. I felt a hassle to your mum who was trying to figure out what to do with me. And I think I might have pushed you out, trying to have Millie all to myself. But I hate seeing Millie so upset, especially with everything else that's going on with her at the moment."

"What *is* going on with her at the moment?" I ask.

"I promised her I wouldn't say."

"Oh, there you go again with your stupid secrets," I say, flopping back onto the pillows. "You just said you were sorry you'd been pushing me out."

"I am," Isabella says. "But you need to talk to Millie."

"I tried!" I say in frustration. "She wouldn't tell me anything. I... I don't think she wants to be my mate any more."

"You're crazy if you think that," Isabella says. "She's just kind of confused. Speak to her, okay?"

"Are you sure you can't tell me what's going on?" I ask.

"I really can't. But I'm sure Millie will tell you."

"I hope you're right," I sigh.

"I know I haven't been entirely fair," Isabella says. "And I should have said thank you for coming to rescue us from the cave. What you did was amazing. Nobody has ever,

ever done anything like that for me before."

"You're welcome," I mutter.

"You're an amazing mate, you know that? I'd... I'd like to be your friend too, Suzy. If you'll have me."

Gosh. Talk about a turnaround. Did I hear that right?!

"You're so funny, and really loyal..." Isabella's continuing. "Mills has said she'll come and stay with me, maybe you could come too? It would be great to know I've got two friends in the country."

As I agree, I secretly cross my fingers that me and Millie will have sorted things out by then.

I really, really hope so.

CHAPTER
TWENTY-SEVEN

Isabella and I are eating cornflakes the next morning when the doorbell goes.

I open the front door and there's an impossibly groomed woman standing in front of me. She's wearing tight jeans, the highest heels I've ever seen in real life, and sunglasses so enormous they practically obscure her whole face. Her blonde hair is immaculate, swishing around her cheekbones as she smiles.

"Suzy? Gosh, look at you. You've grown so much!"

A waft of expensive perfume shoots up my nostrils as the woman sweeps me into a crushing hug. I yelp as my arm gets squished against her.

"Mum?" Isabella says, emerging from the kitchen.

"Darling!" The woman (who I've deduced is Caro – just

call me Sherlock), sweeps inside and gives Isabella an enormous hug too.

"What are you doing here? I thought I was meeting you at Paddington," Isabella says. She returns the hug, but warily. She's not exactly looking overjoyed to see her mum rock up out of the blue.

"We need to talk, sweetie," Caro says, pushing her sunglasses up onto the top of her head.

"What about?" Isabella says suspiciously. "What have you done now?"

"Nothing!" Caro says. "Is there somewhere we can sit down? Have a proper chat?"

"In there," I say, pointing through the doorway towards the lounge. "I'll get you guys some drinks?"

"Coffee for me, please," Caro says. "Filter, if you've got it?"

Filter? She'll be lucky. Value instant is what she's getting. She'll never know the difference.

"Nothing for me, thanks, Suzy," Isabella says.

As I wait for the kettle to boil, the temptation to go and listen at the door to what Caro's saying is overwhelming. But I resist. Although, I do maybe carry the drink through a smidgen slower than I should have done.

When I enter the room it's pretty obvious they've

both been crying – they have red eyes and their make-up's not as perfect as it was a few minutes ago.

"Erm, is everything all right?" I ask, carefully putting the mug down on the coffee table.

"Fine," Caro says, pulling a tissue out of her (designer) handbag. She smiles. "We just have a lot of things to sort out, don't we, darling? But we'll get there."

Isabella nods. "Yeah."

"I'll just go and tell Mum you're here," I say. "She'll be so excited to see you."

"Caro!" Mum says, as she rushes into the room a few moments later. They embrace. "I didn't know you were coming!"

"Needed to see my baby girl," Caro says. "I missed her. We're going to get the train back to London together. Sorry we can't stay longer this time, but we'll be back soon for a proper visit, promise. We want to get unpacked in our new house, don't we, Is?"

Isabella nods. She looks the happiest I've seen her since she arrived.

"Why don't you go and get your bits and pieces and we can make a move?" Caro says.

"I'll give you a hand," I say, following Isabella upstairs.

"Everything okay?" I ask cautiously, once we're safely away from adult earshot. This Isabella-and-me-as-friends thing is taking some getting used to.

"I think so," Isabella says, slumping down onto my bed. "She apologised, which she's never really done before, and said she's done her best to make things better with Luca. She said she doesn't have a problem with me and him keeping in touch, and she's paying for me to go back to Italy before the end of the holidays, so, y'know, all good."

Isabella says the words nonchalantly, but I can see how pleased she is.

I guess they've still got a long way to go, but it's a start.

"Right, we need to take Isabella and Caro to the train station," Mum says, after we've finally dragged Isabella's luggage downstairs.

"Hmm?" I say. I'm distracted fiddling with my phone. I've been trying to get hold of Danny since we got back, but he's not answering texts. Or calls. And when I rang his house last night, his dad answered and got all kinds of weird saying he didn't know where he was.

I'm starting to get suspicious.

"Suzy, are you listening to a word I've been saying?" Mum says.

"Um, no. Sorry," I say.

"We're leaving to take Isabella and Caro to the station," Mum says, with exaggerated patience. "Harry's coming with us, but there's no room for you as well in the car. Amber, I want you to go and put your feet up."

"Stop telling me what to do," Amber says, her eyes flashing fiercely. "I'm not a child."

Since we got home, Amber's been in a major, major grump. I have never seen her like this. My happy, fluffy sister has been replaced by someone so crotchety it's like she sat naked in a wasp's nest.

"I'm only trying to make sure you're all right," Mum says.

"Well, don't. Leave me alone," she says, storming off. Which would be much more impressive if she wasn't waddling like John Wayne.

"It's like living with a stroppy teenager," Mum sighs at Dad. "Two stroppy teenagers," she says, casting a pointed look in my direction.

"Bye, Isabella," I say, deciding to ignore my mother. I give her a hug. Out of the corner of my eye, I can see the parentals giving each other a look of surprise. Mum shrugs at Dad.

They are SO obvious. Honestly.

"That rat's not coming with us, is he?" Isabella asks as Harry skulks into view.

Okay. I have to know. "Are you really allergic to rats?" I ask curiously.

Isabella pauses for a moment, then grins and lets out a snort. "Hah. No."

"I knew it! So what's the deal, then?"

"Honestly? I'm terrified. Completely and utterly terrified."

The thought is so ridiculous, I can't help it. I start to laugh. Then Isabella starts laughing too, and soon we're howling like a pair of complete loons.

Now the parentals are completely baffled.

"I'm worried about leaving Amber," Mum says, as Isabella gives me another goodbye hug and makes me promise for the zillionth time I'll visit. "She said she wasn't feeling all that well..."

"She'll be fine," Dad says, ushering Mum towards the door after Isabella and Caro. "You're only going to be gone half an hour. She'll survive until then."

As the house falls quiet, I sit and watch some TV for a bit, still moping about Millie and keeping an ear out for Amber. She went ape at me earlier when I moved her biscuits, and I don't want to get my head bitten off again. It's like she's got PMT on overdrive or something. Definitely best avoided. It doesn't help that Mark's not around. He's usually the one that helps calm her down, but he left for a meeting first thing.

I try to ring Danny, but there's no answer. Gnargh!

Hmmm. Maybe I will feed my misery. I tiptoe towards the kitchen, and then jump out of my skin as Amber appears in the doorway in front of me. At least I manage not to shriek. I do *not* think that would have gone down well.

Uh oh. Time for a sharp exit.

"I was, um, going to my bedroom... Took a wrong turning," I say, laughing nervously as I step backwards.

"Don't go, Suzy, I'm not feeling well," Amber says. She grasps my shoulders and shuts her eyes as she winces.

"What's wrong?" I say, not too concerned, given all the false alarms we've had over the last few weeks. Although now she's so close, I notice she's gone very pale.

"I've got tummy ache," Amber says through gritted teeth. She exhales slowly and her grip on my shoulder intensifies.

Ouch. She has got serious clampage going on.

"My bump keeps getting really squeezy," Amber says. "I think you can get these pretend contraction things. Maybe it's those."

You *what*?

"You're having contractions?" I shriek.

"Not real ones," Amber says.

Phew. Thank goodness for that.

"Ow, ow, here's another one..." Amber says, then she yelps in agony and clutches her tummy again. There's the sound of water hitting floor and all of a sudden my socks are soaking.

"Uh oh, I think I wet myself," Amber says. "I can't believe I did that. How embarrassing."

"Um, are you sure that's what it is, Amber?" I say. That can't be her waters breaking, can it? I have no idea what to do!

"Owwww," Amber says, doubling over again. "It really hurts."

"Um, do you think you might be in labour?" I say.

"Noooo," Amber wails. "It's too early. And Mark's not here."

Think, Suzy. Think. And think fast, before a couple of babies come shooting out of your sister and skid across the kitchen floor.

"I'll give Mum a ring," I say. "She'll know what to do."

I speed-dial Mum's number with trembling fingers, but get the tinny voice telling me her phone is currently unavailable.

"Can't get through. I'll try Dad," I say. But when I ring Dad's phone, I can hear his Metallica ringtone echoing through from the lounge. He's forgotten his phone. Okay. Mark.

His phone's switched off. I leave a garbled message telling him to call me as soon as he can, and then try Isabella. She's my last hope.

She answers.

"Hey, Suzy, what's up?"

"I need to speak to Mum," I say.

"Sorry, we're already at the platform. The traffic was terrible so they dropped us off and left straightaway. There's been some burst water main or something. The roads are shut and the traffic's all backed up."

Noooooooooooooooo!

"Is everything okay?" Isabella asks.

"Really not. Tell you later, gotta go," I say, and hang up the phone.

This cannot be happening.

"Ooooooh," Amber says. "Do something. It really hurts!"

"Um, maybe I should ring the hospital?" I say.

"Okay," Amber says, staggering over to a kitchen chair. "The number's on the front of my maternity notes."

She shrieks the last bit, and I can see the realisation of what's about to happen is finally sinking in.

"What are we going to do? What are we going to do?"

Her voice is getting more high-pitched by the word and I can tell she's heading for a proper freak-out.

As am I.

But one of us has to stay calm. And as I'm not the one about to deliver two people out of my you-know-what, I guess that has to be me.

"Just chill," I say. "I'm going to ring the hospital, and I'm sure they'll tell us it's something that always happens."

"You think?" says Amber.

"Yep," I say, lying through my teeth. "Stay there and take it easy, and I'll call the hospital and see what they say. Deep breaths, okay?"

My hands are shaking so hard and my brain is so frantic with panic that it takes four attempts to dial.

When I finally get through, the midwife tells me Amber needs to come in immediately, as she needs examining.

Oh God. How am I supposed to get my sister there without any form of transport? Mum, where are youuuuuuuuuu?

I try her phone again. And again. And again. Still no answer.

Deep breath. I can't let Amber know how much I'm freaking.

"Um, well, nothing to worry about, but we need to get you to the hospital." I force a smile as I break the news to Amber.

"I can't go there," Amber replies. "Mark's not here. I'm not ready. I've not packed my hospital bag or anything."

"I can pack it for you," I say. "What do you need?"

"Um, my make-up bag? A towel? I don't know, Suzy, I can't think!"

"Okay, okay, you stay here and I'll go and sort it out," I say. "Um, and I'll call a taxi…"

"What? Why?" Amber asks. "What do we need a taxi for? Where's Mum? Ooooooh owowowowow."

"Please calm down," I beg. "I can't get hold of Mum, so I think we should get a taxi in and meet her there, okay? I'll keep trying her, though."

Amber's leaning back on the chair, hands on her stomach, panting weirdly. I take her silence as consent, so quickly ring the taxi, then run around like crazy grabbing stuff for her hospital bag. I'd be going so much faster without this stupid sling.

Um, what might she need? She said she wanted make-up and a towel. What else? Clean pants! I add a couple of thongs. Shower cap. Negligée. Anything else…? Maybe some lipstick…

"Suuuuuzy, hurry uuuuuuuuup," Amber bellows from downstairs.

I try Mum again from the upstairs phone.

There's still no answer.

CHAPTER TWENTY-EIGHT

"The taxi's here!" Amber shouts, while I'm still rushing about in a mad panic trying to put a bag together.

"Coming," I shout back.

I grab a random selection of clothes, and decide that whatever I've got will have to do. My brain seems to have stopped working.

I race down, risking life and limb on our shiny wooden stairs in my socks, and help Amber along the path to the waiting taxi.

"I'll be back in a minute," I say, running back upstairs and into the bathroom, where I grab all the towels I can get my hands on, throw on some shoes, then dash back outside.

I've no idea what we'll need them for, but in hospital

dramas, they always seem to demand piles of towels at a birth.

"You all right, love?" the taxi driver says warily as I clamber in and pad the seat with towels. Amber's standing outside, swaying and taking deep breaths, wincing in pain every so often.

"We need to get to the hospital," I tell him.

"What's the rush, she's not about to give birth or anything, is she?" He laughs, then sees the expressions on our faces. "Oh God. I don't know about this. I don't want any babies born in my cab. I've only just had it cleaned and——"

"She's pregnant with twins," I tell him. "You have to help us, please, please, take us to the hospital – my mum's not here."

"Ooooowwwwwwww," Amber wails again.

The taxi driver stares at her for a minute, then opens the back door. "Oh all right, get in," he says decisively.

"My missus is pregnant at the moment," the taxi driver continues, as he sets off at breakneck speed. As soon as he pulls out into the main street, I see Isabella wasn't wrong about the traffic. It's moving ridiculously slowly. The problem with where we live is that loads of the roads are one way, so if one bit goes wrong, it all gets backed-up super quickly.

"Keep breathing," I urge Amber, reaching over awkwardly

to pat her arm. Amber's got her head tilted back against the seat and swats me away.

"Is the panting helping?" I ask.

"I don't know," Amber huffs. "I saw it on TV. It still really huurrrrtsssss, owowowow... and what about my make-up? I haven't got any make-up on. I can't give birth without my mascara, Conni G said it's important to look beautiful when you're bringing life into the world..."

Honestly, right now my sister's eyelashes are the last thing on my mind.

"Where's Markymoo? I want my Markymoo," Amber says. "Try him again!"

Obediently, I try Mark's mobile. It's still switched off, so I leave an updated message telling him we're on our way to the hospital and he needs to get there as soon as he can.

"I don't know if I can do this," Amber says. All of a sudden she looks like she's going to cry.

"You can. You're going to be fine," I say.

"But... but... what if I'm a rubbish mum? What if something happens to the babies? What if I drop one?"

"You're going to be great," I say, twisting awkwardly past my cast to pat her knee. "You're amazing. You won't drop them."

Amber still looks worried, but then another contraction kicks in.

It feels like forever before we arrive. We stagger up to the door of the maternity ward and wait to be buzzed in.

"If you could take a seat," a frazzled midwife says, after we get inside.

"Um, I think she needs someone to look at her now," I say nervously.

"We've got quite a few ladies waiting," the woman says patronisingly, then Amber lets out a hideous yowl, and crumples to her knees.

"Make it stop," Amber screams. "Please, please, make it stop."

I second that sentiment wholeheartedly. I don't want to be here for this. I'm supposed to be at home right now, watching a DVD and figuring out how to fix the mess that is my life. Where's my mother when I need her?

"I feel like I want to push," Amber says.

Oh no. Oh no, no, no. No pushing. Pushing means the babies are coming, doesn't it?

"Maybe we should get you looked at," the midwife says. "Sally, can you give me a hand with... what's your name, love?"

"Amber," I tell them as they help my sister to her feet and lead her into a ward. "And it's twins. I'll wait out here."

There's no way I can be there during that. The thought of watching babies come out of my sister's undercarriage makes me feel all kinds of peculiar.

"Suzy, don't leave me by myself," says Amber, twisting around and bursting into tears. "I'm scared and it huuuuuurrrrrts."

"Come on, love," Sally says, urging me to catch them up as she helps Amber onto a bed. There are six curtained-off rooms, and I can hear some seriously weird noises. Someone actually sounds like they're *mooing*.

Lalalalala, I can't hear you, I think, as I surreptitiously try to stick my fingers in my ears.

"Mark's not here, the babies can't come," Amber says, grabbing my hand. Her eyes are wild with fear. "I'm not ready. I forgot to sign up for the birthing classes and I haven't read any of the books. I spent the whole holiday reading magazines. I haven't even got their names picked!"

"All right, love, I'm going to examine you," says the midwife, and as she gets busy, I thank the Lord for modesty-protecting sheets.

"Talk to me, Suzy. Distract me," Amber says.

"Um..." My brain goes blank. What am I supposed to say?

"Anything," Amber says. "Tell me anything."

"Um, I had a huge fight with Millie," I blurt out.

"You did?" puffs Amber, wincing again and then a stream of four letter words come flying out of her mouth. Crikey. I have never heard my sister curse like that before. "Ooooooooooohf! What did you fight about?"

"Um, well, she was spending all her time with Isabella and I was feeling left out," I say. "It seems silly now, I guess. I talked to Isabella and she's had a really hard time moving about and stuff so she wanted someone to talk to. But there's something going on with Millie, I know there is. I'm not sure she wants us to be mates any more."

"I don't think that's true," Amber says.

"I dunno," I say. "Isabella said there was something going on with Millie, but she won't tell me what it is."

"Do you really not know?" Amber asks. "It was kind of obvious on holiday."

It was? How did my crazy older sister notice and I didn't?

"Look, you need to talk to – nnnngggggghhhh!" Amber winces and grits her teeth.

"Right," says the midwife, emerging. "I don't mean to alarm you, but it looks like we're quite close. Your babies are coming, Amber. We're going to move you up to the birthing suite and get you hooked up to a monitor."

All of a sudden I feel faint. There are black spots before my eyes and I grab onto the bed for support.

"Are you okay?" the midwife says.

"Yep," I lie. "I'll, um, just try my parents again."

But there's still no answer. In desperation, I try Mark's phone for a third time and leave another long, garbled message.

Up in the birthing suite, Amber's been attached to a monitor with all these belts wrapped around her tummy. She seems to be getting the contractions more often now.

The midwives give me the task of making sure Amber's got water to drink if she needs it and holding her hand. She squeezes my good hand so tightly I think I can actually feel my bones crunching together. It would be just my luck to end up with two broken hands, but as I'm not really in any position to complain, given what Amber's going through, I keep quiet. It feels like hours have passed, though I've got no idea how long it's actually been. I'm too busy praying that the babies stay in until Mum or Mark gets here.

Then, during a contraction, a terrifying alarm goes off from the monitor and half the hospital seems to be piling in our room.

"What's going on?" Amber pants, leaning back on the pillows. Her face is pale and worried.

"Is everything okay?" I ask, leaping to my feet.

One of the doctors examines the machine and turns around. "The heart rate of baby two dropped, and although it's fine again now, we're going to need to get you prepped for a Caesarean section, Amber. Probably best to get your babies out sooner rather than later."

This goes from bad to worse.

Am I really going to have to see a double whammy of an operation plus babies coming out? *Really?*

They should show *this* in biology class. That'd stop the teen pregnancy problem in an instant.

"Um, I'm really not sure I'm the right person to go in with Amber," I say.

"If you're the only one here, I'd get the scrubs on," the midwife says briskly. "She needs you."

I'm shown into a room where I quickly wriggle into some weird blue trousers and matching top. They're absolutely massive. I force the hat down onto my hair, and as I reach out for the door handle, I catch sight of myself in the mirror.

Huh, check me out. I'd make an excellent doctor.

Then I remember why I'm wearing these clothes, and the fear returns.

I step outside the room and am about to join Amber, when I hear a shout from the end of the corridor.

"Suzy!"

Oh, thank the Lord and all that is holy.

It's Mark.

CHAPTER TWENTY-NINE

Several hours later, I'm peering into the open cot containing the twins.

They're fast asleep and so tiny.

They're wrapped up warmly in blankets and dressed in clothes provided by the hospital, because when I was packing, I neglected to put anything in for the babies. I'd totally forgotten about them.

Oops. Not a very good first act as Auntie Suzy. But in my defence, I had other things on my mind.

Like, not letting my sister give birth on the kitchen floor.

I can't believe that I'm an auntie. Or that Amber is a mum.

To two little girls.

Yes. Two more females to add to the Puttock dynasty.

I can only imagine how delighted Dad must be.

On the other side of the cot, Amber's sitting in a chair, looking shell-shocked but super happy. She didn't need the C-section after all. Things sped up a lot once she got into the operating theatre, and the babies came out naturally. They have to stay in hospital until their due date, though, and be monitored, so they'll be in for a few weeks, but the doctors are really pleased with how well they're doing.

"Aren't they the most beautiful things you've ever seen?" Mum says, putting her hand on my shoulder.

"Um, yes," I lie. Because they're kind of cute, I guess, but also a bit peculiar, with their pointy little heads.

I really am rubbish at this auntie stuff.

But at least I was there for Amber. Mum and Dad had got stuck in the traffic outside the station, with no mobile reception, and couldn't move for ages. By the time Mum picked up my frantic messages, they were still miles from the hospital. Dad made it here in record time, but by then the babies were already out.

"They're lovely, aren't they, Chris?" Mum says. She smiles at Dad, all gooey, and he puts his arm around her waist.

"They really are," Dad says, bowing his head over the cot, but not before I see what look suspiciously like tears glistening in his eyes.

Mum grins knowingly. "See, he loves you all really,

324

whatever he says," she whispers.

"Hmmm?" Dad says.

"Nothing," she replies, quick as a flash.

"I think they look kind of like aliens," Harry announces. She has no qualms about hurting people's feelings. Mum hushes her, but it doesn't look like Amber's heard. She's off in some dream world. The doctor said she might be in shock for a while. I don't know how we'll tell the difference, to be honest.

"So have you chosen names for them yet?" Dad asks.

"Well, we thought we'd name one each," Mark says, putting his arm around Amber and squeezing her to him. "Are you ready to tell?"

"Think so," Amber says.

This should be interesting. Given they called their dog Crystal Fairybelle and all their possible suggestions so far, I can't wait to hear what they've come up with. Let's face it, the name's going to be tainted by the fact they've got a horrible surname to stick with it whatever the first names are. Mycock is not good.

But then, I guess I've survived so far with Puttock. Aunty Suze can help them through the tough times.

"I've picked Lily-Unicorn," Mark says. "She's this one." He points to the smaller of the two babies, still sound asleep.

"And I've chosen Violet-Chihuahua," Amber says. "They're flower-themed names, see? With our favourite animals."

Wow. That I was not expecting. Their names sound normal. Pretty, even. Well, their first names do. We'll ignore the middle ones.

"Oh, they're lovely," Mum says, clasping her hands to her chest and peering down at the babies again. She can't take her eyes off them. "Lily-Unicorn and Violet-Chihuahua. Beautiful names for beautiful girls. I can't believe we're grandparents, can you, Chris?"

"Nope," Dad says drily. "I don't feel old enough."

"You look old enough," Harry says cheekily, and ducks out of the way as Dad gives her a playful swat around the back of her head.

"You were brilliant today, Suzy," Mark says. "I can never thank you enough for being there for Amber."

"He's right," Amber says, smiling. "You were a star."

While we're talking, little Violet-Chihuahua opens her eyes. They're big and blue and she stares at us, like she's sizing us up, before snuggling closer to her sister. Lily-Unicorn doesn't look impressed, and immediately starts bawling, her red face scrunched and cross.

Amber reaches in, picks her up and jiggles her about, but the cries get crosser and crosser. "Mark, help," she says.

"She's not stopping. What am I supposed to do?"

"I dunno," Mark says. "Anyone?" he says, looking around.

Mum's about to take over when Harry produces her wand from her pocket. "Stop crying!" she commands, waving the wand in front of Lily-Unicorn's face.

And to everyone's amazement... she does.

Even Harry looks astonished. But also pretty chuffed.

And it's then, watching the twins, I realise how amazing it must be to have a sister and best friend from birth. Someone you know who'll always be there, no matter what. Someone you share an unshakable, unbreakable bond with.

My sisters may drive me mad, but I guess I wouldn't be without them.

Just like I don't want to be without Millie.

And all of a sudden, I know I have to make things right. Millie's my best friend in the whole wide world, and I need to talk to her properly. Find out exactly what's going on.

"Can we clear the room for a moment, please? We need to do a few checks. Just Mum, Dad and the babies," a doctor says, swishing the curtain aside.

"I'm going to get a coffee," Mum says.

"Sounds good," Dad agrees.

"I'm going to ring Danny," I say. I wander out into the hospital grounds and find a bench.

"You answered!" I say when Danny picks up. "I haven't talked to you for ages."

"Yeah, sorry about that," he says. "How are you?"

"I'm home," I say.

"You are?" he says. He seems alarmed. "As in, back in Collinsbrooke?"

"Yeah. But don't be too pleased to hear from me or anything," I say, sounding more annoyed than I'd intended. What is going on with him?

Danny laughs. "No, no, don't take that the wrong way. It's just I wasn't expecting you back until later."

"We got back yesterday," I explain. "A lot's gone on. I've been trying to call you, but you weren't answering your phone. And your dad said he didn't know where you were when I rang your house."

"Erm, yeah... um, well... I've been kind of busy."

"Anyway, it doesn't matter. I'm at the hospital—"

"The hospital?" Danny interrupts. "What've you done now?"

"Nothing. For once," I say. "Amber had her babies a few hours ago."

"She did? What did she have?" Danny asks.

"Two girls. Lily-Unicorn and Violet-Chihuahua," I say.

"Those are surprisingly normal names," Danny says. "For Amber and Mark, I mean. Not for regular people."

"Yeah, it could have been much worse. I was the only one with her when she went into labour. I've never been so stressed in my life."

"You were?" Danny says. "Nightmare. You weren't actually there at the... y'know... were you?"

"Nah. It was a close call, but fortunately Mark arrived just in time. I'll tell you all about it when I see you. When are you free? Now?" I ask.

"Um, not right now..." Danny says.

And that's it. I've had enough. I've been away for days, I've wanted to see him like crazy, and it's starting to sound horribly like he's not missed me one little bit.

"Danny, what's going on? Why are you being so offish? I could hardly get hold of you at all while I was on holiday, and now I'm back you don't seem to care—"

"Whoa, whoa, whoa, of course I care, silly – I missed you like mad," he says. Immediately I feel a teeny bit reassured. "Look, okay, why don't we meet up tonight?" he says.

"Tonight? But that's hours away," I protest. "Can't I come over? I've got so much to tell you—"

"Um, the thing is, I'm not at home right now,"

Danny interrupts. "And I've got some stuff I need to do before then."

"Stuff? What stuff?" I protest, ignoring his question. I really want to talk to him about Millie.

"Trust me, okay?" Danny says. "Meet me at seven at Bojangles?"

"But isn't Bojangles closed?"

"Just meet me there then."

"Okay," I sigh, giving in.

"All will be revealed later," Danny says, hanging up the phone and leaving me utterly confused.

What's he up to?

I've no idea. And tonight's ages away. So I think for now I'll go back into the hospital and hang out with my new nieces some more.

CHAPTER THIRTY

Later that night, I'm walking to Bojangles when I see someone familiar on the other side of the road, slightly ahead of me.

I recognise the turquoise hair streak and slow down, suddenly unsure.

It's Millie.

She's listening to her iPod, head bobbing away to the music. I bet she's listening to The Drifting. Gotta be.

I want to sort things with Millie. She's my best friend. I know everything about her, down to what she's probably listening to on her iPod, for goodness sake. But... but what if she doesn't want to make up?

I guess one way or the other, I have to find out for sure.

As Millie waits at the crossing, she sees me and immediately her hand goes up in a wave.

Then she obviously remembers that we had a fight,

as the smile disappears from her face and her arm falls down by her side. Now she looks unsure, too.

Should I wait for her, or keep walking?

Wait? Or walk?

I dither indecisively and the green man comes on at the crossing. Millie heads over and removes the headphones from her ears.

"Hi," she says quietly.

"Hey," I say, fiddling with the button on my coat.

"I wanted to—" Millie starts at the exact same time I say, "Can we talk?"

And then we laugh, and the tension eases a bit.

"I hate that we had that stupid fight," Millie says.

"Yeah, me too," I say.

"Isabella texted and said she'd spoken to you. She said you ended up feeling pushed out on the holiday," Millie says. "I'm sorry. I never meant for that to happen."

"You two were always together," I mumble. "Getting ready to go out, sharing your private jokes... and I was really upset when you didn't get me to come with you to the cave, you know."

"I am so sorry," Millie says. "I honestly thought I was doing you a favour by not making you come."

"I had a long chat with Isabella before she left," I say. "She explained a lot."

Millie's face instantly becomes guarded. "She did? What did she say?"

"Stuff about how difficult she's found things, mainly. But she also told me to talk to you. Millie, what's been going on?"

Millie takes a deep breath, but doesn't answer.

"It just feels like you've changed," I blurt out. "I thought we shared everything. Why didn't you want to come home and why was I complicating things?"

Millie looks baffled. "What?"

"I heard you and Isabella talking in the cave. You said you didn't want to come home and——"

"Suze, I wasn't talking about you!" Millie interrupts. She stares down at the pavement and chews on her lip. Then it all comes spilling out. "I was talking about Mum. The reason Mum came on holiday and Dad didn't had nothing to do with Dad needing to work. It was because they were having a trial separation. They needed time away from each other to see if they still wanted to be married or not. That's why I didn't want to go home. It's been all kinds of stressful there for ages."

"You *what?*"

I couldn't be more surprised if Millie had smacked me in the face with a haddock. But I suppose, thinking about it, that explains *everything*. Although I'm majorly relieved it wasn't me Millie was talking about in the cave, it doesn't stop me feeling heartbroken my friend's had such a tough time.

"Mum's been a stress-head since she lost her job and Dad's working all the time to make sure we've got enough money. They kept fighting and it was getting really bad before we went away," Millie says sadly. Her eyes fill with tears and I lean in to give her a hug. She squeezes back gratefully.

"So, um, did the trial separation work?" I say.

"Well, they had a huge talk last night," Millie says. "I overheard them saying they're going to go and see some counsellor to try to help sort things out, which I guess is good. Plus, Mum got back to an email offering her a job, which she was really chuffed about."

"That's great," I say. "But why couldn't you talk to me about it all? You spoke to Isabella and you hardly know her."

"Because she was the only person that got it. I didn't think you'd understand. Your parents are solid. And yes, I know your family drives you crazy," she says quickly, seeing my expression, "but you guys are always there for each other."

"You and I are *best friends*, though," I say. "We're supposed to tell each other everything. Couldn't you have said something?"

"I tried," Millie says. "I honestly did."

And when I think back, I realise maybe she did. I'd dismissed her parents fighting as just silly arguing, when Millie was trying to tell me it was something more than that.

"I'm really sorry," I say. "I should have listened."

"Yeah, well, I probably could have tried harder," Millie says. "But I was embarrassed. I didn't want to admit things were really that bad. Like, if I didn't talk about it, it wasn't really happening. Stupid, right?"

"Not really," I say. "I get that. Sort of. But the fact you talked to Isabella and not me sucks."

"I know. I'm sorry," Millie says. "I really, really am. But Isabella understood, she knows what it's like."

"I thought you wanted Isabella to be your best friend instead of me," I mumble.

"What?" Millie says. "Why?"

"I dunno... because you seemed to really like hanging out with her and I'm not a Mulberry girl."

"A Mulberry girl?" Millie frowns. "I don't even know what that is."

"You know. Like, one of those girls who are all groomed and glossy and carry designer bags. Someone like Isabella. I'm not like that. I'm scruffy. My hair's mad. Even my bag broke in five minutes. Plus I do stupid things and end up breaking bones."

"You fell off your bike," Millie protests. "That could happen to anyone. And why do I care that you're not a Mulberry girl? I think you're amazing and flipping hilarious to boot. You're my BFF, I wouldn't change you for the world. Come here."

And with that, Millie gives me another tight squeeze.

I'm so glad we're okay. So, so glad.

As we're hugging, I remember there's something huge I need to tell Millie.

"Amber had her babies!" I say excitedly, and Millie screams.

"She did? What did she have? Girls, right?"

I nod and Millie claps with glee. "It had to be. I wish I'd seen your dad's face when he found out."

"Actually, he was kind of okay about it."

"What did she call them?" Millie says.

"Violet-Chihuahua and Lily-Unicorn," I say.

"Cute. I can't wait to meet them," Millie says, linking her arm through mine. "So where are you off to now?"

"I got this weird message from Danny," I say. "He wants me to meet him at Bojangles. I don't know why, that sign said it was going to be shut indefinitely or something, didn't it?"

"I got the same message from Jamie, asking me to meet

him there," Millie exclaims. "They probably forgot, you know what they're like. We can still go and meet them, though. We'll just go somewhere else when our divvy boyfriends realise that the place is still closed. As long as it's not Tastee Burga."

"Definitely not Tastee Burga," I agree, and we grin at each other happily.

Outside Bojangles, there's nobody to be seen.

"They're not here," Millie says.

"We were right, though, Bojangles is still closed. Look, the sign's still up." I cup my hand up against the glass door, trying to see inside. It's pretty dark, but I think I can see what looks like flickering lights.

Just then, the door opens, and I nearly fall flat on my face into the café.

"Whoa!" Danny says, grabbing me as I fly forwards.

Danny.

It's Danny.

I sink into his arms as he pulls me close. Mmmm, he smells so good. He drops a kiss onto my head, before gently putting his hands on my shoulders and moving me away slightly.

"Hey, you," he says, with a small smile. My body melts as I stare into his brown eyes. "Nice cast. Suits you."

"What are you doing inside if this place is shut?" I ask, still drinking him in.

"Shhhhh," Danny says, laughing. "All will be revealed. But first..." Danny pushes my hair back from my face, and tips his forefinger under my chin so I'm looking up at him. Slowly, he leans down to give me a kiss. His lips are tender and soft, and totally worth waiting for.

Mmmmmm.

"Is Jamie in there?" Millie asks impatiently, prodding my back. "Would you two shift so I can see my boyfriend, please?"

Danny breaks away from me and laughs. "Yeah, he's here. But wait..." He grabs Millie's arm as she tries to push past. "We've got a surprise for you two," he says. "You need to shut your eyes before you go in."

"Eh? Why?" Millie says suspiciously.

"Just do it," Danny says, putting his hand over Millie's eyes as she tries to peer over his shoulder into the café. "You, too, Suze," he says. "In you come..." He gently steers Millie and me into the café. I'm staggering all over the place.

What's Danny doing? I fall over at the drop of a hat when I can see where I'm going, for goodness sake.

Millie and I bump into each other, and what feels like several chairs and tables, as we slowly walk forwards. I sniff the air. It smells of paint.

"Ooof," I exclaim, as a table jabs me in the hip. "Can we open our eyes now? What's going on?"

"Nearly there..." Danny says. "Okay, now you can look."

As my eyes open, I gasp in astonishment. The café's beautiful. The ceiling has been repaired, and the walls are freshly-painted, although the pictures haven't been put back yet. The tables and chairs have been pushed to the sides of the rooms, apart from one table for four, which has been left in the centre. There are little tea-lights flickering on it and tiny posies of flowers on two of the place settings. Around the room, fairy lights twinkle prettily, turning the café into a magical wonderland.

"What did you... How did you... What is all this?" I ask. "Is this for us?"

"Certainly is," Jamie says, emerging from the door that leads to the kitchen.

Millie squeals and flies at him, leaping into his arms.

"Why don't you come and sit down?" Danny says.

"It's so good to see you," Millie says, covering Jamie's face in kisses.

"Cool it, you two," Danny says, but his hand grabs hold of mine under the table and as his thumb gently strokes my palm, I smile to myself.

"What is all this?" I say again.

"We wanted to give you a surprise to welcome you back," Jamie explains. "It's a good one, right?"

"Totally!" Millie and I chorus.

"But I thought they were going to be closed for ages," I say.

"We bumped into Hannah the day you left," Danny says. "That's who we were with when you rang, Suze. She'd found a plasterer, but she was having a nightmare getting a painter and decorator who could come before next month."

"So we said we'd do it," Jamie says. "It's not like we had anything else to do. You guys were away and it was kind of boring on our own. No offence, mate," he adds to Danny quickly.

"None taken," Danny replies.

"We only finished, like, an hour ago," Jamie says. "We've been working non-stop for days."

"But you don't know anything about decorating," Millie exclaims.

"It's not that hard to paint a wall, thanks very much," Danny says. "Give us some credit."

"And I found all these fairy lights and stuff for cheap at the same place you get the ones for your bedroom," Jamie explains.

"Hannah's crazy grateful," Danny says. "She paid us, but as a thank you she let us have the place to ourselves, to treat you two when you got back. She's cooking us a meal and everything, which should be here in a minute... Look, here she is."

Hannah emerges from the kitchen balancing plates of food up her arms. She smiles broadly as she approaches the table.

"Welcome back!" she says, putting plates of freshly-made pizzas and garlic bread and bowls of salad into the middle of the table. Then she sets down four hot chocolates, complete with cream and marshmallows.

My mouth waters.

"Thank you so much," I say to her.

"Mmm, tank oo," Millie says, her words barely understandable – her mouth's already full of pizza.

"It was the least I could do, especially as I'm reopening tomorrow now, weeks before I thought we'd be ready," says Hannah. "You're a lucky pair, having these two around. They've saved me a fortune."

"Listen to this woman. She speaks a lot of sense," Jamie says, waggling his slice of pizza in her direction.

"There are ice cream sundaes with chocolate brownies for pud," Hannah says. "I'll leave you guys to it. Knock on the kitchen door when you're finished."

"So, would you rather we'd taken you to Tastee Burga?" asks Jamie, with a cheeky glint in his eye.

"No way!" Millie and I chorus.

"This is amazing, thanks," I say, moving my chair closer to Danny so that I can snuggle into his side while we eat. The meal is perfect. My friends are perfect. Bojangles is perfect.

Everything is perfect.

I don't think I've ever been happier.

And you know what? I don't need to be a Mulberry girl.

Because most of the time, it's pretty blimmin' fantastic being me, Suzy P.

ACKNOWLEDGEMENTS

Roll up, roll up, it's time for the list of thank yous to people who helped in one way or another during the writing of this book. *readies pompoms* Cheers, whoops and shout-outs for the following utterly amazing bods...

Adrian Hughes, Oliver Hughes, the rest of my family, Catherine Sparrowhawk, Gill McLay, Ali Abedelmassieh, Lindsey Fraser, Sara Starbuck *holds aloft friendship balloon*, the lovely, lovely team at Templar – especially Emma Goldhawk, Will Steele, Helen Boyle, Jayne Roscoe, Jess Dean and Annie Godfrey, Jo Nadin, Kay Woodward, Marie-Louise Jensen, Lucy Spedo-Mirandola, Zoe Davis, Claire Park (excellent obs and gynae advice, any mistakes completely my own), Neil Griffiths for the photos (visit him online at www.griffithsphotography.co.uk), the amazing bloggers and reviewers who were so super-lovely about *Me, Suzy P.* and last, but by no means least, YOU. Yes, you! I cannot thank you enough for picking up and reading this book. I hope you enjoyed it.

FIVE FACTS ABOUT

1) I was taken camping every year as a child. The last night I spent in a tent there was a huge storm, my tent leaked and I was ill. I vowed never to camp again.

2) I'm shorter than you'd think.

3) I'm a walking disaster area. I gave myself concussion getting into a car, and ended up with my arm in a plaster cast after opening a window.

4) My eyes change colour.

5) My favourite foods are cheese, chocolate and potatoes. Not together. That would be weird.

You can find me online at: www.karensaunders.co.uk

f facebook.com/karensaunderswriter

🐦 @writingkaren

Suzy tweets too: @suzyputtock

Do come and say hello!

DON'T MISS BOOK ONE...
OUT NOW!

I'm Suzy Puttock (yes, Puttock with a <u>P</u>), fourteen years old and a total disaster magnet.

My life's full of ups and downs. My loved-up big sister Amber's getting married and wants lime green bridesmaids' dresses. I'm not happy about that.

But there's this hot new guy, Zach, just started at my school. I <u>am</u> happy about that. Only… I've had a boyfriend since forever, Danny.

So now I'm all kinds of confused!

'A must-read.' *Girl Talk*

'It's immensely likable and absolutely hilarious! I look forward to reading more by this fab author.' *Bookster Reviews*

'A lively, heart-warming story, sure to put a smile on your face.' *Luisa Plaja*, author of *Diary of a Mall Girl*